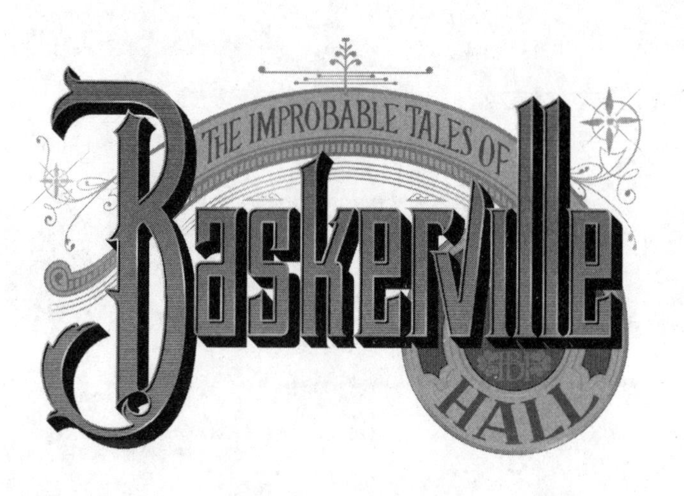
THE IMPROBABLE TALES OF
Baskerville
HALL

By

ALI STANDISH

In Partnership with the Conan Doyle Estate Ltd.

HARPER

An Imprint of Harper Collins*Publishers*

The Improbable Tales of Baskerville Hall Book 1

Library of Congress Control Number: 2023932493
ISBN 978-0-06-327557-7

Typography by Torborg Davern
23 24 25 26 27 LBC 5 4 3 2 1

First Edition

To Luka, Emma and Eva, Paige and Will,
Anna and Haley, Ava Katherine,
and all the cousins yet to come.

"Once you have eliminated the impossible,
all that remains—however improbable—
must be the truth."

—SHERLOCK HOLMES

Contents

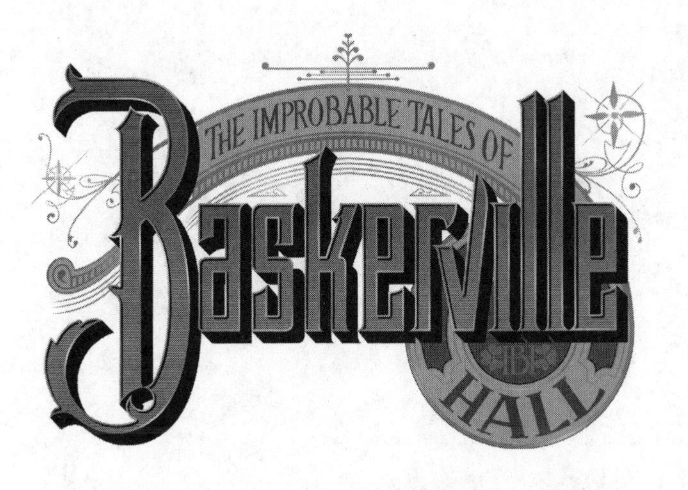
THE IMPROBABLE TALES OF
Baskerville
HALL

ONE

A Study in Scarlet

ARTHUR WAS A BOY WHO WAS ALMOST NEVER wrong. At school, he had the *most* annoying habit of working out the answer first, and getting it right, too. His classmates knew this wasn't his fault—it was simply the way his mind worked.

But if you had asked Arthur Conan Doyle if something was stirring in the air that crisp September day, if he could sense adventure—and danger—drawing near, he would have quickly pegged you for a fortune-teller trying to trick him out of a half penny.

Even Arthur, as it turned out, could be mistaken now and again.

"Is that all?" he asked that fateful afternoon, frowning at the cut of mutton Mr. Fraser had set on his butcher's scale. Split seven ways, it would barely add up to a mouthful each.

"I'm afraid that's all your money will buy today, Arthur," Mr.

Fraser replied with a sad smile. Arthur noticed the dark circles beneath the butcher's eyes.

He glanced at the far end of the sawdust-strewn shop, where Mrs. Fraser usually worked, but she wasn't there. Her sight had been getting worse lately—he could tell from the way she squinted to see him when he greeted her. Perhaps it had become so bad she could no longer see well enough to work. That meant she would need a doctor, and that Mr. Fraser would have to hire someone to take her place.

In other words, Arthur deduced, Mr. Fraser could no longer afford to give him a bit more than what he could pay for.

"Yes, sir," Arthur said, and—remembering his manners—"thank you."

As he moved toward the door, carrying the mutton wrapped in paper, he studied the other customers waiting in line. There was a man who must have been very preoccupied, for he didn't seem to notice that he had stepped in horse manure on his way to the shop. There was a woman who had patched a tear in her skirt rather shabbily. And a boy who, judging by the bulge in his boot, was concealing a knife.

Better to notice those things than the mouthwatering cuts of veal and pork behind Mr. Fraser's counter, waiting for other families to come claim them.

They're not for us, Arthur told himself. *Not today, at least.*

It was a relief when he stepped out into the sloped cobblestone streets of Edinburgh, which bustled with shoppers and paperboys, horses and girls selling posies of flowers on the corners.

The air smelled of fresh ginger cakes from Barrowclough's

Bakery and was cooled by a southwestern breeze that whispered of autumn. The leaves on the few trees along the road were rattling pleasantly, waiting for their turn to fall.

For young Arthur, there was usually nothing more wonderful than a September afternoon. September heralded the start of a new school year. New lessons. New subjects.

Today, though, the wind brought only a chill to his heart.

Before he knew where his feet were carrying him, he found himself crossing the street to W. Scott Books, where he watched a bookseller arranging her display. He couldn't make out any of the titles from this side of the glass, but the volumes were every bit as appetizing as the butcher's finest meats had been—maybe even more so. To think of all the places that lay inside of them, far away from Scotland, all the adventures waiting to be had.

He let out a sigh, fogging the window with his longing.

They're not for me, he reminded himself again. *Not today.*

If his family couldn't afford enough food to fill their bellies, they certainly couldn't afford books to fill Arthur's mind.

As if in agreement, the sharp rap of knuckles from the other side of the glass shook Arthur from his thoughts. The iron-haired bookseller was scowling at him from inside, gesturing for him to move along.

As he stepped back onto the crowded sidewalk, Arthur came to a decision.

He remembered Mr. Crabtree, the surly headmaster at Newington Academy whose breath smelled like sour milk, telling Arthur that with a mind as sharp as his, he could truly make something of himself in this world.

But Arthur was not going to be able to test Mr. Crabtree's theory, for he had decided he would not be returning to Newington Academy next week.

Someone needed to earn for the family, and with his father working less and less, that someone would have to be Arthur. The thought filled him with dread but also determination.

Perhaps he would return to the butcher's the following day and ask Mr. Fraser for a job as an apprentice. He didn't much fancy chopping cuts of meat all day, but it beat sweeping chimneys or—he shivered—digging graves.

For now, though, he was needed at home, where his mam would be waiting to make a start on supper.

As he turned, Arthur nearly ran into a woman pushing a baby in a pram up the winding hill.

"Excuse me, ma'am," he said.

But the woman barely seemed to notice him.

Strange, thought Arthur.

He looked at her more closely. She was a pretty woman, but her expression was slightly pinched, as if she were in pain. Her face was a pale moon above the bright bouquet that burst from a satchel at her side, and the rich scarlet fabric of her dress. The dress stood out in the crowd of passersby, most of them clothed in drab shades that had half faded to gray.

For an instant, the woman froze.

In that same instant, Arthur put three things together.

First, the woman's dress was very new.

Second, the baby in the carriage was very small—no more than two months old.

Third, the woman's breathing was *very* shallow.

In a flash, the woman's eyes fluttered, and she tipped forward like a teakettle.

Dropping the parcel of mutton, Arthur threw his arms out as she swooned, catching her just before her head hit the pavement.

Relief filled him as he awkwardly set her down. He had read the signals correctly. Once she had recovered her senses from her fainting spell, this woman would be able to return home safe and sound with her baby.

Her baby!

Arthur's head whipped around just as the pram began to roll down the sloping sidewalk. He shot out a hand for it, but he was too late. It picked up steam as the hill steepened, moving faster and faster.

His heart gave a leap as the pram jolted over an uneven stone and veered sharply toward the road . . . where a carriage drawn by four enormous horses thundered straight toward it.

TWO

A Rather Strange Encounter

THE BABY'S PRAM WAS ABOUT TO BE TRAMPLED by the horses, but Arthur was too far away to reach it! His eyes scanned the street and then he bent, his fingers finally finding a small stone on the ground.

"Oi!" he shouted with all his might, hurling the stone and praying that it would find its target.

It hit the man walking in front of the pram square in the back of the head, just as Arthur hoped it would. The man whipped around, searching for the culprit, and instead saw the pram hurtling toward the road. He lunged forward and managed to grab its handle just in time. A second later, the carriage pounded past.

Arthur slumped with relief. A small crowd had gathered to see what the commotion was, craning their necks to get a look at the man with the pram. He walked back up the hill, one hand pushing the baby, the other holding fast to the head of a cane. Arthur was surprised to see how elderly the rescuer was—he had made such a sprightly leap.

"Did you throw that rock?" he asked Arthur in a crisp, flat accent.

Arthur couldn't help but stare as the old man tucked the cane under one arm and adjusted his top hat so he could rub the back of his head. His age wasn't the only thing Arthur found surprising. The man's lined face was deeply tanned, as though he'd recently been in the tropics, and his snowy white beard was perfectly groomed. He had a long, narrow nose and gray eyes, and he was dressed in a sharp tweed suit and waistcoat. His cane, Arthur saw now, was a shining mahogany staff topped with a silver raven's head. Why would an English gentleman like him be in a neighborhood like this?

"I'm very sorry, sir," Arthur said. "Only, I knew if I called out, you might not realize I was calling to *you*. You wouldn't have turned around in time."

The gentleman considered Arthur for a long moment before his beard gave a little twitch. "Well, I suppose there are worse reasons to inflict a head wound upon a stranger."

The grouchy bookseller had emerged from her store to help the baby's mother to her feet. The woman pulled her baby from his nest of blankets and held the child close to her chest.

"I'm told I have you to thank for breaking my fall," she said to Arthur. Then she turned to the gentleman. "And you for saving my baby."

The Englishman shook his head. "That was down to the boy, too. If not for his quick thinking, the outcome may have been quite dire. Quite dire indeed."

After that, there was a bit of a hullabaloo with the mother insisting on Arthur taking the flowers she had just bought from the market and strangers coming up to shake his hand. It was quite dizzying for Arthur, who mostly just wanted to go home. Finally, when the mother and baby had taken their leave and the crowd had dispersed, it was just Arthur and the curious gentleman left behind.

The man leaned against the bookshop window, tapping an unlit pipe against his lips in a thoughtful way. His eyes were piercing when they met Arthur's.

"You broke that woman's fall, eh?" he said. "Fast reflexes, I suppose?"

"No, sir," Arthur replied, unnerved by this stranger's watchful eye. "I could see she was going to swoon."

"Oh? How's that?"

"Well, I could tell her dress was new, and I saw she was quite pale and seemed to be having trouble catching her breath. She had just had a baby, but her waist was very trim. So I thought to myself that while she was out dress shopping, she might also have stopped in to purchase a"—here Arthur lowered his voice to a whisper—"*corset.*"

He hoped the gentleman wouldn't think it odd that he knew about such things, but he *did* share a room with five sisters, after all, and his mam had only just had Baby Constance a few months ago.

Arthur cleared his throat. "But apparently whoever put it on had laced it too tight. And such undergarments have been known to restrict airflow and cause—"

"Fainting spells," finished the gentleman. "Quite."

The bell in nearby Newington Church began to chime the hour, and Arthur gasped.

"Please excuse me," he said, stooping to pick up the package of mutton he'd dropped earlier. "I must be getting home."

The man tipped his hat to Arthur. "Your powers of observation served you well today," he said. "Perhaps even better than you know."

Before Arthur could think of anything to say to such a strange parting remark, the man had faded into the crowd. But not before Arthur had time to notice another odd detail about him. He had come up the hill with the cane in his right hand. Yet as he walked away, he gripped it firmly in his left.

THREE

The Greatest Thing

THE SUN WAS JUST DIPPING BELOW THE horizon when Arthur burst through the door. His five sisters spent the evening hours curled up like cats in every corner of their front room, so it was no surprise when he was immediately pounced upon. Mary threw her little arms around his neck while tottering Caroline latched onto his leg and gave his knee a friendly—but painful—bite.

Ann and Catherine, his elder sisters, were darning socks by the fire, Baby Constance snug in her bassinet between them.

"You're late," Ann said, flinging aside her work. She hated sewing. "We've been worried!"

"Catherine said there was probably just a line at the butcher's," Mary crowed, "but *I* said it was more likely you'd been kidnapped by highwaymen. Wouldn't that have been ever so wonderful?"

"Why *are* you late, Arthur?" asked Catherine, firelight illuminating her serious face. "And what on earth are those?"

"Flowers!" Caroline chirped, jumping to try to reach the gifted bouquet of bell heather and thistle. "My flowers!"

The baby began to giggle at the sight of Caroline, which set Mary off laughing in turn. Arthur grinned. He hadn't even been able to remove his boots yet.

"I'll tell you everything at supper," he said. "But I'd better get this to Mam."

He held up the package the butcher had given him. Kicking off his boots, he handed the flowers to Caroline and went to find his mam in the kitchen. Her cheeks were flushed from the steam billowing out of the pot on the stove, her dark hair falling out of its braid.

"Oh, Arthur!" she said, her face breaking into a warm smile. "Just in time."

"It's not much," said Arthur as he handed over the small cut of meat. "I'm sorry I couldn't get any more."

His mam's smile did not waver, though something in her eyes shifted. "I'm used to making a little go a long way," she said. "And besides, Mrs. Gillies stopped by with a handful of potatoes they had going spare. We'll have a feast!" Then, lowering her voice, she said, "Why don't you see if your pa will be joining us?"

Arthur did his best to sound at ease. "Of course."

As his mam turned back to her steaming pot, Arthur tiptoed along the corridor toward a door that was open only a sliver. He peered in and saw his pa seated at his desk, head in his hands. His hair was uncombed, his shoulders slumped. Pasted to the wall were all kinds of newspaper clippings he kept for inspiration, along with his own sketches of fairies and goblins and other fantastical creatures. Strewn around him on the floor were crumpled-up balls of paper, and several empty glass bottles.

On a nearby easel stood a sketch of a monstrous creature, its teeth bared above its waistcoat. Mr. Doyle was an illustrator of children's books and was completing his work for a new edition of *Beauty and the Beast*. Or at least, he was supposed to be.

What Arthur's pa suffered from wasn't an illness like chicken pox or consumption, which affected the body. Rather, it was an illness of the mind, which left Mr. Doyle a shadow of the man Arthur had once known and still loved.

"Pa?" he asked. "Will you join us for supper?"

"Not tonight, my boy." Mr. Doyle didn't move an inch. "I have much work and little appetite."

Arthur had been expecting this answer, but he still ached for his old pa back. He withdrew, shutting the door quietly behind him.

And so there were only six Doyles—seven if you counted the baby—seated at the table, all of them with tumbling chestnut hair, sandy skin, and each with a lone dimple in their left cheek. Mrs. Doyle ladled out the watery stew into bowls and tore off a morsel of bread for each of her children. Arthur noticed that she saved none for herself.

Though the stew was thin and the bread stale, supper was indeed a feast. Arthur was filled near to bursting with the laughter ricocheting around the table, the smiles of his sisters in the flickering candlelight, and the way his mam gasped when he told them about the runaway pram.

"Say again," said Catherine, eyebrows furrowed, "how you knew the woman was about to faint?"

"Tell the part about the horses!" demanded Mary, who loved nothing more than a good disaster. "Are you *sure* no one was injured?"

It was almost possible to forget about the empty seat at the head of the table, a silent ghost in the shadows.

When supper was done, Ann and Catherine returned to their darning while Arthur carried Caroline and Mary up the rickety stairs to the bedroom the children all shared and tucked them into their bed. Then he sat down next to them and told them the next chapter of *The Swashbuckling Tales (and Terrible Tragedies) of Timothy Tay, Chivalrous Squire and (Sort of) Swordsman*, a story Arthur had made up one night to help Mary fall asleep, just as Mam used to do for him.

When Caroline was softly snoring and Mary's eyes had fluttered shut, Arthur returned to the kitchen, where his mam was washing up, and took a deep breath.

"I'm going to ask Mr. Fraser for a job tomorrow," he said. "It seems he needs help in the shop."

Arthur thought this would be welcome news to his mam, but instead she stiffened. When she turned to him, her round face was pained, but her eyes were fierce.

"Arthur," she said forcefully. "You mustn't. I know you want more for yourself. *I* want more for you. You deserve to stay in school."

"*You* deserve to have bread with your supper," he argued. "And Ann and Catherine deserve new stockings. Someone in this family has to make money."

She shook her head. "But you, Arthur—*you* are destined for something great."

Arthur nudged her shoulder with his own. "But, Mam, family is the greatest thing of all."

He meant what he said. Still, as he lay in bed that night, his head quickly filled up with all the things he had tried so hard to push away during the day. Questions about a world filled with mysteries begging to be solved.

Those questions are not for you to answer, he told himself sternly. *Not now. Maybe not ever.*

Finally, he fell asleep.

But it was a troubled sleep that was cut short at dawn the next morning when there came a noise so loud, it shook the whole house.

FOUR

An Invitation

BANG! BANG!

Someone was knocking at the door like they meant to break it.

BANGBANGBANGBANGBANG!

Arthur threw back his covers and tumbled down the stairs.

"What's going on?" came his mam's voice.

"I don't know," said Arthur warily.

Drawing her nightgown close around her, Mrs. Doyle slowly stepped toward the door and cracked it open. After a moment she opened the door wider.

There was no one there.

"Someone playing a trick?" he suggested.

His mam bent down and picked something up off the doorstep. "Maybe not." She held out her hand to Arthur, and he saw she was holding an envelope.

It was addressed to him.

"But . . . I've never had a letter before."

Even the rare correspondence that occasionally arrived in expensive, foreboding envelopes from his father's brothers and sisters in London was never addressed directly to Arthur—only ever to his mam.

"Open it," urged Mrs. Doyle.

Arthur took the envelope and broke the wax seal to pull out the first of two papers inside. It was a letter, written in black ink on fine white paper with a gold border, the letters swooping across the page as though they were dancing. Was it his imagination, or did the paper smell vaguely of gunpowder? He suddenly felt a bit breathless.

"Well?" said Arthur's mam. "What does it say?"

Arthur read it aloud.

To Young Master Arthur Doyle:

I am pleased to inform you that you have been accepted as a student at Baskerville Hall for the 1868 school year. Baskerville Hall is the most rigorous and innovative school in these British Isles and has produced some of the finest minds of our time. However, because of the highly sensitive and rather unconventional nature of our studies, we guard our secrets closely from the outside world. As such, you must tell no one about your acceptance, barring immediate family.

So—are you ready to challenge all that you know?

Sincerely,

Professor George Edward Challenger,
Headmaster, Baskerville Hall

P.S. Term begins tomorrow.

FIVE

The Finest Minds of Our Time

THE FRONT DOOR STILL GAPED OPEN, AS though the house itself were stunned by the astonishing letter. Arthur ran his hands over the golden crest at the top of the page, feeling its ridges beneath his fingers to make sure he wasn't dreaming.

Baskerville Hall. The words sent a thrill through him.

"But this is wonderful!" his mam cried. "Let me see!"

When she reached the end of the letter, she peered inside the envelope. "Look, there's another page! Oh, it has more information about the teachers. Let's see. Dr. J. H. Watson, Anatomy and Physiology; Dinah Grey, Professor of Theoretical Sciences; Brigadier Etienne Gerard, Languages and Equestrian Arts . . ."

Arthur's heartbeat quickened. The words began to stir images in his mind of polished oak desks and chalk dust suspended in sunbeams.

But why had he been admitted to this school? He hadn't even applied.

His thoughts were interrupted by the sound of the study door creaking open. Mr. Doyle shuffled out, still in his clothes from the night before. There were charcoal stains across his left cheek from where he must have fallen asleep against one of his sketches.

"What's all this fuss about brigadiers?"

"Oh, my dearest," Arthur's mam said, "Arthur has been accepted into a school."

Bewilderment hardened into suspicion on Mr. Doyle's face. "A school? But Arthur already has a school."

"This is a *special* school. It's called Baskerville Hall. It sounds wonderful. I was just reading about his teachers."

His teachers. As though they already belonged to Arthur.

"Brigadier Etienne Gerard," muttered Arthur's pa, reading over Mam's shoulder. "I know that name from somewhere. But it can't be. . . ."

Mr. Doyle dashed back into his study. When he returned a moment later, he clutched a scrap of newspaper that he must have pulled off his wall. The suspicious lines on his face had melted away, and his eyes were wide with a wild delight Arthur hadn't seen there in a long time.

"Look here," said Mr. Doyle, stabbing a finger at the sketch of a mustachioed man whose broad chest was crowded with medals. "Brigadier Etienne Gerard! He fought in the Crimean War. He's a hero. Why, he practically led the Siege of Sevastopol!"

"Think of what he could teach Arthur!" his mam trilled.

"But he won't," Arthur said, finally shutting the front door against the chill creeping in.

His parents turned to look at him.

"What do you mean, Arthur?" his mam asked.

Anatomy . . . Theoretical Sciences . . . Equestrian Arts. Such wonderful words. *But not for me*, he thought. "We can't possibly afford a school like that," he said.

Mrs. Doyle laid a gentle hand on her son's arm. "But, Arthur, look."

She handed him the second sheet of paper.

Beneath the list of teachers and subjects was a note written in a different hand from the first, its lettering small, tight, and orderly.

Dear Mr. Doyle,

In his haste, it seems Headmaster Challenger has forgotten to mention a few key details. Kindly report to the chapel ruins in Holyrood Park at 6 a.m. sharp tomorrow morning. Only bring with you the essentials. Everything else will be provided.

Finally, all expenses will be taken care of by the school. As our students almost always go on to attain great success in their chosen career paths, the generosity of past generations allows us to offer you tuition free of cost.

We look forward to your arrival.

Sincerely,

Mrs. Louise Hudson

Deputy Headmistress, Baskerville Hall

"Don't you see?" Mrs. Doyle said. "This is your chance to go and make a name for yourself!"

Hope tugged at Arthur's heart, but he still couldn't allow himself to give in to its pull. "I can't leave," he murmured, looking up at his mam. He didn't dare look at his pa. "Even if the school is free, the family needs me here."

From the corner of his eye, Arthur saw Mr. Doyle's cheeks flush and wondered if he was angry. But when his pa spoke, his voice was choked.

"My boy," he said, gripping one of Arthur's shoulders. "I admit I haven't been the father any of you deserved. But I won't allow you to sacrifice your chance at success because of my shortcomings. This school will give you the opportunity to do more for this family than I ever have. I will do my best for your mother and sisters. But you . . . you must go."

Arthur hesitated for only a moment. Then he threw himself into his pa's arms. Mr. Doyle returned his son's embrace, first stiffly, then with a warmth Arthur had sorely missed over the past months.

"Go where?" Mary asked.

Arthur turned to see his sisters gathered on the steps.

"Arthur has been accepted to a wonderful school," his mam exclaimed. "He's going to study with the finest minds of our time!"

Only then did Arthur allow himself to believe it. He was

really going . . . to Baskerville Hall!

Chaos erupted. Mary began wondering aloud how Arthur would get to the school, and if his journey would be dangerous. "Perhaps you'll go by boat and meet terrible pirates," she mused happily. "Or perhaps by a train that derails. Promise you'll write and tell me all about it!"

Baby Constance, having been roughly deposited in Arthur's arms, was now drooling with open-mouthed wonder at the commotion.

Arthur cried out as Caroline sank her teeth into his kneecap in protest. Constance burst into a fit of giggles as Arthur hopped around, trying to free his leg. Drool flew through the air.

"Enough!" called Mrs. Doyle, wiping a glob from beneath her eye. Though her cheeks were still glowing with the thrill of the news, her voice was firm. "Arthur leaves tomorrow. We must prepare!"

Arthur's last hours before leaving seemed to be the shortest in his life. While he couldn't wait to set eyes on his new school, he wanted to savor his final day with his family. He wanted to hold fast to each moment, but it was like trying to catch sunlight. The hours passed by in a blur, as though the hands on the mantel clock had started spinning unnaturally fast.

Just before supper, Mr. Doyle pulled Arthur into his study and handed him a sketch with a trembling hand.

"Thought you might like to take this with you," he mumbled.

The drawing was of the Doyle family sitting around the table, the way they did on his pa's good days. Instead of a stuffy portrait, Mr. Doyle had drawn them all grinning and laughing with one another, as if they had just shared a wonderful joke. He had captured all their curls, their smiles, their dimples, perfectly.

Arthur stared down at the picture. "I love it."

"It's so you don't forget us," his pa said. "Nor how proud we are of you."

Arthur didn't know which meant more—his pa's drawing or his words.

For her part, Mrs. Doyle presented Arthur and the others with a ginger cake, his favorite, which Mr. Barrowclough the baker had given her for half price since it was slightly burnt.

One moment, Arthur was falling into bed, the taste of sugar and ginger still on his lips. The next, his mam was gently shaking him awake.

"Get up, my boy," she whispered. "It's time to go."

SIX

Arthur's Seat

THE WINDING STREETS OF EDINBURGH WERE still dark and empty when the two Doyles set out. Arthur clutched the carpetbag that held his most prized belongings, all except for the warm woolen coat his mam had stayed up late into the night mending. That, he pulled tight against the early morning chill as they neared Holyrood Park.

Even in the darkness, the park wasn't hard to find. Its craggy, gorse-covered slopes loomed over the city, or rather, Arthur's Seat did. That was the name of the peak in the middle of the park, which was named for King Arthur. Arthur *Doyle* had spent many a summer morning there, waving imaginary swords and pretending to be the legendary king with whom he shared his name—and who had been the subject of many of his mam's bedtime stories.

"There it is," Arthur said, looking up from the base of the hill. "Come on, Mam, or we'll be late!"

The ancient chapel ruin, which the letter said would serve as their meeting point, sat on a crag about halfway to the top of the peak. Arthur scrambled up, craning his neck to glimpse who might be there.

When at last they reached the ruin, pink clouds to the east had announced dawn's arrival, which meant it had to be nearly six o'clock. But even in the meager light, Arthur could see that there was no carriage waiting for him at the ruin. There was no one at all, except a few sheep that eyed Arthur and his mam from a distance.

Had the Doyles misread the invitation? Or worse, had the school decided not to accept him after all?

"There's no one here but us," Arthur said, a breeze ruffling his hair.

"They're coming. I'm sure they're just running a wee bit late," replied his mam.

"But what if—"

Arthur stopped short as the breeze surged into a wind that howled through the gaps in the ruin wall. Three things suddenly became obvious to him.

First, though the wind blew more fiercely by the minute around the chapel ruin, the trees on the next slope over were completely still. For some reason, the wind had confined itself to this patch of hillside.

Second, there were far more convenient places to meet a coach, and certainly to meet a train or a boat. Which meant he must be traveling some other way.

Third, the enormous cloud approaching them wasn't a cloud at all.

"It's an *airship*!" he cried.

Sure enough, an enormous, oblong balloon was sailing swiftly toward them, like a white whale that had suddenly taken flight. Hanging from the bottom of the balloon were dozens of thick red ropes, which tethered it to a gleaming wooden ship below. It barreled closer and closer, until Arthur could see the emblem from his letter emblazoned on the ship's side. It was a shield decorated with an ivy-covered chalice and a golden key crossed with a sword.

Below the crest were the words: *Scienta per Explorationem.*

"It's going to land right on top of us!" Arthur's mam exclaimed, gripping his arm.

Indeed, the ship was directly overhead now, just a stone's throw from flattening them.

But then it came to a sudden stop. It hovered in the air for a moment before something was hurled over the side. A rope ladder unfurled, the bottom rung landing just in front of Arthur's knees.

"Splendid," he whispered.

A face appeared over the rail of the ship. Arthur couldn't make out any details, as the sun behind cast it in shadow. "Morning, Mrs. Doyle," called a deep voice. "I won't come down to introduce myself, if you don't mind. My knees aren't what they used to be. If young Mr. Doyle could climb up, we'll be on our way."

His mam craned her neck to squint at the man, amazed. "I didn't expect—I mean, an *airship*. Is it safe?"

"I assure you, it is quite safe," replied the man firmly but politely, though Mrs. Doyle had barely spoken above a whisper. "Arthur will be in good hands."

"Then . . . then I suppose this is goodbye," she said.

Before Arthur could reply, she had pulled him into an embrace so tight it nearly knocked the wind out of him. "Take care, my boy," she murmured in his ear. "Write to us."

"I will, Mam," Arthur wheezed. "Goodbye for now. Make sure to tell Mary about this. She'll love it."

Then he turned and started up the ladder to the airship and all the places it might one day take him.

SEVEN

Flying

ARTHUR'S INSIDES TWISTED AS HE CLIMBED, and he couldn't tell if it was from his frayed nerves or the frayed rope, which swayed madly beneath his fingers. Every time he thought he'd found his balance, his carpetbag crashed into the ladder, sending it swinging again.

Despite the morning's chill, his palms were beginning to sweat, making it harder to keep his grip.

Only three rungs left . . .

Two rungs now . . .

Arthur's sweaty palms slipped.

"Ahh!" he cried out, feeling himself arching backward in the air, with thirty feet separating him from the hard ground below.

Then he felt a tight grip on his wrist and a jerk upward, and he was dropped roughly onto the ship's deck.

"Are you all right, boy?" asked the man. Arthur blinked up at him. His rescuer was peering down at him with fiery eyes. His skin was a deep, bright bronze. He wasn't very tall, but he had a proud barrel chest and an impressive mane of dark curls atop his rather large head to match his similarly impressive beard. The angles of his face were sharp enough that they might have been chiseled from stone.

"Well?" the man demanded.

"Y-yes," Arthur stammered. "Yes, sir, I'm all right."

"Then what are you waiting for? On your feet and pull up the ladder. We're late."

The man stomped off toward the helm of the ship as Arthur followed his orders.

Just as he finished with the ladder, a sudden jolt sent him staggering backward. By the time he had regained his balance, all he could see were the clouds that had suddenly enveloped them.

A new, wild feeling filled Arthur, crowding out his fear. This was not a bedtime story, or a page from *Gulliver's Travels.* He could reach out and skim the clouds with his own fingers. He was flying—really *flying*!

"Boy!" the man called. "Come and help me drive this airbag!"

The sun appeared through the clouds, warming Arthur's cheeks. He could hardly believe this gruff fellow was the same one who had spoken so cordially to his mam. Still, a grin spread over his face. "Yes, sir!"

He made his way past four enormous anchors—two stowed on each side of the ship—to the prow, peering in awe at the vast belly of the balloon above.

"Good," the captain said as he approached. "You take over from here. I've been up all night. Need to catch a few winks before we arrive at the school."

He stepped back to reveal a complicated system of pulleys and levers, with a spoked wheel at its center. "Take . . . over?" Arthur asked. "But I don't know how."

Ignoring him, the captain wrenched open a trapdoor in the ship's wooden floor. "We're headed due south," he called out as he climbed down the steps to the cabin below. "Wake me when we cross into England."

"But—"

The trapdoor slammed closed, leaving Arthur alone on the deck of the airship. He gulped.

From belowdecks came a loud snore.

Was this some kind of test, or was the man simply mad? Either way, Arthur was going to have to fly the airship. He took a steadying breath and then stepped to the helm. "You can do this," he whispered.

He took a moment to assess his surroundings. There was a large compass hanging above the wheel. It was pointing southwest. He shifted the wheel slightly to the left, and the compass needle moved to point south.

Well, that had been easy enough.

A hand-drawn map had been stuck to the side of the wheel, with landmarks labeled in the swooping handwriting Arthur recognized from his acceptance letter. He squinted to make them out. Edinburgh was marked, and Liverpool and Manchester and London. And there, in the northwest corner of England, tucked into a painted forest, was a sketch of a little building labeled "Baskerville Hall."

Arthur's gaze went northward. Between England and Scotland crept an uneven line marked "Hadrian's Wall." Arthur had read about this ancient wall, a defense constructed by the Romans in the age when they still ruled Britain. Relief filled him. When he saw the wall, he would know they were close to England and that it was time to wake the captain.

To the other side of the wheel were assorted pulleys and levers, some of them labeled, others not. One large lever was attached to the ropes that secured the ship to the balloon, and Arthur figured that it must control the distance between the two. Another lever was labeled *H*. But Arthur couldn't work out what that one would be for.

For a long while, he stood like a skipper looking out at a brilliant sea, marveling at the moors and mountains passing below. Towns no bigger than shillings appeared here and there.

His heart quickened when he caught sight of a dark, snaking object. The wall? A river? No, it was a set of tracks, with a steam train chugging along them. The airship seemed to be moving faster than the train, though, which was strange. Airships were supposed to be slow. And now that he thought about it, they didn't normally travel more than a few miles at a stretch, either. . . .

Something on the horizon caught his eye. Dark clouds gathered up ahead, and a bolt of lightning shot through them, a bright needle piercing through gray wool.

Arthur's eyes returned to the lever labeled with an *H*. He had just realized what the *H* stood for.

Hydrogen.

Hydrogen was the lightest element of all—lighter than air.

That's why airship balloons were filled with the stuff. It was cheap, light, and *very flammable.*

Another bolt of lightning flashed through the sky as thunder shook the ship. They were headed straight into the storm. If lightning struck the balloon, it would explode into a ball of flames.

"Oh, dear," whispered Arthur. He thought about calling out to the captain for help, but if this was supposed to be a test, that might mean he'd fail. And besides, he doubted he had enough time to go belowdecks and rouse the man anyway. He had to act fast.

Think, Arthur. The storm stretched out over the entire sky before him. There would be no going around it. He could turn the airship back and head north, but the clouds would still swallow them in no time.

The only way to go was down. If Arthur could get the ship to dive quickly enough, it could skirt beneath the lightning's reach.

That part would be simple enough. The more hydrogen in the balloon, the lighter it was, and the higher they flew. Less hydrogen, in turn, would cause them to fall. But fast enough to avoid the lightning?

Arthur had no choice but to find out. Another flash tore through the sky. It was close enough that Arthur smelled the crackle of its electric charge. He reached out and jerked the hydrogen lever down as far as it would go.

For a long moment, he felt suspended in air.

Thunder snarled from all sides, like a pack of hungry wolves closing in.

Arthur gulped.

Then he felt a sudden swooping sensation in his stomach as

the ship began to plummet through the clouds.

"Yes!" cried Arthur. "It's working!"

The ship fell—down, down, down—until the sky grew lighter and the rain faded to a gentle patter. When the next lightning strike came, he could just make out its muffled light through the cover of the storm clouds high above.

He'd done it!

But his relief was punctured by another realization.

The ship was still falling, and faster now.

Arthur shot out a hand to push up the lever, hoping to pump more hydrogen back into the balloon.

But the lever wouldn't budge.

They were above a farm. Arthur could make out the tiny cows grazing there, blissfully unaware of the giant balloon rapidly crashing toward them. He pushed against the lever again, putting all his weight behind it. Nothing.

He backed away and took a running start, thrusting his shoulder under the stubborn lever.

But the lever didn't move, and now Arthur's shoulder throbbed.

At least Mary will get her disaster story, he thought. *Only I might not be around to tell it.*

Just as Arthur was thinking this grim thought, his eyes fell on one of the four iron anchors he'd passed when he boarded the airship.

If he couldn't make the balloon more buoyant, perhaps he could make the ship weigh less. He scrambled across the deck and unclipped the first anchor from its mooring. It took all his might to thrust it over the rail's edge. There was no time to watch it fall, as the ship, suddenly off-balance, tilted starboard. Arthur slid down the deck to the opposite anchor and heard a loud *THUD* as the first one hit the ground, followed by several moos of protest from the cows below.

He heaved the next anchor over the other side of the ship, then moved to the stern to loosen the anchors there. The ship was rising now, but not fast enough. A large barn was ahead. If they stayed on course, they would smash into it.

Just as Arthur flung the last anchor over the ship's side, he heard the screeching sound of wood against wood. He was too late. They'd struck the barn! He sank to the floor, waiting for the worst.

He had always dreamed of a life full of adventure. He'd just never imagined it being quite this short.

Suddenly, the noise stopped. Then they were climbing higher. Arthur was dizzy with relief. They must have just grazed the barn's roof!

Before he'd had time to take so much as a breath, the trapdoor slammed open, and the captain appeared once more.

"What in the name of Pythagoras?" he roared.

He took one look at their surroundings and lurched toward the helm, throwing his substantial weight under the hydrogen lever to fling it up, sending them soaring back toward the clouds. The storm, like the barn, had disappeared behind them.

"Well, boy," said the captain, turning his blazing eyes on Arthur. "You nearly crashed my ship. Worse, you woke me up."

"There was a storm," Arthur explained. "I knew if we were to be struck by lightning, we'd catch fire, so I dropped us below it. But the lever got stuck, and I couldn't get the ship back up. I had to throw the anchors over."

Arthur held his breath. Would this explanation be enough for the captain? Or would he turn his airship around and take Arthur straight back to Edinburgh?

The man glared at him for a long moment. Then he sighed. "That blasted lever," he grumbled. "Been meaning to get it fixed. I suppose I'll have to send someone to collect those anchors. Where are we, anyhow?"

Arthur pointed through the clouds to a tumbledown wall that had just appeared, snaking across the land below as far as the eye could see. *Hadrian's Wall!*

"We've just made it to England, sir."

"Have we now?" The captain shrugged his wide shoulders. "Well, that's better than being a pile of smoldering ash, I suppose. But perhaps it's best if I take it from here."

"So I passed the test?"

"What test?"

Arthur blinked and had to suppress a giddy laugh. He was going to Baskerville Hall after all. *And* he had single-handedly flown an airship.

"Sir?" Arthur said. "I saw a steam train a little while ago. It seemed we were moving faster than the train. But that's not possible, is it? Not in an airship?"

For the first time, the man's face broke into a grin. One of his front teeth, to Arthur's astonishment, seemed to be made of silver. "*My* airship can," he said.

"But how?"

"You'd need advanced knowledge of dynamic physics to understand, and you'd have to be accepted into the Circle of Lightning to learn that."

Arthur had no idea what the "Circle of Lightning" was, and after narrowly escaping death by fire, he thought he would rather not hear anything more about lightning just then. "But . . . what will people think if they see us?" Arthur wondered aloud.

The man gave a loud guffaw. "That they're mad, probably," he said. "And most of them will be right—about time they realized it!"

Arthur wondered again if his companion mightn't be the mad one.

"Do you live at the school, too?" Arthur asked. He hoped the question didn't sound rude, only he couldn't imagine someone so gruff being a part of such a prestigious place. More likely he was the equivalent of a coachman, running secret errands for the school in his airship.

The captain snorted. "I should think so, considering I run the place. Or didn't I introduce myself, Doyle?" He looked at Arthur, grinning once more, the sun glinting off his silver tooth. He held out a large calloused hand. "George Edward Challenger," he said. "Headmaster of Baskerville Hall."

EIGHT

Baskerville Hall

ARTHUR DIDN'T HAVE MUCH TIME TO GET over his shock before the airship began to dive.

"Hold on, Doyle!" the headmaster crowed.

He seemed to be following the course of a river that snaked through the valleys. Below them, shadows of clouds blew over gentle emerald hills. Between these, patches of autumn forest gave way to amber moors.

They were close enough to the ground now that Arthur could see the tiles of the roofs on the houses in a small village below. Then they veered sharply into a thick forest. A narrow road through the wood eventually led to a gravel drive lined with arching Lebanon cedar trees. The drive spilled out into a wide, rolling estate that was presided over by an enormous stone manor house.

From the sky, the manor looked like a square that was missing one side and boasted soaring gables and too many chimneys to count. It was covered in creeping vines that blazed crimson and orange. And on one side, a giant twisted tree burst inexplicably from a glass-domed roof, its uppermost branches wrapped in a vise grip around one of the house's chimneys. The manor's windows winked at Arthur in the crisp sunlight.

"That's it, isn't it?" he exclaimed. "Baskerville Hall!"

"Indeed," muttered the headmaster as he consulted his pocket watch. "With not a moment to spare."

As they flew closer, Arthur saw that a long chain of glass-houses sprouted from the manor's west wing. Behind these was an elaborate garden with a maze of gravel pathways that meandered through the hedges and flower beds.

Beyond the manor a patchwork of cottages, stables, and other outbuildings of various sizes and states of repair had been scattered across the lawns. One of them had bright puffs of green and purple smoke rising from its chimney.

Challenger was bringing the airship to land outside an enormous barnlike structure that was mostly hidden by the forest. As they neared the ground, a large bird with a hooked beak and very short wings waddled frantically across their path, causing Challenger to jerk the wheel to the left. Arthur had seen an illustration of a bird like this before, in a book called *Alice's Adventures in Wonderland.* But it couldn't be. . . .

"Didi! Out of the way!" Challenger called.

"Sir, is that a *dodo*?"

"She's the closest living thing you'll find to it. As far as we know, she is the last of the entire family of didine birds."

They hit the ground with a sudden *thump!* that Arthur felt

vibrate through his whole body.

"Here we are," said the headmaster. "Baskerville Hall. Now if you'll excuse me."

"Um, Headmaster?"

Arthur had just caught sight of a large sign posted nearby. KEEP OUT! it read. EXTREMELY DANGEROUS BOG AHEAD. TURN BACK NOW TO AVOID PEAT PETRIFICATION. IT REALLY IS A NASTY WAY TO GO.

The headmaster followed Arthur's gaze. "Nothing to worry about, Doyle," he said. "We have to keep prying eyes away somehow."

"Challenger!"

A man dressed in foreign military garb, including a sword slung from his hip, was striding toward the airship hangar.

"Brigadier?" Challenger replied, jumping down from the ship and landing roughly on the ground. He swore beneath his breath and rested one hand on the small of his back.

"You are urgently needed," barked the man, speaking in the same accent as the French teacher at Newington Academy. He caught sight of Arthur and did a double take. "Oh. I thought you were unaccompanied."

"Clearly, you are incorrect," Challenger barked back. "What is it, Etienne?"

Arthur realized this must be Brigadier Etienne Gerard, the hero of the Crimean War whom his pa so admired. He felt his breath catch in his throat.

The brigadier glanced up at Arthur again. Then, in a much lower voice, he replied, "There has been . . . *another incident.*"

Challenger's face darkened. The two men strode off as Arthur scrambled to collect his bag and climbed clumsily down from the ship. By the time his feet found the ground, the headmaster and the brigadier were already approaching the steps that swept up to the manor's front door. *Strange*, Arthur thought to himself. *I wonder what that was all about?*

As he approached the manor, he saw it was guarded by a legion of gargoyles. Some were in the shape of panthers or lions. But others looked like sea monsters or fierce goblins. Another was most certainly a monkey picking its nose.

Arthur's gaze moved above the front door, which had just slammed closed behind the headmaster and the brigadier. He saw the same crest from his letter carved in stone. And those Latin words . . .

"Scienta per Explorationem," Arthur murmured.

"Through exploration, knowledge," came a nearby voice. "It's the Baskerville Hall motto."

Arthur was startled to see a person—a *girl*—standing next to him. She was lugging a large trunk covered in labels behind her. She was a bit shorter than Arthur, with broad shoulders, a round face, and skin that was chestnut brown. Her eyes were big and bright, and under her hat her hair was black—curled in the front and twisted into an elegant braid in the back.

"Are you a student here?" Arthur blurted.

She looked at him coldly. "Of course I am."

Arthur had never considered that girls might also study at Baskerville Hall. But it made sense, of course. If the school truly accepted only the finest young minds, many of those would belong to girls. He thought of his own sisters—Catherine with her faultless logic and Mary with her bottomless imagination.

Arthur introduced himself and held out a hand for the girl to shake. As she reached out her hand to take his, Arthur caught a whiff of something that reminded him of home.

"Irene," she said. "Irene Eagle."

Irene spoke with an unfamiliar accent. Her wardrobe was strange to him, too. She wore a fitted red dress with golden buttons at the cuffs and a tiered, ruffled skirt. Curiously, the skirt was hemmed at her knees in the front, and trousers were visible underneath, tucked into her shining black boots. A golden pocket watch was pinned to her bodice.

Arthur was suddenly self-conscious of his carpetbag and recently mended coat. "You've obviously had a long journey," he said. "You have been in America, I think?"

Irene frowned. "You *think* correctly. How did you guess?"

He gestured at her luggage. "Well, you've got a steamer trunk," he said. "That means you've probably come by steam train or boat. But your hand smells of ginger, which is a common cure for seasickness. That means you came on a boat. And your watch is set to the wrong time. Five hours behind. You must have been *really* seasick not to think to change it on your journey."

She touched her pocket watch instinctively. "You have no idea. I've never been so glad to be on dry land in all my life."

Arthur grinned, thinking of his own journey. "I know what you mean."

"Did you come by ship, too?"

"You could say that."

They started up the steps together, Arthur taking hold of one end of Irene's heavy trunk. "Are your parents diplomats or something?" he asked.

"Why would you think that?" She peered at him sharply.

"All the labels on your trunk. You must travel a lot."

"They're opera singers, actually. I go with them on their tours, but they decided it was time for me to settle somewhere for a while. So here I am."

"Opera singers," repeated Arthur, who had never been to the opera himself. "Wow."

"It's not as glamorous as it sounds, trust me."

Arthur was distracted by a movement he detected out of the corner of his eye. Barely visible through the trees on the edge of the grounds, someone sat astride a black horse. The rider, clad in a dark green cloak, was strangely stiff and still. Only the swish of the horse's tail gave them away. Even with a hood drawn low over the rider's face, Arthur had a prickling feeling that the figure was staring straight at him.

"Look," he murmured, turning to Irene. "Who do you think that is?"

"Where?" she asked.

Arthur blinked in surprise. In the instant he had turned away, the horse and rider had melted into the shadows.

Before he could say anything more, the manor doors were thrown open. There stood a pale, plump woman with flushed cheeks, a shining brow, and frizzy gray hair that had mostly refused to stay in its bun. She was dressed entirely in yellow. "If you'll kindly leave your bags here," she said breathlessly, "they will be taken to your rooms. You're the last to arrive, and I'm afraid we're on a tight schedule."

Arthur and Irene stood open-mouthed, staring at the woman's companion. Peeking out from behind her skirts was an enormous gray animal.

"Is that a—"

"Wolf?" finished Irene in a small voice, as the animal opened its jaws to yawn, revealing teeth as long and sharp as coffin nails.

"Oh yes, this is Tobias," said the woman. "Toby for short. The headmaster takes quite an interest in zoology. You should see some of the creatures he's brought back over the years."

"Like Didi?" Arthur asked.

"Indeed. I've come to be particularly fond of Toby. Such a dear little lamb. I'm Mrs. Hudson, by the way, the deputy head. You must be Miss Eagle and Mr. Doyle. Now come this way, please. We're meeting in my parlor."

She turned on her heel and, to Arthur's relief, Toby got up and silently followed behind her. He was tall enough that Mrs. Hudson could have rested her forearm on his back as she walked.

"Ladies first?" Arthur asked, still thinking of those very un-lamblike teeth.

"Not a chance," Irene replied with a wolfish grin of her own.

NINE

Grover and Pocket

ARTHUR STEPPED INTO THE WIDE OAK-paneled hall. A sweeping staircase was straight ahead, but Mrs. Hudson and her "dear little lamb" were disappearing through a doorway on the left. Arthur and Irene followed her into a large sitting room.

There were perhaps twenty other students already gathered there, talking in little groups on the sofas or by the fireplace. Most of them were dressed in much finer clothes than he was.

But I bet none of their mothers stayed up late mending their coats, Arthur thought, smoothing his hands protectively over the wool.

Mrs. Hudson's parlor was lavishly decorated in shades of yellow, with swarms of saffron roses patterning the wallpaper. A silver tea service had been set out at the back of the room, and there were plates of biscuits and tarts. Arthur's stomach rumbled.

He and Irene made their way back to the tea table, where he eyed the tarts, which were also yellow.

"I'm sensing a theme," he said to Irene. "Lemon, do you think?"

"Pineapple, I'm afraid," came a droll voice.

An extremely tall, extremely scrawny, and extremely gloomy-looking boy was standing on his own by the table, dressed in all black. His hair was black, too, and shiny as a raven's wing. His skin was tawny, and he wore small round spectacles low on his nose.

"Pineapple?" Arthur echoed. He'd heard of pineapples but had never tasted or even seen one before.

"Yes, they grow them in the glasshouses," replied the boy. "Along with other tropical fruits. I prefer lemon myself. I'm Grover Kumar, by the way."

"Irene Eagle." Irene extended a hand, which Grover shook limply. "And this is Arthur . . ."

"Doyle," supplied Arthur. "And . . . that's amazing! This whole place, it's unlike anything I've ever seen before. When do you think we start classes?"

Grover shrugged. "I don't think much about time," he said. "Each second is simply another step in the march toward our inevitable end. Speaking of ends, would you like to see my collection of grave rubbings?"

He held out a notebook stuffed with papers of all sizes. Irene and Arthur glanced at each other.

"You . . . collect grave rubbings?" Arthur asked.

"Yes," said Grover. "Ever since Mother made me stop collecting animal bones. I was terribly disappointed, you know."

"Perhaps you can show us some other time," Irene said politely.

"We were just about to get a bit of food."

Grover shrugged, then reached into his pocket and popped a lemon drop into his mouth. He wandered off.

Arthur turned to Irene. "I've never met anybody quite so—"

"Grover's a bit strange, all right," said a girl who was helping herself to one of the mismatched china tea mugs. "But he's a barrel of laughs once you get used to him."

The girl's ruddy, freckled face was framed with wiry red curls, and she spoke with what Arthur recognized as an Irish accent. She wore a strange dress that seemed to be made entirely of various pockets sewn together. Some had things spilling out from them—orange yarn, a sprig of rosemary, a silver coil.

"I'm Mary," she said. "But my friends call me Pocket."

"I can see why," said Irene.

She reminded Arthur a bit of his own Mary at home. He wondered, with a pang, what the rest of the Doyles were doing that very moment.

Pocket laughed. "Girls should have pockets, too, don't you think? Where else are we supposed to keep toads and worms and our other important things?"

"Like mice?" added Arthur with a grin, pointing to the tiny pink nose sticking out from one of the shoulder pockets.

"Exactly." Pocket handed the creature a biscuit crumb, and it disappeared again.

"How long have you been here?" Irene asked.

"Since yesterday. Did you know you were coming, or was it a surprise when you got the invitation?"

"It was a surprise for me," Arthur replied. "I only got my letter yesterday."

Pocket's eyes widened. "Yesterday? Goodness, I got my letter weeks ago. Complete surprise, though. I didn't even think the headmistress at my last school liked me very much, or at least she didn't like the inventions I brought to class, but she must have put my name in."

Arthur frowned. Why had he gotten his letter weeks after the other students? And who had given the school his name?

"I had some idea," Irene said. "My parents told me they had put my name forward."

"Oh, just like Jimmie over there," Pocket said, pointing to a short boy with charcoal hair, olive skin, and slumped shoulders, who was standing with a tight knot of students. The boys were all dressed in smart jackets, the girls in glossy dresses. "His father actually went here. He's some bigshot businessman, so Jimmie was a shoo-in."

Arthur was still looking at the boy across the room when Jimmie suddenly turned to meet his eye. They held one another's gaze for a long moment, each one considering the other.

They nodded at the same time.

"He's standing with the London crowd. Actually, none of them would have been surprised to get their invitations. Harriet Russell's mother is a duchess and a lady of the bedchamber! She claims that her pillowcase once belonged to Queen Victoria. And then there's Sebastian Moran. His father is in Parliament."

Pocket was now pointing to a blond boy with a jutting chin who loomed over the others in their group. Even from here, Arthur could see that he had broken his nose at some point, though it looked to have been set well.

Sebastian, too, turned to glance at the newcomers. He smiled at Arthur, but there was something sly about the look in his eyes.

Arthur thought of his own pa, hunched miserably over his desk at home. "Does everyone here have parents that are rich or famous?"

"Not mine!" Pocket replied. "And not Grover's. Lots of us are from completely ordinary families. Oh, look—there's Ahmad Sayyid. Apparently, *his* father saved Dr. Watson's life on his last trip to Afghanistan. He's mad about geology. Rocks this and rocks that."

A slight boy in a long white tunic and blue vest waved at them. Pocket continued around the room, pointing out their new classmates. Ahmad and Irene weren't the only students who had come from abroad, and everyone seemed to have an important family, a wonderful talent, or an interesting passion. Arthur had wondered why his letter had arrived late, but now he was beginning to wonder why it had arrived *at all*.

"Are you all right?" Irene murmured. "You look as if someone's just walked over your grave."

"Fine," replied Arthur brightly. "Just tired."

"Did someone say *grave*?" Grover asked, wandering back over.

Then the parlor door burst open again, and Headmaster Challenger plunged into the room. Mrs. Hudson clapped her hands for silence.

"Headmaster!" cried Ahmad. "Your jacket!"

The headmaster looked down. His pocket had erupted in flames. He grunted, patting it out. He seemed entirely unbothered, as though looking down to find his jacket on fire was a regular occurrence. Irene stifled a laugh.

"Right, then," he said, his voice booming through the prim parlor. "Welcome to Baskerville Hall. You'll find that we do things very differently here than at other so-called *schools*. We will not waste time on grammar lessons, and we do not concern ourselves with etiquette."

A nervous giggle rippled through the students. Mrs. Hudson gave a frazzled sigh, sharing a glance with a thin, pale, straight-backed man who sat nearby in a wheelchair. He gave her a knowing look, amusement dancing in his eyes as he stroked his modest mustache.

"At this school, innovation and creativity are rewarded. There are no clucking governesses or needling tutors to watch over your shoulder. We understand that risks must be taken in the service of knowledge. We *expect* you to take those risks."

Arthur couldn't be sure, but he thought the headmaster had nodded briefly in his direction. His heart lifted. Perhaps Challenger had been more impressed with Arthur's performance on the airship than he'd let on.

Mrs. Hudson cleared her throat.

"Yes, yes, I'm getting there," said the headmaster. "Even at a place like Baskerville, however, there are rules, and you will be expected to follow them. We do not engage in the paddling of bottoms, the boxing of ears, or any other type of corporal punishment. We don't need to. If you break the rules here, you do so at your own peril."

His eyes roamed the room, as though daring someone to challenge him. Arthur saw the boy next to Sebastian elbow him with a grin. Sebastian kept his eyes trained on the headmaster.

"Now I shall introduce you to some of our esteemed faculty," said Challenger. "Dr. Watson, Professor of Anatomy and Physiology."

The man sitting next to Mrs. Hudson bowed his head.

"Brigadier Gerard . . ."

The portly man who had whisked the headmaster away from the airship was about to step forward when—

BOOM!

An explosion rattled the parlor windows. Students gasped, and a few screamed. Grover raised his eyebrows, looking interested for the first time.

"Blast . . ." Challenger growled. "Not again!"

And without another word, he strode from the room.

TEN

Into the Ring

"I THINK I'M GOING TO LIKE HIM," SAID Pocket after the headmaster had gone.

"And I like the sound of no pesky governesses or tutors," replied Irene, smiling.

"I liked what he said about taking risks," Arthur added. "Nobody ever tells children to take risks."

Mrs. Hudson clapped her hands to call them to order. "Well, as the headmaster has been detained by one of his, ah, experiments, let us proceed with a tour."

As they were herded from the room, Arthur grabbed a pineapple tart and stuffed it into his mouth. He closed his eyes as the sharp sweetness danced on his tongue. It was like nothing he had ever tasted.

When he opened his eyes again, Mrs. Hudson was flinging

open a set of double doors down the hall from the front entrance.

"This is our library," she said. "You will all become acquainted with its many treasures in due course."

Arthur's heart leapt as he peered in and saw a sprawling room stuffed with rows and rows of books, stretching from floor to vaulted ceiling high above. A globe the size of a carriage was mounted in one corner, and the ceiling had been painted with a gilded mural of the stars. Narrow staircases led up to the second and third stories, where students in dark purple uniforms were scattered about. The space between the third story and the ceiling was divided into increasingly shorter floors, like layers in a cake that had been squashed by something heavy, and were accessible by winding staircases that looked none too sound. An old man with untidy silver curls slept in an armchair behind a long wooden desk.

"This is Mr. Underhill, our esteemed librarian. Mr. Underhill?" called Mrs. Hudson. When there was no response, she called again, more loudly this time. The old man's eyes fluttered, then shut once more.

Mrs. Hudson sighed in defeat. "Oh, never mind. Let's go."

Arthur turned to speak to Irene, but instead he found the boy called Jimmie standing next to him, staring into the library with a hungry expression.

Then Irene was tugging him along, for Mrs. Hudson was already guiding them off into the east wing. As Arthur followed, his attention was caught by a detail he hadn't noticed before. One of the manor's front doors was missing its windowpane, as though the glass had been smashed from it.

He turned away when he noticed Jimmie watching him.

"Lessons are all taught here," Mrs. Hudson called as she led them deeper into the house. For a woman with short legs, she was very fast. "Except for biology and equestrian courses, which are taught in the conservatory and on the grounds. The buttery, where your meals will be served, is located at the end of the west wing. Curfew is at sunset. . . ."

Arthur was only half listening. Through the passing windows, he spotted glimpses of odd and wonderful things. There was a room full of strange specimens—a crimson-and-turquoise moth the size of a hawk pinned inside a glass case, shelves full of creatures preserved in jars of formaldehyde, and a human skeleton that, though it had long been without eyes, seemed to watch them nonetheless. Another room was blanketed in mist. Two people inside sat across a round table, holding hands and chanting.

"Are they having some kind of a séance?" Irene whispered.

Grover stood so close to the window that his breath fogged the glass. Then a scowling boy appeared on the other side, and a heavy curtain was yanked across it.

In the next room, an older woman in a long white smock with black buttons up the side was working to untangle various wires. She looked up and smiled, brilliant blue eyes shining from her pallid face. Above her, glass bells had been suspended by ropes from the ceiling. Tiny bolts of lightning flickered inside them.

Arthur gasped. "Is that—"

"Electricity," breathed Irene.

The next thing Arthur knew, he was being pushed from behind. He spun around to find that Toby had nudged him with his long snout. The wolf was staring at Arthur expectantly.

"I guess we're supposed to stay with the group," Arthur muttered.

"And finally, here is our auditorium," Mrs. Hudson was saying when Arthur and Irene caught up, "which we use for—ah, Professor Stone, there you are."

Mrs. Hudson ushered the students into a large dark room, with rows of seats leading to a stage. Onstage was a boxing ring. A hulking man stood inside it, wearing boxing gloves and jabbing at the air. He turned to face them, and Arthur saw that purple scars ran up and down his florid face, which bore quite a resemblance to a bulldog's.

"Ah, Hudson, you've brought me new blood!" he shouted merrily. "Wonderful, wonderful. Bring 'em 'ere where I can take the measure of 'em."

The students shuffled forward nervously.

"*He's* a professor?" Harriet—the girl with Queen Victoria's pillowcase—whispered.

Professor Stone wiped the sweat from his brow and peered down at them.

"Are we going to learn boxing?" Pocket squealed. She was trembling with excitement.

"Of course you will," Professor Stone answered.

"But . . . *why*?" Harriet asked.

The professor leaned against the rope and grinned. "Boxing ain't all about strength and speed, little miss. Oh, I know what people say. Boxers are just a bunch of brutes. But to survive in the ring, you need to have your wits about you. Thrive under pressure, see? Learn to box and you'll be able to keep a cool head in any tight corner."

"Some of us simply avoid tight corners," muttered Harriet.

"In fact," said the professor, his grin widening, "I believe we might have time for a match or two before Mrs. Hudson takes you to your rooms. Then you can see for yourselves."

"I'll volunteer, sir," came a smooth voice. Everyone turned to look as Sebastian Moran stepped forward, wearing an amused expression. No wonder, since he stood nearly a head taller than the rest of them. Who could possibly hope to beat him in the ring? Arthur wondered if Sebastian's broken nose had been the result of a previous fight.

"Excellent!" cried Professor Stone. "And who will volunteer to fight in our other corner?"

Silence fell over them. Not even Pocket was bold enough to step forward.

Arthur leaned over to Irene. "What kind of school *is* this?" he whispered.

"The kind where you either make it or you don't, I expect," she whispered back.

Just then, Arthur felt someone shoving him from behind. He lurched forward and spun around, expecting to see Toby again. But it was the group of Londoners standing there. They were all staring straight ahead, but a few of them sniggered. Jimmie stood a few feet apart, staring at the ground.

"Bravo!" Stone called. "Another volunteer."

Arthur froze, then slowly turned to look back at the stage, where Professor Stone was staring straight at him. So, he realized, was everyone else.

Grover, who was standing on Arthur's other side, gave a little bow. "I sincerely look forward to reading your obituary," he said.

ELEVEN

A Match Met

ARTHUR GULPED. HE HAD BEEN IN HIS FAIR share of fights with the boys from the opposite end of his road, who insisted on picking on the younger, poorer children that lived on his end. Sebastian reminded him of those smug boys.

Irene gave his shoulder a squeeze. "I'm rooting for you," she whispered.

"Me too!" Pocket said. "Show them how it's done!"

Shaking off his doubts, Arthur stepped into the ring.

"Queensberry Rules," barked Stone, tossing a pair of padded gloves to Sebastian and then Arthur. "Gloves on. Three rounds, each lasting for three minutes or until one of you is down for ten seconds. Take your corners, men."

As Sebastian took his corner, he held his arms out in front of him in a fisticuffs stance, smiling coldly at Arthur. Arthur, his heart racing, raised his own hands, too, but kept them tight to his face, elbows bent. He wondered what it would feel like to be knocked out by a punch to the chin. But he pushed that thought out of his mind before it could take root. *Concentrate!* he told himself.

Stone strode to the middle of the ring. "Ready, men? And . . . *fight*!" He rang a bell before springing out of the way.

Sebastian and Arthur edged toward each other, sizing one another up. Sebastian's outstretched stance was meant to keep his opponent at a safe distance. But it would make him slower to draw back his own hand for a blow. Unfortunately, Sebastian seemed to be amazingly fleet of foot for his size, and kept moving back and forth around the ring, making it difficult for Arthur to approach for an attack. Suddenly, Sebastian darted forward, jabbing Arthur in the shoulder. Winded, Arthur was knocked off-balance for a moment before straightening into a hook meant for Sebastian's right temple. But light-footed Sebastian easily flitted away, shooting Arthur a slippery smirk.

"There's no shame in losing," Sebastian murmured as they continued to prowl around each other. "Well, not much anyway. Look here, I'll even give you a free punch so you can save face."

He loosened his arms, dropping them low and away from his head. "Come on, Doyle," he coaxed. "It might be the only chance you get."

Arthur could see in his mind just what Sebastian wanted to happen. If he took the bait, Sebastian would wait for Arthur to jump up and swing for the taller boy's jaw, leaving his own midsection exposed. Then Sebastian would land a hard blow to Arthur's stomach, possibly knocking him to the ground where he would be at Sebastian's mercy.

Sebastian was playing a game, so Arthur would play along.

"One free punch?" he asked.

Sebastian nodded. "Go on, then."

Arthur sprang up as if to hook his opponent in the face. Then, even more quickly, he ducked down and to the side, just in time to feel Sebastian's fist fly over his left shoulder. In the moment Sebastian was left exposed, Arthur landed a blow to his ribs.

Sebastian winced and flung his elbows down to protect his rib cage. It gave Arthur an idea, but he only had a moment to think about it. Then—

Wham!

Arthur had only been distracted for a split second, but that was enough time for his opponent to swing hard for his face. Luckily, Arthur's tight stance meant that his gloves took most of the power from the blow. Still, the impact of the punch rattled his brains for a few seconds. The crowd *ooh*ed as Arthur wavered on his feet, but he kept his balance. If he could just stay upright until—

Suddenly, a bell was clanging, and Stone rushed into the ring. "That's round one," he called. "Nice clean fighting, men. Take your corners and get ready for round two."

Sebastian grinned at the cheering crowd. Arthur forced his attention away from the pain in his shoulder to Sebastian's left hand, which was still protecting his ribs.

Arthur smiled.

By the time Stone rang the bell to begin the second round, he had a plan.

There was no circling this time. Arthur dove straight into the

fight, aiming for Sebastian's midsection. Sebastian blocked the punch, but only barely.

When Arthur threw the same punch again, Sebastian blocked it more easily. And when he did it the third time, Sebastian seemed almost relaxed. "I'm getting bored," he said, before jabbing with his right arm. Arthur ducked, narrowly missing the blow. "But then, I've never much enjoyed a Scotsman's company."

Arthur forced himself to ignore the slight and kept his eyes trained on Sebastian's ribs. Time after time, he aimed his hooks there, and each time Sebastian blocked him and struck back with glancing blows. By the end of the second round, Arthur was red-faced and panting with the effort, while Sebastian sauntered back to his corner looking as though he might be on his way to a grand afternoon tea.

"Third and final round!" Stone called.

Arthur and Sebastian edged toward one another. "You should have taken my offer in the first round," Sebastian muttered. "I'd have dropped you then and there and saved you some embarrass—"

Before he could finish, Arthur had drawn back his fist as far as it would go, preparing for another hook to the ribs. Sebastian brought his arms down to block the blow that he'd clearly been expecting, and, quick as a flash, Arthur shifted his aim and struck Sebastian square in the temple. The boy's eyes widened for just a moment before his legs crumpled beneath him and he fell to the ground.

Stone was next to him in an instant, yelling out the count. When he reached ten, Stone grabbed Arthur's hand and lifted it into the air. "We have a winner, ladies and gentlemen!"

Arthur felt the thrill of victory course through him, and he smiled, raising one padded glove into the air. He was exhausted and in pain, but somehow, he still felt fantastic.

The onlooking students clapped, though some did so more enthusiastically than others.

Letting Arthur go, Stone smacked him on the back with one of his enormous hands, nearly sending him sprawling. Arthur extended a hand to Sebastian to help him up.

"Are you all right?" he asked.

For a moment, Sebastian stared at Arthur. Then he raised an arm and let Arthur help him to his feet. He held out his other hand for Arthur to shake. "Well fought," Sebastian said, loud enough for the crowd to hear.

But when Arthur tried to pull his arm away, Sebastian squeezed it in an iron grip.

"I suppose that's what growing up in a gutter will teach you," he muttered through his perfect teeth. "I've got some lessons to teach you myself."

Mrs. Hudson, whom Arthur had quite forgotten was still in the room, stepped from the back of the crowd. "Well, if we're done here—"

Before she could finish, someone else stepped forward from the crowd and lifted a hand into the air.

It was Jimmie.

"Yes?" Mrs. Hudson asked, a touch impatiently.

"I'd like a turn," he said quietly. "In the ring. With him."

He gestured toward Arthur.

Arthur studied the other boy as he wondered why Jimmie had made this request. He didn't seem hostile. In fact, he seemed to be studying Arthur right back.

"That's the spirit!" cried Stone. "Want to take on our reigning champion, eh? Prove your mettle?"

"How about it, Hudson?" Stone asked. "Do we have time for one more match?"

"Not really, no," said Mrs. Hudson curtly.

"Then we'll go one *round*! Anyone can spare a mere—yet perhaps momentous!—three minutes."

Mrs. Hudson sighed in defeat and dropped herself back in her seat. Stone waved Jimmie into the ring, and the next moment he was ringing his bell once more.

Jimmie crouched closely behind his fists, like Arthur, in a coil of energy that seemed ready to spring at any moment. He was shorter than Arthur, with a narrow frame and small gray eyes that studied Arthur intently.

His tongue flicked across his lips. It was Arthur's only warning before Jimmie leapt forward, and it gave him just enough time to dodge the blow Jimmie hoped to land.

Their eyes locked once more, and Arthur felt an odd connection, like an electric current, running between them. They circled one another.

"You wanted Sebastian to see you getting tired, didn't you?" asked Jimmie in a soft voice. He jabbed, and Arthur blocked it.

"Sometimes people underestimate me," Arthur replied. "And sometimes that works in my favor."

Now it was Arthur who aimed a punch for the stomach. Jimmie seemed to sense it coming and hopped back so that Arthur's fist merely grazed him.

"You kept aiming for the same spot, over and over, like you'd forgotten there was anywhere else to aim for. But you didn't forget. You made *him* forget."

"I didn't *make* him do anything. I just . . . encouraged him."

Jimmie smiled, but it wasn't a smug smirk like Sebastian had worn. It was a smile of appreciation.

The next moment, he struck again, this time with his left fist. A murmur stirred like a wind through the crowd. The boys had both changed stances at the same time, and now began to circle in the opposite direction.

It felt more like a dance than a fight.

All the while, they kept their eyes trained on one another. Their three minutes must be nearly over, and neither had even struck a proper blow. It was almost like Jimmie had been drawing Arthur closer and closer in order to—

In the moment that Jimmie jabbed with his left, Arthur shot his own left fist forward. He felt his glove connect with Jimmie's cheek just as a blow to his own face knocked him sideways. The next thing he knew, his head was hitting the ground. He lay there for what seemed like a long time but was probably only a couple of seconds, seeing stars. When his head stopped spinning, he groaned and forced himself to sit up.

To his surprise, he saw that Jimmie was on the ground, too. They had each landed a blow at the exact same time. The boys looked at each other, both blinking with shock. Then Jimmie's serious eyes brightened and he grinned.

The crowd was cheering—clearly it had been a great show.

"That's some left hook you've got," Jimmie said.

"I could say the same about yours."

"I don't think we've been properly introduced," said Jimmie,

once they were back on their feet.

"I'm Arthur Doyle," said Arthur, pulling off his gloves and holding out a hand.

"And I'm James, but my friends call me Jimmie," said Arthur's formidable opponent. "Jimmie Moriarty."

TWELVE

A Room with a View

"THAT'S QUITE ENOUGH FOR ONE DAY, STONE," Mrs. Hudson announced. "We certainly don't want a repeat of the Squashing Incident of 1857."

"Ah, it weren't so bad," Stone replied. Then, a frown crossing his face, he added, "Well, except for the lad they landed atop of. He never was quite the same. . . ."

An hour before, this statement might have alarmed Arthur. But he understood now that Baskerville Hall was a place unlike any he'd ever known. And he found that he had already begun to love it.

Mrs. Hudson rushed them back through the sprawling manor house so they could tour the west wing, but when they reached her parlor, the headmaster's booming voice summoned her inside. There was a note of worry in it that Arthur hadn't heard before.

As Mrs. Hudson ushered the others outside, Arthur hung back. Through the crack in the parlor doorway, he could just make out the figure of Headmaster Challenger huddled together with Dr. Watson and Brigadier Gerard. They were discussing something in low voices. Arthur leaned closer.

He caught the words *security measures* and *anything taken* before he heard an insistent yelp and looked down to see Toby staring up at him with his accusing yellow eyes. Arthur didn't need to be told twice. When the wolf turned and moved lightly toward the front steps, Arthur followed close behind. He brushed his fingers over the ornately carved oak of the front door as he passed, eyeing the broken windowpane closely.

While Arthur rejoined his classmates, Mrs. Hudson was busy accosting a passing boy who looked to be about sixteen. He wore large spectacles over an expression of wide-eyed surprise and had an unruly tuft of blond hair. Each strand stood on end, giving him the overall appearance of a giant, baffled dandelion clock.

"Just show them to the tower," Mrs. Hudson was instructing him. "Tell them how it all goes. They're only first years, Bruno. Surely you can handle them."

"Of c-course," said the boy called Bruno. "I'm your man."

Though he didn't sound at all sure that he was.

"Good." Mrs. Hudson turned back to the rest of them. "Bruno here will show you to the tower now. You'll settle in, then report to the buttery for supper."

She swept past them and back into the manor.

"Ah," Bruno said, still blinking in apparent shock at the group in front of him. "Yes. Well. Off we go."

"What's the tower?" asked Irene.

Bruno pointed to a looming stone structure that stood at the westward edge of the grounds and drooped alarmingly toward the wood. "First years and some second years live in the tower. That's because you aren't allowed to choose a Circle yet."

"A Circle?" Irene asked.

Bruno nodded. "A Circle of study. There are five—Iron, Dawn, Lightning, Spirit, and the Citadel. If chemistry, metallurgy, or engineering interest you, you'd join the Circle of Iron. The Circle of Dawn is one of the bigger groups, and it includes all the life sciences. Biology, anatomy, zoology—those sorts of things. Brainy students who like maths, physics, and astronomy join the Circle of Lightning. The Circle of Spirit is the smallest—and strangest, if you ask me. They study the unexplained, ghosts and fortune-telling and such. And everyone else, the girls and boys who go on to run businesses and governments, they join the Circle of the Citadel. It's a bit of a catchall Circle—they study languages, music, military history, equestrian science, and more. Everything you'd need to know about to make conversation with the King. Most of the wealthy lot, dukes' sons and the daughters of Parliament, end up in the Citadel. Not me, though. I'm a coleopterist, so I'm in the Circle of Dawn. Once you're accepted into a Circle, you move into a different dwelling with the professor who heads it up."

"What's a coleopterist?" Arthur asked.

Bruno turned to give Arthur an affronted look. "Why, someone who studies beetles, of course. They are infinitely more interesting than humans."

Irene bit her lip to stifle a giggle.

Arthur thought about the Circles with growing excitement.

They all sounded so fascinating. How could he choose only one? Even the Circle of Spirit, strange as it seemed, held a certain attraction. The rest of his friends, however, seemed eager to make their choices.

Irene and Jimmie immediately started talking about how practical the Circle of the Citadel sounded. Grover began pelting Bruno with questions about the Circle of Spirit, and whether they had ever succeeded in contacting the dead.

"The Circle of Iron," Pocket said dreamily. "That's got to be the one for me. Although there's something about the Circle of Lightning that sounds exciting, too. . . ."

"You could do both," Bruno said. "Some students end up crossing Circles in their later years and joining more than one. It's not easy, though. The amount of homework alone . . ."

Maybe that will be me, Arthur thought. He wanted to learn it *all*.

Instead of taking the winding path, Bruno plunged into the tall grass, cutting directly for the tower. Even if the tower didn't lean to one side, it would still have been a strange-looking building, and even stranger out here in the country. It was round and covered with ivy, so that it might at first be mistaken for the trunk of some enormous tree. Several chimney stacks cropped up from its crown, which held no clock or bell.

They had come to the base of the tower and an ancient-looking wood plank door with an iron handle. "Well, must dash," Bruno said. "I really can't keep my dissection specimen waiting any longer. Nice to—that is, I hope—well, do stay in touch."

Bruno swept into an odd bow and took several long strides before breaking into an ungainly sprint back toward the hall.

The door was low enough that most of the students had to duck to make their way inside the tower. Irene shivered as they entered the dark antechamber. It was furnished with nothing more than a threadbare rug, a table with a gas lamp, and a velvet chaise covered in long silver hairs. In front of them was a door with an engraved nameplate, but Arthur didn't need to read it to know it would say Mrs. Hudson. The hairs on the chaise clearly belonged to Toby, which meant that the wolf probably slept there. And why else would he do that, unless he was guarding his mistress's door?

"It feels like a tomb in here," Irene said, crossing her arms over her chest. A dark-haired girl next to her looked around with wide, frightened eyes.

"Not really," Grover said from behind them. "Tombs are much more interesting. I once locked myself inside one for three days."

"Why am I not surprised?" Arthur asked.

To their left, a staircase rose up in a spiral. One by one, they started up the stone stairs, the clatter of their shoes echoing around them. Soon they found themselves on a round landing with a door on either side. One of them was ajar. Inside, a girl was sitting on her bed, using a magnifying glass to examine something in the thickest book Arthur had ever seen.

"Oh," she said, looking up. "You must be the new first years. Looking for your rooms?"

A few people nodded.

"You've got to keep climbing," she said. "Your rooms will all be on the top floors, above all the second years."

They carried on climbing, examining the little engraved plates on the doors they passed to find their own names.

"Is it just me," huffed Irene, "or does the tower keep getting narrower and steeper?"

On the next landing, Ahmad and Grover found their room, which was across from Sebastian and a horse-faced boy called Roland Stanley.

Harriet and the nervous dark-haired girl—whose name, Arthur learned from the nameplate on the door, was Sophia De Leon—peeled off on the next landing. There weren't many of them left now.

When he reached the next landing, Arthur strode to the solitary door to peer at the names.

ARTHUR DOYLE
JAMES MORIARTY

He turned and smiled at Jimmie, who was peering over his shoulder. "Looks like it's you and me," he said.

Jimmie nodded. "Looks like it."

Irene and Pocket continued up the next flight of stairs. "See you for dinner," Arthur called.

"If we ever actually find our room," Irene replied as they continued climbing.

"I suppose we'll have to get to know each other as friends now," Jimmie said, "rather than as opponents."

Arthur laughed. "I'm just glad it's you and not someone like Sebastian."

He immediately wished he could take the words back, remembering that Jimmie *was* someone like Sebastian.

But Jimmie didn't seem bothered. "My family has known his

for years," he replied. "He's a terrible snob, all right. Especially to outsiders. I mean—not that you're a—"

"It's all right," said Arthur, relieved that they were even now. "I *am* an outsider. It's my first time in England."

Jimmie's eyes widened. "Your *first* time?"

"I have family in London," Arthur added hastily. "My aunts and uncles."

"But you've never been to visit?"

Arthur felt his cheeks beginning to warm. "They're . . . very busy," he said.

He couldn't tell his new friend the truth—that his father's well-to-do brothers and sisters no longer wanted anything to do with Mr. Doyle. That they felt he'd brought shame on the family by succumbing to his spells of illness.

"We'd better go in," he said, before Jimmie could ask any more questions. "Mrs. Hudson said something about dinner, and I'm starving."

And besides, he couldn't wait another moment to see his new home.

It was a small half-circle room with a pair of windows. A desk had been shoved under each one, and there was one narrow bed on either side of these. Next to the door, there was a washbasin, a modest coal fireplace, and two skinny wardrobes, each supplied with a plum-colored suit, a matching tie, and a white shirt. The room was hardly three paces wide and six long. It was what Arthur imagined a ship cabin might look like, only instead of blue ocean out the window there was a sea of green creeping vines.

Curious about the view, Arthur went to the window and pushed it open. He cleared away the ivy to see the sun setting

on the overgrown fields and winding paths, making the manor's windows glow.

"Not bad," Arthur breathed. At home his only view had been of flapping laundry lines.

"Not bad at all," Jimmie agreed. "What do you think *this* is for?"

He pointed down between their desks, where a thick coil of rope was tied to some kind of iron anchor that jutted up from the floorboards.

Arthur, still leaning out the window, had only just begun thinking through the possibilities when he felt a shadow overhead and looked up to see something barreling down from above, straight for his head.

"Arrrrr!" cried someone in a gruff voice. "Prepare yerselves to surrender . . . or DIE!"

A Curious Kind of Thief

ARTHUR SHOT BACK FROM THE WINDOW just as a thick coil of rope plummeted down from somewhere above. The next instant, a pair of boots came into view, followed by a purple skirt. Then a roguish smile and a single glittering eye.

"Pocket!" Arthur cried as she climbed in through the window.

"That's Captain Pocket to you," she said, winking the eye that was not covered by a black eye patch.

No sooner had Pocket deposited herself onto the floor than another set of boots appeared, and Irene was climbing into the room, rather more gracefully than Pocket had. They had both changed into their new uniforms, which matched the ones hanging in the boys' wardrobes. Pocket wore a skirt, while Irene had opted for trousers.

"Well, at least we know what the rope is for now," muttered Jimmie.

"Whoever built this place must have been afraid of fire," said Irene. "And no wonder. Can you imagine trying to escape down all those stairs?" Her gaze landed on Jimmie. "I do hope we're not interrupting."

"Not at all," said Arthur. "I suppose this means you found your room."

"Conveniently located right above yours," said Pocket, removing her eye patch.

"Jimmie, this is Pocket," said Arthur.

"Yes, we met this morning," Jimmie replied. He was staring at Pocket with what might have been either amusement or confusion.

"Oh, right. And this—"

"I'm Irene. Irene Eagle."

She extended a hand, which Jimmie shook. "You're American," he said.

"Half," Irene clarified, looking intently at him. "My mother is American. My father is Welsh."

"Well, you certainly don't *sound* Welsh."

"Perhaps because I've never been to Wales. Have you any other observations to make?"

The pair fell silent but continued to study one another with suspicion. Arthur cleared his throat, anxious to put an end to whatever tension had arisen between his two new friends.

"Jimmie and I better get changed for supper," he said. "Mrs. Hudson might send Toby to fetch us if we're late. And I'd really rather not make an enemy of something with such . . ."

"Sharp teeth?" finished Irene.

"Exactly."

Arthur and the others caught Ahmad and Grover just as they were leaving their room. Arthur introduced himself to Ahmad and spent the walk back to the manor listening to the tale of Ahmad's journey from Afghanistan to Baskerville Hall, which included passage on a ship that had nearly capsized; long, dangerous trips on camel and horseback; and a stopover in Italy to see the excavation of Pompeii.

He listened with fascination, but also with growing jealousy, as Ahmad spoke of all the places he'd been and adventures he'd had. A few steps behind, Jimmie and Irene seemed to be competing over who had traveled to the most far-off destinations. Chicago and Warsaw and Istanbul—places Arthur had only read about in books, if he'd ever heard of them at all. The chill between them thawed instantly when they discovered that they had both dined at the same hotel restaurant in Paris, where they had been served by the same oily waiter, who picked his earwax when he thought no one was watching.

Jimmie had called Arthur an outsider, and that's exactly what he felt like as Irene and Jimmie laughed together. He didn't have interesting stories to share like the others. He'd never even left Scotland until that very morning.

He was relieved when they reached the manor steps. As he approached the top, he stopped, finally realizing what was bothering him about the broken windowpane in the front door.

He had never stolen anything himself, though he had considered it in a few desperate moments. But he *had* known plenty of

thieves. And whether they were picking pockets or locks, they all knew that the most important part of the job was not to attract attention.

Irene and Jimmie paused next to him.

"What is it, Arthur?" Irene asked.

"Right after I arrived, Headmaster Challenger was rushed off by the brigadier," he explained in a low voice. "He said there had been another 'incident.' And then I saw them talking on the steps here and pointing up at the window. After our tour, I overheard some of the teachers talking about increasing security and whether anything had been taken."

"A break-in," said Jimmie and Irene at the same time.

Arthur nodded. "That's what it sounds like. But . . . what kind of thief breaks in through the front door?"

FOURTEEN

The Buttery

THE BUTTERY WAS ALIVE WITH CHATTER AND awash with delicious aromas. It was a large room with high oak panels and an arched ceiling that was pinched at the top. Wood beams ran across the ceiling, over the tables full of students passing around steaming dishes. A mural at the back of the room depicted Prometheus stealing fire from the gods.

"First years sit at the far end," barked a red-faced woman in an apron—clearly the cook—who had suddenly appeared next to them. "And you can take these while you're at it."

She shoved several covered dishes toward Arthur and Jimmie.

The other first years were sitting at the far end of a table that ran the length of the room. Smaller tables were scattered about the rest of the hall. Little jam jars with sprays of wildflowers adorned the surface of some, and stacks of books or strange, glinting instruments had taken up residence on others. The kind of students, too, changed depending on which table he was looking at. Some sat in deep, focused silence, while others played cards. The students at a table toward the back of the room—which had hay strewn beneath it—burst into laughter at something the brigadier had just said.

"I bet the different Circles all sit at their own tables," said Irene.

Arthur nodded and pointed out five large heraldic pennants hung around the room near the different groups of tables, each one with a different symbol and Latin phrase embroidered in white on deep purple velvet. Closest to them were a half circle with rays of light blazing from it, a triangle split by a lightning bolt, and a tower with a star above it. "Look," Arthur said. "Those must be the symbols for the Circles of Dawn, Lightning, and the Citadel. And the students all have little patches with those same symbols sewn on the shoulders of their uniforms."

Sebastian called to Jimmie as they walked past him and two other boys. They were sitting closest to the second years, who occupied the other half of the long table.

"There's room here," Sebastian said. He glanced at Arthur and Irene, then back to Jimmie. "Room for *you*. Roland was just telling me about the foxhunts at Ragsby Hall. They're legendary. I'm sure the subject wouldn't be of much interest to your . . . companions."

"No," Irene replied. "It would not be."

Jimmie blinked. He was silent, and for an awful moment Arthur was sure he was about to sit down. "Thank you," he said finally. He held up the bowl Cook had given him. "But I've got to take this to the other end anyway. I'll see you around, Sebastian."

Sebastian shot Jimmie a thin smile while Arthur suppressed his own victorious grin. He, Irene, and Jimmie took their seats at the end of the long table.

Arthur opened the lid on his bowl to reveal bread rolls and took one before passing them around. They landed with unpromising thuds against their plates.

"I wish they would let us choose our Circles now," said Pocket. She was staring wistfully at a table where the woman in the white lab coat who Arthur had glimpsed during their tour sat with a group of students. They seemed to be passing conversation back and forth at a rapid speed, as though it were a blazing ball of iron, hot from the forge. On the shoulders of their uniforms was a patch with a hammer crossed with a glass flask.

That must be the Circle of Iron table, Arthur thought.

"That's Professor Dinah Grey," Pocket explained. "I've read all about her. She's working on creating electric lights. Not only that, though! Electric *everything*. Carriages and bicycles and ovens . . ."

Arthur tried to wrap his mind around this idea as he spooned out a helping of mushy peas. But he was having trouble concentrating on anything except the food. He couldn't remember the last time he'd had a meal so big.

"What about you, Grover?" Irene asked. "Do you know what you want to study?"

"I want to be a necrologist," he said.

"What's that?" Ahmad asked.

"Someone who writes obituaries."

Jimmie frowned. "So you want to study . . . dead people?"

Grover blinked. "What's more fascinating than death?" He

glanced longingly at a nearby table, which was smaller than the others, covered in a lace cloth, and lit with spindly taper candles. In the middle of the table, he recognized the pair of students he had seen chanting together in the foggy room during their tour of the school. Empty seats had been left on either side of them, and they were huddled in conversation. The boy on the left was tall but stooping, with very pale skin and dark features. The other one had short brown hair and looked younger, but that might have been down to his rose-colored cheeks and a small upturned nose.

"Circle of Spirit," Grover said, seeing that Arthur was staring, too.

"We saw those two earlier," Arthur said, pointing to the pair. "Having some kind of . . . ritual?"

Unlike the rest of the students, the pair was dressed all in white with patches on their shoulders that showed an open hand with an eye on the palm.

"A second year told me they're called Thomas Hood and Ollie Griffin," Grover said. "They keep themselves to themselves, but there's all kinds of rumors about them, apparently. That they've got some kind of *powers*. That they can see beyond the veil."

Arthur felt a shiver run down his spine and tore his gaze from the strange boys.

"Well," said Jimmie, looking skeptical, "I guess you really can study pretty much anything you want here."

"Your dad went here, didn't he?" Arthur asked. "What does he do now?"

"He's a businessman," Jimmie said vaguely. "What about yours? What does he do?"

"He's an artist," Arthur replied.

"What kind?" Irene asked.

"An illustrator. He's working on an edition of *Beauty and the Beast* right now."

And had been for some months, with very little to show for it.

"That's exciting!" said Pocket. "My da's a sheep farmer. He may not be rich or famous, but our sheep make the warmest wool in Ireland!"

Jimmie's and Arthur's eyes met across the table. There was something dark in Jimmie's expression that Arthur could feel mirrored in his own. An understanding of sorts passed between them. Arthur might be avoiding the truth about his father, about how poor his family was. But there were things Jimmie didn't want to speak of, either.

"That kind of thing doesn't matter here, does it?" Ahmad asked. "We can be anyone we want in this place."

Arthur found himself nodding. Ahmad was right. What did it matter that he didn't come from a wealthy home full of fancy things? He had ideas and dreams the same as the others. And perhaps he hadn't traveled the world, but that was going to change one day. He was sure of it. He would *make* sure of it.

His story would start right here, right now, at Baskerville Hall, and no one was going to write it but him.

FIFTEEN

Dr. Watson Plays a Trick

THE NEXT DAY STARTED NOT WITH A BANG, but with a blast.

Arthur and Jimmie both shot up from their beds, bleary-eyed in the early light.

"What's going on?" Jimmie mumbled.

Arthur threw back his covers and went to the window. He spotted a figure in military dress galloping on horseback across the grounds, blowing into a French horn. Brigadier Gerard might have been attempting a song, but the bleating notes made Arthur want to cover his ears. He slammed the window shut.

"I think it's our wake-up call," Arthur said.

Jimmie groaned and pulled his covers over his head.

"Get up, or we'll miss breakfast," Arthur said. "And I'm almost certain I smell bacon."

❧

There was a jittery air of excitement at breakfast that morning. Everyone had either slept like a baby (or the dead, in Grover's case) or gotten no sleep at all. Pocket, who had been up half the night adding pockets to her uniform, was literally on the edge of her seat. The quiet girl who was roommates with Harriet—Sophia De Leon—kept her head bowed over her plate.

At the end of the meal, Mrs. Hudson bustled to the head of the long table, holding an open notebook.

"Your timetable for this term is as follows. Ten pounds of sugar, followed by five gallons of—no, no, that's not right at all." She began flipping through the notebook's pages. "Ah, yes, here we are. Immediately after breakfast, you will report to Dr. Watson's room for Human Physiology. . . ."

She went over their schedule for the day, which included lessons with Professors Grey and Stone, plus an Introduction to the Natural World with someone called Professor Loring.

"Does anybody know where we are going?" Ahmad called out, after Mrs. Hudson had shooed them from the buttery with no further instructions.

Arthur remembered catching a glimpse of a skeleton in one of the classrooms. Surely that would be Dr. Watson's room?

"I think I know," he said.

He led them through the halls, past classes already full of students, until they came to the classroom with the skeleton. The door was wide open, and Dr. Watson was sitting behind a desk, dipping a pen into his inkwell.

Arthur cleared his throat. "Hello, sir."

Dr. Watson looked up. "Ah," he said with a gentle smile, "there you are. I was about to send for the brigadier to organize a search party. He does so love those. Do come in."

He pushed his wheelchair out from behind his desk and moved to the center of the room as Arthur and the others took their seats, gazing around at the murky jars lined up on shelves. One contained a human hand.

"Better not misbehave, everyone," Ahmad called. "We're being watched!"

He gestured to a collection of jars at the back of the room that contained *eyeballs.*

Arthur was aware of his own eyes widening and felt suddenly very grateful to have them safely in his head.

"You'll become used to them over time," said Dr. Watson cheerfully. "They may seem gruesome to you now, but the study of specimens like these helps us understand how the human body works and the marvels it is capable of."

Arthur studied his classmates, who looked in turns horrified and fascinated. But . . . wasn't someone missing?

"What kind of marvels do you mean, sir?" asked Sebastian.

"I have met women who performed unexplainable feats of strength in moments of crisis," said the doctor. "Men who have survived injuries that should surely have been fatal. Each of us in this room has a mystifying ability to sense impending danger. Think of the hairs that stand up on your arms when you feel you are being watched. Why, my own knee can predict with great accuracy when a storm is brewing. It all comes back to the uncanny connection between the mind and body."

Just then, the door opened, and Sophia De Leon appeared looking pale and breathless. She had some kind of ivory scarf wrapped around her neck.

"I'm very sorry, sir," she squeaked. "I . . . got a bit lost."

"In fact, I believe you're just in time," Dr. Watson replied, his gaze landing on her scarf. "I was just about to introduce the class to the theories of Franz Mesmer. Has anyone heard of him?"

Arthur put up a hand. He had read about Mesmer in one of the books he'd borrowed from the library at his old school. "Franz Mesmer invented the idea of animal magnetism," he explained. "He thought there was a force inside every living thing, and it could be channeled to heal illnesses. But he was—"

"Indeed," Dr. Watson agreed. "Which brings us back to—What was your name?"

Arthur frowned. Why had Dr. Watson cut him off?

"Sophia De Leon," the girl answered.

"Lovely. Now, Miss De Leon, might I ask you to remove your scarf so I can examine that rash?"

Sophia looked up, startled, then nodded slowly.

Arthur leaned forward. *How had Watson known she had a rash?*

She unwound the scarf to reveal red blotches blooming on her neck.

"You get such rashes from time to time?" Dr. Watson asked. "When you are anxious? Like on your first day of a new school?"

Again, Sophia nodded.

The class was silent as Dr. Watson pointed to what looked like a cauldron with iron rods sticking out at odd angles, which sat beneath the chalkboard.

"A common ailment," said Dr. Watson. "Now, if you'll allow

me, I'd like to perform a demonstration of Mesmer's methods and help you get rid of that rash. All I need you to do is take hold of one of the rods."

He gestured to the strange instrument between them. Sophia took a cautious step forward and reached out a hand. Arthur noticed Dr. Watson's own hand disappearing into the cauldron for an instant before taking hold of another of the rods.

"Lovely. Now simply train your gaze down, that's it, and take a deep breath for me. Keep your gaze focused on the iron baquet here, as I use the magnets inside to channel the energy between us."

Watson cleared his throat. When he spoke again, his voice was slower and deeper.

"You are safe and welcome at Baskerville Hall," he murmured. "You are about to embark on the most wonderful years of your young life. Isn't that right?"

As Dr. Watson continued speaking, Sophia's eyelids began to droop.

"Yes," she said dreamily.

"No need to feel anxious about being here, is there?"

"No."

Next to Arthur, Irene gasped. He followed her gaze to Sophia's neck, where the skin was fading from red to pink.

"You are feeling quite relaxed then?" Watson asked.

"Yes," Sophia said again.

The pink faded to olive. Murmurs spread throughout the class as others noticed.

"Very good, Miss De Leon. I think that's enough. You may drop your hand."

Sophia's hand slid away from the baquet, and at the same instant, Dr. Watson snapped his fingers. Sophia blinked a few times, looking around as though she couldn't quite remember where she was. She brushed her fingers against her neck. "Is it gone?"

"Indeed it is," Watson replied.

"You . . . you cured me!" she exclaimed.

Her voice no longer quavered.

"You may take your seat," said Dr. Watson, nodding warmly.

Arthur furrowed his brow. Dr. Watson had stopped him just before he was about to say that the idea of animal magnetism had been widely disproven in the decades since Mesmer came up with it. Surely Watson would know that!

And yet, they had all seen Sophia's rash fade with their own eyes. Earlier, she had been anxious and fearful. Now she sat with a serene look on her face as she inspected the rows of gruesome jars lining the room.

"Does anyone have any questions about my little demonstration?"

"There's some kind of trick to it," Ahmad said, "isn't there?"

He'd taken the words right out of Arthur's mouth.

A smile played on the doctor's face, and he waved Ahmad up. "Come," he said. "See for yourself."

Ahmad grinned as he strode up and took hold of one of the baquet's rods.

"Now, keep your eyes down, please. Listen closely to my voice."

Arthur watched carefully as the professor's voice slowed and deepened, and Ahmad's eyes began to glaze over. Again, he

spotted Dr. Watson's hand reaching into the baquet for just an instant before it returned to the iron rod.

"Now, Mr. Sayyid, do you recall the day we first met?"

Ahmad nodded. Arthur remembered that Ahmad's father had known Dr. Watson back in Afghanistan.

"I sang you a song. The first one you learned in English, I believe. Could you please recall it for us now?"

There was a moment of silence, and then Ahmad burst into song.

"TWINKLE, TWINKLE, LITTLE STAR! HOW I WONDER WHAT YOU ARE!"

Everyone laughed. Even Dr. Watson gave a chuckle.

"That will do," he said, when Ahmad came to the end of the first verse. He snapped his fingers, and Ahmad froze, his mouth still gaping open. Dr. Watson began to applaud politely. Some of the class joined in, and Ahmad swept into a bow.

Arthur's eyes remained fixed on the baquet.

"Sir," he said, when Ahmad had returned to his seat, "could you show us what's inside the baquet?"

Dr. Watson looked at him with interest. The corners of his mouth twitched as he reached into the great cauldron and pulled something out.

He held up a large black-and-white whirligig. Dr. Watson gave it a lazy flick so that it turned faster, the black and white sections blurring together in a way that was . . .

"Mesmerizing," Arthur said. "That's what you were doing!"

"Indeed I was," said the professor, smiling broadly now. "How did you know?"

"I saw you fiddle with something inside the baquet," Arthur

said. "Plus, I know that Franz Mesmer's ideas were disproven a long time ago. But some of the techniques he used *do* work, like hypnosis, also known as mesmerizing. That's where the word *mesmerizing* came from—his name!"

Every gaze in the classroom was now trained on Arthur, and suddenly he felt heat creeping up his own neck.

"So wait," said Pocket. "Dr. Watson hypnotized them?"

"Yes," Arthur replied. "He made us all think that the baquet had some kind of mystical healing powers, but it was Dr. Watson's *words* that had power. The power to get Ahmad to sing in front of the class, and to get Sophia's body to make the rash go away."

"So it wasn't a trick, really," Jimmie said. "It was the connection between body and mind, just like Dr. Watson said."

Now everyone turned to look at Sophia, who appeared surprised but not unhappy.

"Oh, very good, Dr. Watson!" she said, clapping her hands.

The professor gave a bow of his head. "Mr. Doyle is right. Franz Mesmer's ideas of animal magnetism were discredited long ago," he said. "And yet, no one could deny that he *did* help his patients. Eventually, scientists realized that his power came not from his strange instruments but from his ability to put his patients into a hypnotic state in which the mind was more open to suggestions. He used a deep, calming tone of voice and some kind of visual aid to make their eyes tired. Once they were in this state, Mesmer would suggest that the patient heal, and they would take his suggestion without ever knowing they had."

"What about Ahmad?" Pocket asked. "There was nothing wrong with him!"

"No," Dr. Watson said with a fond look at Ahmad. "But I

know him to be a natural-born performer. I trusted he would need only the slightest encouragement to put on a show."

Ahmad grinned.

"It is an important thing to remember, as you start your studies here at Baskerville Hall. The mind is more powerful than we know. The only limitations it has are the ones we set on it. Now, if you'll kindly turn your attention to my friend Napoleon here. . . ."

Dr. Watson pushed his wheelchair over to the skeleton in the corner and began a lecture on the musculoskeletal system as the class scrambled to take notes.

At the end of the lesson, he waved Arthur over to his desk.

"Well done for seeing through my little trick, Mr. Doyle. Too often we are distracted by life's stage props." He gestured to the baquet. "We miss the truths they are trying to distract us *from*."

"Thank you, sir," Arthur said. "It was a pretty excellent demonstration."

"You flatter me," the doctor replied. He hesitated. "You know . . . you do remind me of a very dear friend."

"Who, sir?" Arthur asked. "And how—"

He'd been going to ask how Dr. Watson had known his name. After all, he'd had to ask Sophia for hers.

But at that moment, Sophia herself arrived at Arthur's side to thank Dr. Watson, and Arthur was left on his own to wonder.

SIXTEEN

Magic Made Knowable

WHEN THE CLASS FILED INTO PROFESSOR Grey's laboratory, Pocket seemed on the verge of nervous collapse.

"Breathe, Pocket," Irene said. "It's not as if she's a god."

"But she *is* like a god," Pocket retorted, finally exhaling. "She understands electricity, which is like a sort of magic power."

"Gods don't practice magic," said Jimmie. "Witches do."

"I suppose I've been called worse things in my day," came a deep, velvety voice.

Jimmie paled as they all turned to see Professor Grey sitting on a stool beside the door. She was slender and sat very straight, giving her a spry appearance despite her wrinkled face. Her blue eyes flashed at them.

"I'm very sorry, Professor," Jimmie said. "I didn't mean—"

"Please forgive my friend," Pocket interrupted. "Well, he's not really my friend. We only met yesterday. In fact, I'm not even sure if I like him. Oh, by the way, I'm Mary. Mary Morstan. Most people call me Pocket. You can call me whatever you want."

She finished off her strange introduction by teetering into a curtsy.

"I'm sure Pocket will do very nicely," said the professor. "And you need not cast aside your friend just yet. Science is simply magic made knowable. So, you might say that witches were some of the earliest scientists. Take a seat, please."

Where Dr. Watson's room had been brimming with specimens in jars, Professor Grey's laboratory gleamed with hulking contraptions that Arthur couldn't even begin to fathom. In front of each seat was a glass bottle partially filled with water and stoppered with a cork. Through each cork, a wire poked out.

"What do you see?" Professor Grey asked as she glided up to the front.

"Just a glass bottle," Irene said, "with some water inside."

"Anything else?"

"There's a wire coming through the cork," Harriet called.

"I'm going to count to three," Professor Grey said. "On my count, you will take a gentle hold of the end of the wire. One . . . two . . . *three*."

No sooner had Arthur pinched the wire than he felt a sharp burst of pain in his hand. He jerked it back. By the yelps of his classmates, he could tell that they had all felt the same thing. Grey didn't even blink.

"Now," she said, "who can tell me what else is in that bottle?"

Pocket raised a shaking hand. "It's electricity," she said. "They're Leyden jars."

"Very good. And can you tell us what that means?"

Pocket lifted her chin. "A Leyden jar is a container that stores static electricity. The wires conduct that electricity into the glass bottle, where it remains trapped, ready to discharge into our fingers as soon as they come in contact with the wires."

"Very good," said Professor Grey, and Pocket beamed. "Electricity is one of many invisible forces that exist all around us, shaping our lives in countless ways. We've only just started to dream of the ways *we* might shape *it.* In this class, we will learn about such forces. We will study the process of alchemy—the transformation of something ordinary and unseen, like friction, into a something extraordinary, like a sudden lightning strike. In this class, you will learn to dream, because no purely rational mind could ever conceive of the future in which we might one day live—where we can use knowledge to reshape the world in infinite ways. That future is coming, if only we are lucky enough to live to see it."

As she spoke, Arthur found that he was hanging on her every word. He remembered what Pocket had said about a world with electric lights and carriages, and he imagined going back to Edinburgh to find it whizzing and whirring with fantastic machines. He envisioned the skies crowded with airships like Headmaster Challenger's, and the streets bustling with people who were no longer burdened with illness, because their minds had healed them.

It was a spectacular dream.

Later, when the rest of the class left for lunch, Pocket stayed to ask Professor Grey to autograph a copy of a pamphlet she had published years earlier on the work of female scientists, which Pocket had read several dozen times. She reappeared in the buttery as Arthur was blowing the steam from his first bite of steak-and-kidney pie.

"You'll never believe it," Pocket said, slumping down between Irene and Grover. "Professor Grey is *leaving.* She's going to retire after this term!"

"Well, she is very old," Irene said. "So yes, I can believe it."

"But can you believe my luck?" Pocket moaned. "I've wanted to meet her for years. Now I'm here, and she's going. Is there any pie left?"

Irene slid her plate over to Pocket. "You can have mine. Honestly, steak-and-kidney pie? I'd give my left arm for a ham sandwich."

"At least she invited me to be part of her research group," Pocket said, tucking into Irene's portion of pie. "I'll get to assist her with her experiments after classes. So I'll just have to learn as much as possible before she goes."

"That's the spirit," Arthur said.

"Speaking of spirits," Grover droned, "when do you think we'll get to take Psychical Sciences? I'm very eager to begin my communications with the dead. I've already come up with an extensive list of questions for William Shakespeare and Catherine the Great."

Arthur's and Jimmie's eyes met across the table. Then they looked away just as quickly, for fear they would both dissolve into laughter.

"Welcome to the conservatory," Professor Loring said half an hour later, as the class filtered inside. Loring was a small, wiry man with a balding pate, unruly hair, and dirt under all his fingernails.

"How spectacular," Irene murmured, taking in the cavernous room. In front of them, an enormous, gnarled tree had erupted from the jade floor tiles and stretched up past the glass dome ceiling that its branches had mostly shattered. The rest of the room was inhabited by clumps of man-sized ferns and snarled webs of vicious-looking vines.

"As you can already see," Loring went on, "Baskerville Hall is home to hundreds of species of plants, trees, fungi, and animals, some of them found nowhere else in the world."

Arthur remembered Didi the not-quite-dodo, who Professor Challenger had said was the last of her kind.

Loring spoke very quickly, as though his tongue couldn't quite keep up with his thoughts.

"All the animals—that is, the dangerous ones at least—are kept in our vivariums, so you needn't worry about a crocodile popping out for an afternoon snack." He let out a loud *AHA!* that Arthur took to be a laugh. "However, many of our plants are poisonous, even lethal. Most are confined to the poison garden, but some must be grown in other areas. They look innocent, mind you. Even the most poisonous, like hemlock, can often be confused with parsnip or carrot plants."

"That's very . . . inconvenient," said Pocket.

"Unless you have an enemy you need getting rid of," muttered someone. Arthur turned to see Sebastian staring straight at him.

Jimmie rolled his eyes. "Don't pay attention to him," he said. "He's still sore you beat him in the match yesterday."

"I'm not worried," Arthur said. In fact, he was surprised it had taken Sebastian this long to continue their battle outside the

ring. He had been expecting it all day, but Sebastian had seemed entirely focused on their lessons. "But . . . if Sebastian ever asks me round for tea, I think I'll pass."

Professor Loring was gesturing for the class to follow him through a narrow passageway that connected the conservatory to the glasshouses. He wore rubber boots that squeaked as he walked and left faint muddy footprints in his wake.

When they emerged from the dark tunnel, Arthur felt as though they had landed on a different continent. The air was thick and steamy, lush with the scent of greenery. They were still standing in a corridor, but this one had walls made entirely of glass. At regular intervals, doors off both sides led into a series of glasshouses.

"The glasshouses are each set up to mimic a different environment," Professor Loring explained, "or cater to a specific type of species. We have tropical and subtropical houses, desert houses, orchid houses, swamp houses, carnivorous plant houses. There are thirty in all."

"Carnivorous plants, sir?" Ahmad repeated. "Like plants that eat . . . meat?"

"Insects, mostly. Some can eat mice and even shrews. That's only the species we've discovered, mind."

Arthur was trying his best to pay attention, but he was distracted by the glimpses of all the tiny glasshouses they were passing. Here was one taken up almost entirely with an enormous vat of water, its surface covered in water lilies of every imaginable hue. There was one that was home to all number of spindly plants with needles sticking out in all directions. Some houses were a riot of color. The air in another rippled with hundreds of translucent butterflies, each wing like a tiny glass window.

"And these are our vivariums," Loring said. "Home to animals rather than plants. Here you can see one of our most interesting occupants."

He came to a stop in front of a particularly large glasshouse. Arthur glanced in, then did a double take. Between clumps of palms sat a heavyset girl with frizzy hair. Sitting across from her was a hulking figure with wide amber eyes, a snub nose, and reddish-brown hair covering its body.

"Meet Lucky," said Loring, his chest swelling proudly. "Our resident chimpanzee. We call him that because he was rescued from a circus, where his keeper had beaten him within an inch of his life."

The poor animal would have been much luckier if he'd never had to be rescued at all, Arthur thought sadly.

There was something laid out between Lucky and the girl.

"Sir," Arthur said, hardly believing his eyes. "Are they playing *cards*?"

Loring nodded. "Sinead here has been Lucky's closest companion ever since he arrived. He was only a baby then. She has been making a study of his intellectual capabilities. Lucky is exceptionally good at playing Memory, though he hasn't gotten the hang of whist just yet."

"Can we meet him?" asked Irene.

"Certainly not," Loring said, pointing to a sign on the door that said KEEP OUT. "In addition to possessing an astonishing intellect, chimps are five times stronger than a human man. When provoked, they can become quite aggressive. That's why I always keep Lucky's habitat locked except when Sinead is in with

him. Now, if you'll turn your attention this way—"

Arthur turned reluctantly to join Grover at the back of the group when he heard a cry behind him.

"Lucky, NO!"

Everyone whirled around at the same time. The door to Lucky's habitat was now wide open, and the chimpanzee was standing in the doorway, his eyes darting back and forth.

"Who opened this door?" Professor Loring hissed, edging toward the front of the class.

"*Tsk tsk*, Arthur," murmured a voice in Arthur's ear. "How could you do something so reckless?"

Sebastian was standing there, looking the picture of concerned innocence, while Roland smirked next to him.

"I didn't—" Arthur spluttered. "Wait. *You* opened it, didn't you?"

"We saw you do it with our own eyes," Roland said. "So it's two against one."

Arthur felt rage rising in his chest. He took a step toward Sebastian, but as he did, he accidentally knocked into Grover, who dropped his notebook to the ground.

"My grave rubbings!" he cried as the papers flew everywhere.

Irene tried to take hold of his arm. "Grover, leave them!"

But before she could grab him, Grover had darted forward.

Lucky bared his teeth at the boy, who was now kneeling just a few feet from the chimpanzee, desperately trying to collect his papers. Grover looked up and whimpered, clutching his rubbings to his chest.

If someone didn't do something, and quickly, Grover would be the one in need of an obituary.

SEVENTEEN

A Lucky Break

"PEOPLE WHO DIE SUDDEN DEATHS OFTEN can't fully pass over to the spirit world, you know," Grover whispered, his lips trembling. Then he let out a noise that was something between a squeak and a moan.

"Be quiet, boy," Professor Loring muttered through gritted teeth.

"Lucky, come back inside," called Sinead. All the color had drained from her face.

But Lucky didn't seem to hear. He took another step forward and bared his teeth.

Irene gasped. Grover whimpered. Even Sebastian was now looking a bit afraid.

Think, Arthur, think.

He didn't believe the chimpanzee really wanted to attack

Grover. But when he darted forward, Grover had scared the animal, who already had plenty of reasons to be scared of humans. If only there was a way to calm Lucky down and make him understand he was safe.

That's it!

He tried to remember exactly what Dr. Watson had said about Mesmer's tactics. *He used a deep, calming tone of voice and some kind of visual aid to make their eyes tired.*

"I need your pocket watch," he said to Irene.

"What? Why?"

"Just trust me."

Irene unclipped the watch from her lapel and handed it to Arthur. If chimpanzees could play cards like humans, could they be hypnotized, too?

He was about to find out.

"Lucky!" he called, trying to keep his voice low, firm, and calm.

The chimpanzee turned to bare his teeth at Arthur.

"It's all right," Arthur spoke slowly. "You are safe. You are not in danger."

As he spoke, he held up the pocket watch and let it swing from its chain.

Lucky didn't look convinced. In the next instant, he was charging toward Arthur.

Run! screamed a voice in Arthur's head.

But there was nowhere to go. Lucky was blocking the way they had come. He would have to stand his ground.

He kept swinging the watch.

"No one here is going to hurt you," he said, doing his best

impression of Dr. Watson. "No human will ever hurt you again."

Arthur braced himself as the chimpanzee closed in on him. It was now or never.

"Slow down now," Arthur murmured. "Stop, Lucky."

At the sound of his name, the chimpanzee came to a sudden halt. Arthur could feel the animal's hot breath on his cheek. Lucky had finally taken an interest in the watch. He narrowed his eyes, curious. Arthur kept swinging it back and forth, back and forth. The chimpanzee's eyes followed.

"Good, Lucky," he said soothingly. "Keep looking at the watch. That's it."

The snarl fell away from the animal's face. His eyes began to glaze. *It was working!* Meanwhile, Sinead was inching out of Lucky's habitat and toward him.

"Come on, Lucky," she cooed. "Let's finish our game, shall we? I'm sure you were about to beat me."

"Go with Sinead," Arthur said. "You want to go with her."

Lucky blinked, then slowly turned and walked back to the door, where Sinead gave his arm a gentle stroke.

As soon as Lucky was back in his habitat, Professor Loring shut the door behind him, then quickly locked it.

Grover stood, then went limp. Ahmad rushed to catch him.

Arthur finally allowed himself to breathe a shaky sigh of relief.

Loring turned back to face his students. His face was beet red. He trained his eyes on Arthur. "You . . ." he started. "That . . . that was . . ."

"Completely BRILLIANT!" Pocket exclaimed.

"But, sir," Sebastian cut in. His jaw was twitching madly. "Arthur was the one who—"

"Saved Grover's life," Irene finished as she took back her pocket watch with a bit more force than Arthur had been expecting. He remembered that it had been given to her by her father. And judging by how heavy it was, it was likely quite valuable.

Lucky and Sinead were once again sitting across from each other, as if nothing had ever happened. Sinead looked up and gave Arthur a weak smile.

"You . . . you saved me," Grover said, blinking his wide eyes at Arthur. "If not for you, I would be but a shade wandering the land for eternity."

"Well, you're welcome," Arthur said, his cheeks flushing.

"Three cheers for Arthur!" Ahmad called.

"Absolutely not," Loring snapped. "We won't disturb Lucky any longer. Class is over. Dismissed."

"But, sir!" Roland tried.

The crowd of students was already pushing him and Sebastian back down the corridor.

"First years," Arthur heard the professor mutter to no one in particular. "It's always something with first years."

EIGHTEEN

The Unsolved Mysteries of the *Baskerville Bugle*

WORD OF ARTHUR'S RECKLESS BRAVERY spread quickly, so that by the next morning, it seemed everyone had heard. At breakfast, the second years made Arthur sit at the middle of the long table so they could hear him repeat the story. Arthur—who didn't even like giving a speech in front of the class at his old school—was relieved when Headmaster Challenger interrupted to ask him for a word and Ahmad took over. Many pairs of eyes followed them as they strode from the room. When he chanced a look up, Arthur was surprised to see that even the strange pair from the Circle of the Spirit—Thomas and Ollie, who usually seemed to be lost in their own world—were staring at him as he passed.

"Doyle," the headmaster boomed, once they had reached the hall. "I hear you hypnotized Loring's chimp just before it ripped Kumar to shreds?"

"I did, sir," said Arthur.

"I'd better never hear of you doing something so foolish ever again," he said. Then, in a lower voice, "That's what Loring and Hudson have told me to say, anyway. But you've saved me from writing a very awkward letter to the boy's parents. I only wish I'd been there to see it myself."

The headmaster was already striding away when a strikingly tall girl with dark, curly hair cropped close to her head approached Arthur. "Hey, could I borrow you?" she said. "For an interview. You'll only miss a few minutes of first period."

"An interview?"

"I'm Afia, Circle of the Citadel. I work for the school paper," she explained. "Sinead told me you're the one who hypnotized the chimp. I want to write a story about you."

Arthur wasn't sure. But then he had a sudden vision of Sebastian's face as he read a newspaper article all about Arthur's heroism. Even better, he thought of his father pinning it up on his study wall with the rest of his clippings. Perhaps it would remind him of the promise he had made to take care of the family while Arthur was gone.

"All right," he said. "As long as it doesn't take too long."

The girl grinned. "Follow me."

She led Arthur up to the second floor, where he hadn't yet been. They passed the doors of a few faculty offices, including one with dried herbs hung above it, whose nameplate read *Agatha Fox*. Under the name, someone had stuck a sign to the door that read: *Professor Fox is away with the fairies*.

"Is that sign . . ."

"Serious? Oh yes," said Afia. "Professor Fox teaches Psychical

Sciences—she's the head of the Circle of Spirit. She's often away for weeks at a time and comes back claiming to have traveled *beyond the veil*. I tried to use that once as an excuse for skipping class with Professor Loring, and he made me bathe the porcupines as punishment. Still, her Circle seems to grow larger every year, though it's still tiny compared to the other four. You'll see them around. Some of them like to wear white."

Arthur was about to reply when a sudden din of clanging and bonging made him jump. Afia laughed. "That's just the horology clubroom," she explained, opening the door on her left to reveal a room packed full of clocks, each marking the hour with its own distinct noise.

"Horology?" Arthur repeated.

"People who like to fix clocks," Afia said. "Apparently, Lord Baker—the original owner of the school—was a bit obsessed with them, and there's some condition that his collection has to be kept here forever. So we have a horology club, even though I'm sure no one's been a member in at least thirty years."

Arthur took in the rows and rows of clock faces. There were elaborately carved cuckoo clocks and dusty ship clocks, golden mantel clocks and silver pendulum clocks, and even a large sundial in the center of the floor. Every bit of space had been taken up with clocks except a large gap in the middle of the far wall.

Just as the last one stopped chiming, Arthur heard a whistle and turned to find Afia halfway down the hallway, waving him on impatiently.

He joined her as she strode into a large room. Inside, Arthur's eyes were immediately drawn to an enormous black machine in one corner. It was shaped a bit like a sculpture of a horse made by

someone who had never actually seen a horse. There was a tray with a lever to one side and some kind of wheel underneath. Atop it perched a golden eagle.

"That's our printing press," Afia said. "It's an American design. They love their eagles, don't they? We'll just sit over here."

She jerked her head toward the opposite end of the room. There were several long wooden desks, each with its own gas lamp. Most of them were strewn with papers. Atop one, a large curly-haired boy rested his feet while reading a magazine called *The Spectator*.

Afia plopped down at the last desk and began searching the drawers. "Let me just find my favorite pen. I'm lost without it."

As she shuffled through her things, Arthur took in the back wall, where old editions of the *Baskerville Bugle* had been pinned to a corkboard. Above them, someone had pinned a page with one word written across it: *UNSOLVED*.

He stepped closer, scanning the articles. One was about multiple reported sightings of a will-o'-the-wisp in the woods surrounding the school. Another concerned a mysterious explosion that detonated in Professor Loring's prized peony bed ("PEONY PRANK GONE WRONG OR SINISTER PLANT PLOT AT PLAY?"). Two of the articles were pinned together. Though one had been written back in 1789 and the other in 1825, the headlines bore a strong resemblance to each other. "SECOND YEAR STUDENT ON MEDICAL LEAVE AFTER BEING CLOBBERED BY FALLING PORTRAIT," read the first. "PROFESSOR LEAVES IN 'ADDLED STATE' AFTER NARROWLY ESCAPING DEATH-BY-PAINTING," announced the second.

"Fascinating, isn't it?" said a boy's voice. Arthur turned to see the boy with the magazine staring at him. He spoke with an Irish lilt and wore an amused smile. "What are the odds that the same painting would fall on not one but *two* different people passing by, over thirty years apart?"

"It was the same painting both times?"

The boy nodded. "It's a huge portrait of Lord Baker. Apparently, he hated the likeness when it was done. And he had a point. It's not a very good painting at all."

Afia laughed. "Oscar's right. His eyes look like they're staring in two different directions, and he's making a face like someone just stepped on his toe. But legend has it that if you say anything bad about the painting as you walk by, his ghost will push it off the wall to get revenge."

"That's it?" Arthur asked. "That's the explanation for why two different people in two different decades were nearly crushed by the same portrait?"

Oscar arched an eyebrow. "Don't let his lordship hear you dismissing his spirit like that."

Arthur had always been interested in the idea that ghosts might walk among the living. The idea that one might be out to seriously injure anyone who insulted his portrait, however, seemed rather unlikely.

"Neither of the victims ever returned after they left," Afia said. "They weren't as lucky as your friend Grover. No one was there to save them. Speaking of which . . ."

She had finally found her favorite pen. She dipped it into her inkwell and began taking notes, as Arthur recounted the story once more.

After he had answered all her questions, Afia set her pen down and sat back in her chair. "I think I've got all I need," she

said. “Unless there’s anything else?”

Arthur hesitated. Something had been niggling at him, something that would have occupied his mind more if he hadn’t been so busy settling into life at Baskerville Hall. Of everything that fascinated him, the one thing that topped them all was an unsolved mystery. “Actually,” he said, “there is something else.”

“Oh?”

“Have you heard anything about a break-in?” he asked. “Something that happened just a couple of days ago?”

Afia and Oscar exchanged a look. “How do you know about that?” Afia asked.

“Well, the window on the front door was smashed, for one thing.”

“But that could have been anything,” said Oscar. “A cricket ball. A directionally challenged robin.”

“I heard some of the professors talking about it, too,” Arthur admitted.

Afia’s face cleared. “Oh,” she said. “Well, keep it to yourself for now, will you? I’m working on an investigation, and I don’t want the story getting out before we go to print.”

So Arthur *had* been right. “Was anything taken?” he asked.

Afia leaned in closer. “Well, that’s the strange thing,” she said. “Nothing has been reported missing. Why go to all the trouble of breaking in if you’re not going to steal anything?”

Arthur frowned, thinking. “Unless they were looking for something they couldn’t find?”

“Possible, I guess.” Afia shrugged. “Anyway, they’re still taking it pretty seriously.”

“What do you mean?”

She pointed at the windows, which had a pair of iron bars fitted over them.

"Someone installed them last night. Over every window in the manor."

Arthur stared at the bars, wondering how he hadn't noticed this before.

Just as they reached the doorway, the door flew open, and a familiar face appeared.

"Grover!"

"Oh, hello, Arthur," said Grover.

"Grover Kumar?" Afia asked. "So you're the one Arthur saved! I was going to find you later, but this is even better. I can interview you now."

"Interview me? But I haven't even applied yet."

Afia frowned. "Applied for what?"

"I was coming to ask if the *Baskerville Bugle* was in need of a necrologist," Grover replied.

Afia's frown deepened.

"It's someone who writes obituaries," Arthur supplied.

"Oh . . . Well, we're pretty well staffed already," Afia said. "Tess does our 'Dear Tess' column, Winnie does Opinions, and Oscar here does Arts and Culture."

Grover hung his head with a sigh. Arthur shot an imploring look at Afia. *"Please,"* he mouthed.

"Fine. I suppose you could bring us a writing sample," she said reluctantly.

Grover straightened again. "Thank you!" he cried. "I will write you the best obituary you've ever read!"

Then he sprinted from the room, giving what Arthur thought

might have been a shriek of glee. Arthur watched as he ran down the hallway and straight into a tall boy in white coming out of Professor Fox's office. The boy glared at Grover and seemed about to give him a telling off when Oscar intervened.

"Leave the little tykes alone, Thomas," he called out. "You've only yourself to blame anyhow. Should have seen it coming in your crystal ball."

The boy sneered at Oscar, while Grover squeaked out an apology before scampering away.

"Wait!" cried Afia. "What about the interview? Oh, never mind, he's gone." She turned back to Arthur. "He's a little *strange*, isn't he? Who does he think he's going to write an obituary for? I mean, nobody's died yet."

She laughed at her joke, but a shiver snaked up Arthur's spine as he glanced out the barred window. The bars were meant to protect the school from someone on the outside. But what did that someone want? And how far were they willing to go to get it? He thought of the rider in green atop a dark horse he had seen in the forest when he'd first arrived. Were they part of this puzzle?

The words echoed in Arthur's head. *Nobody's died . . . yet.*

NINETEEN

The Clover

SOMETHING WASN'T RIGHT.

When Arthur awoke at dawn the next morning, there was a strange charge in the air, as though someone had just been there. And what had awoken him? The brigadier hadn't yet started with his horn.

As Arthur sat up, he heard a crinkling noise. He shifted his pillow and found, to his astonishment, something that hadn't been there the night before.

It was a note addressed to him.

Arthur squinted to make out the words in the gray light. The letter was written on stiff parchment in emerald-green ink.

For the second time in under a week, he found himself in possession of a quite unexpected invitation.

You are cordially invited to appear before the members of the Clover tonight at midnight. Bring a three-leaf clover with you to obtain entry. Tell no one.

"You got one, too, huh?"

Arthur looked up from the invitation to see that Jimmie was also awake, and staring down at an identical piece of paper.

"What's the Clover?" Arthur asked.

"It's a secret society," Jimmie replied. "It's like a shortcut to success and power. My father was a member, so I knew I would get an invitation. I just wasn't expecting it to come quite so soon."

He nibbled on a hangnail as he spoke, as though he were anxious about something.

"A *secret society*?" Arthur echoed. "Like with passwords and rituals? What do you mean it's a shortcut to success?"

"Well, members graduate and many of them go on to be politicians and generals and judges—things like that. Then they help the members who graduate after them to become the same. And so on."

This didn't sound like an exactly fair way to choose who became powerful members of society, thought Arthur. But . . . a shortcut to success was exactly what he needed to help his family.

"Why do they want *me*?" he asked.

"Maybe they heard about you saving Grover," Jimmie replied, sliding his legs out of bed and stretching. "But don't get ahead of yourself. They haven't decided if they want you *or* me yet."

"But the invitation—"

"Is a test," Jimmie said. "And it's only the first. Notice how they didn't tell us *where* to meet?"

Arthur frowned. In his excitement, he hadn't noticed this missing detail.

"Well then, we'd better figure out where this meeting is," Arthur said. "And find a clover on the way to breakfast."

But someone beat them to the task. When Arthur and Jimmie emerged from the tower a few minutes later, they spotted a familiar figure at the edge of the lawn, crouched down in the tall grass.

"Irene!" Arthur exclaimed. "Did you get—"

Her head shot up. "Stop shouting!" she hissed.

"You're looking for a clover, aren't you?" Arthur murmured, when they were beside her.

Irene glanced over her shoulder. It was still early, so no one else was around. "We aren't supposed to talk about it."

Arthur grinned. "So you *did* get an invitation!"

He was relieved he wouldn't have to keep his own invitation a secret from his friend.

"Have you found any yet?" Jimmie asked, running his boot over the grass and peering down.

"Not a single one," Irene said, annoyed. "They've let the grass grow too high for clover to grow. I've been searching for a while now."

"There's got to be some around here," Arthur said. "We'll find them."

"That'll be the easy part," said Jimmie. "The hard part is figuring out where to go tonight."

"I bet they have some kind of hidden clubhouse," Arthur

mused. "Your father didn't tell you where?"

"He wouldn't tell me anything," Jimmie muttered. "Only that I had better be accepted."

Arthur suddenly understood why his friend seemed so anxious.

"We'll find it," he said. "Don't worry. I need to get in, too. I'll have to provide for my family one day soon, so I need all the help I can get."

Jimmie and Irene both looked up in surprise.

"Surely your father will provide for them?" Jimmie asked.

Arthur was quiet for a moment. He had been careful not to share too much about his family with his new friends. Could he really trust them?

He thought of Irene squeezing his shoulder before he followed Sebastian into the boxing ring on their first afternoon. Then of Jimmie refusing to sit with Sebastian and Roland later that evening.

"My father is ill," he said finally. "He . . . drinks quite a lot. It interferes with his work. So there's not much money. And there won't be, unless I find a way to make it. That's the reason I'm here. To ensure that one day I can get a job that will allow me to take care of my family."

Irene took hold of Arthur's arm and gave it a gentle squeeze. "I'm sorry," she said. "I didn't know that about your father."

"And it's noble of you," Jimmie added, "to want to take care of them all."

"Yes," Irene agreed. "But you're wrong about one thing. That's not why you're here."

"What do you mean?"

"You're here because you have the ability to do something wonderful in the world. Someone saw that and decided it couldn't go to waste. So they invited you."

Arthur felt a wistful smile on his lips. Irene had just reminded him of his own mother's words. *"I've always believed you were destined for greatness."*

"You'll find a way to take care of your family *and* do something brilliant," Irene went on. "I mean, you've only been here a few days and already you've saved Grover's life."

"And at least there's no one forcing you into the family business," Jimmie said, kicking a rock.

Arthur was going to ask what exactly the family business *was*, but before he could get a word in, Jimmie spoke again. "What about you, Irene? Do your parents want you to follow in their footsteps?"

"No," Irene replied, crouching down again. "Which is a good thing because I'm no nightingale when it comes to singing. They just want me to do what makes me happy."

"Where are they now?" Jimmie asked.

"Paris. They said they would write every week. AHA!"

She parted two clumps of grass to reveal a bunch of three-leafed clovers trying to grow between them.

She had just handed Arthur and Jimmie each a clover when Arthur detected a flash of movement through the trees close by.

"Did you see that?" he asked the others.

The next instant, something came hurtling out of the forest.

SQUAAAAAAWK!

Didi the not-quite-dodo flapped her feeble wings and jutted her long neck out at him in protest. Arthur let out a laugh.

"I thought there was someone there. But it was just Didi."

He explained to the others what Challenger had told him about the bird.

Irene shook her head. "It's quite sad if you think about it," she said. "It must be lonely to be the last of your kind. What's a nest without an egg inside it?"

Until that very moment, Arthur had not realized how lonely *he* had been, carrying around his father's secret. Now Irene and Jimmie knew, and he felt as though a veil between them had been lifted.

"Speaking of eggs," Jimmie said, "I'm starving."

And so, with his clover tucked securely in his pocket, Arthur headed for breakfast, shoulder to shoulder with his new best friends.

They spent the first half of breakfast quietly exchanging ideas about where the Clover's headquarters might be. The old boathouse? The stables? An attic or a cellar somewhere? Meanwhile, Pocket was trying to explain some complicated electrical drawing she had made to Grover, whose eyes were following a fly that buzzed from place to place across the table. In other words, they both seemed completely normal. Arthur took this to mean that they probably hadn't received invitations.

So, he thought miserably, *I'm going to have to keep secrets from my friends after all.* Well, there was nothing he could do about that. He had to put his family first.

Their hushed conversation was interrupted by the doors banging open and Headmaster Challenger appearing. Everyone quieted and turned to look. His face was streaked with soot, and when he opened his mouth, he gave a great yawn.

"I won't keep you from your breakfasts for long," he said. "I have no wish to enter into Cook's bad books."

Cook gave a tight smile from the corner.

"I just came to announce the arrival of Valencia Fernandez."

A few people, including Irene, gasped. Arthur had no idea who Challenger was talking about.

"Dr. Fernandez is a renowned paleontologist," the headmaster continued, "meaning she specializes in the study of dinosaurs. She has conducted digs all over the world and has just returned from an expedition through islands off her native Argentina. I have offered her use of our facilities to carry out her studies on the artifacts she uncovered, and in exchange, she will be teaching a few classes and giving a presentation later this term."

The headmaster opened his mouth as though to say something else but seemed to think better of it. "That's all," he said. "Please return to your porridge before it congeals."

The hall filled with an excited buzz. Even Irene and Jimmie were exchanging tidbits of information they had gleaned about Fernandez from newspaper articles and pamphlets. Her visit sounded exciting to Arthur, too, but he knew he would have to set thoughts of meeting a real-life explorer aside for now if he wanted to have any chance of figuring out where the Clover would be meeting that night. He cleared his throat.

"We've got work to do," he said. "And not a moment to lose."

TWENTY

The Green Knight

HALFWAY THROUGH DR. WATSON'S CLASS, when they were taking turns finding their pulses and listening to one another's chests with stethoscopes, Jimmie suddenly had an idea.

"What we need," he murmured, "is a map of the school. Or even better, the plans from when it was originally built. We could see if there's anything in the plans that isn't on the map. Some kind of secret room or structure."

"Good idea," Irene said. "But where would we find something like that?"

"Like what?" murmured a voice.

They all turned to see Dr. Watson sitting just behind them, a pleasant smile on his face.

"I'm sorry, Dr. Watson," said Arthur quickly. "We were just

discussing, um, whether there are some shortcuts in the school we don't know about. So we can get to our classes more quickly."

"Is that right?" asked Watson, with an arch of his brow. "My, how industrious of you."

Arthur tried to will the flush from creeping up into his cheeks.

"We were wondering where we could find maps of the school," Irene went on. She spoke with admirable confidence, but Arthur noticed that her fingers were fidgeting with the chain of her pocket watch.

"I see," said Watson. "Well, in that case, you'd better look in the map section of the library. Top floor, I believe. Now, how are you getting on with your stethoscopes? Have you all found your pulses? Let's see."

Before Arthur knew what he was doing, the doctor had taken a gentle hold of his hand and placed a finger on the inside of his wrist.

"Goodness," he said. "Your pulse is quite fast, Mr. Doyle. You'll have to try to keep yourself calmer if you want to get away with lying to your teacher. Mind over matter, remember? Now I suggest you return to your studies. Have you taken a listen to the intestines yet? They are a surprisingly musical organ."

The library was nearly empty when they arrived during their lunch hour. The higher floors of stacks were accessible by rickety, winding staircases much like the one in the tower, except steeper and narrower. The more they climbed, the mustier the air smelled. Arthur inhaled the scent of a thousand old leatherbound books. It was most delightful.

When they were nearly to the top, Irene stopped.

"What's wrong?" Arthur asked.

"I just got a bit dizzy. Haven't these people ever heard of a normal staircase? Let me just—"

But she was interrupted by the sound of footsteps above, coming their way.

"I'm telling you," came a distressed voice, "I've looked at these maps a hundred times."

"And I'm telling *you* that the Green Knight made it clear how important it was to find it quickly and keep it safe," replied a much deeper voice. "If we don't secure it before *he* returns—"

"You don't have to remind me," the first voice—a girl's—murmured. "But I can't simply discover something that doesn't exist. We're just going to have to keep looking."

The staircase groaned as the two speakers stepped onto it. Jimmie, Irene, and Arthur scrambled back down as soundlessly as they could, then ducked onto the first landing they came to. Arthur badly wanted to see the speakers, but he didn't want to be seen himself. They sprinted to the end of the nearest bookcase—ducking to keep their heads from grazing the low ceiling—and crouched behind it just as they heard the pair go by. Arthur poked his head out in time to see a dark crop of hair disappearing down the stairs.

Arthur, Jimmie, and Irene stared at one another. Once the sound of footsteps had faded, Arthur peeked over the side of the staircase, hoping to catch a glimpse of whoever they'd overheard. But no one appeared below.

"There must be another way out," Irene said, leaning over the railing next to Arthur. "What do you think that was all about? Were they trying to find the Clover's headquarters, too?"

Arthur shook his head. "I don't think so. They talked about 'securing' something for the Green Knight . . . before someone else returns."

"And who on earth is the Green Knight?"

"Haven't you read *Sir Gawain and the Green Knight*?" Jimmie asked.

Irene stared at him blankly. "Sir who?"

"It's a poem," Arthur explained. "The Green Knight is a character from the King Arthur legends."

"I suppose you *do* know King Arthur?"

Irene rolled her eyes at Jimmie. "I've heard of him, yes. But as you know, we aren't big on kings and knights on my side of the Atlantic."

"Oh, but the stories are wonderful," Arthur said. "My mam used to read them to me before bed. They're full of adventure and chivalry. I dreamed of being a knight when I grew up."

"But there aren't any knights anymore," Jimmie replied. "Not that kind, anyway."

"Right. So the Green Knight must be some kind of a code name for someone," Irene said.

"But for who?" Arthur asked, his mind racing.

An image came to him of a cloaked figure on horseback, deep in the shadows of the forest.

The cloak he'd been wearing was green.

He told the others about what he'd seen. "Could *that* have been the so-called Green Knight, do you think?"

"Maybe," Irene said. "But what is it that he wants? What are they trying to keep safe, and from who?"

Arthur gasped. "The break-in!" he exclaimed. "Maybe whoever

did it was trying to steal the thing that the Green Knight—whoever he is—is trying to keep safe."

"It's a thought," said Jimmie. "But they could have been talking about any number of things. And we've got our own mystery to solve, remember?"

"Yes," Irene agreed. "We need to get to those maps."

Arthur knew they were right.

But he also felt certain that the Green Knight and the break-in were connected. And he was going to find out how.

Arthur, Jimmie, and Irene spent the rest of their lunch hour poring over every map they could find of the school and its grounds. The plans for the original manor house were so old they curled at the edges and felt as though they might crumble in Arthur's hands. They revealed a priest hole behind the first-floor east corridor, which would have been used to hide a Catholic priest during Queen Elizabeth I's Protestant reign. But that was far too small for an entire secret society. Even one priest wouldn't have been comfortable there for very long.

There was a vegetable cellar beneath the buttery, but surely that was no secret. Cook would be down there all the time. And a secret society would want somewhere to meet where they didn't risk being covered in potato peelings.

"They would need somewhere private but roomy," Arthur said.

"Probably somewhere that nobody else would want to go," Irene added.

"Look at this," Jimmie said.

He spread a large, faded scroll across the table they had been using for their research. It seemed at first glance to be a map.

On second glance, however, it revealed itself to be *two* maps.

There was a map of the grounds, recognizable by the pond and the shape of the clearing in the trees. But there were no buildings on it. Overlaid on the first map was a second one, drawn on translucent onionskin paper. This one marked a series of tunnels and chutes leading to a large central chamber.

"It's a *mine*!" Arthur said. "Baskerville Hall is sitting on top of a mine!"

"I wonder what kind of mine it was," Jimmie said. "It's obviously abandoned now."

"So it's private," Arthur mused. "Plenty of space. And nobody else is going to want to go down there. Could *that* be where the Clover's headquarters are?"

"Actually, I don't think so," Irene said. "I'm pretty sure it's right here."

She had carefully peeled back a corner of the school map that had curled in on itself and was pointing to a drawing of a hut just on the edge of the forest. Below the drawing, someone had written something in small green lettering.

Domum Trifolium Incarnatum

"It's Latin," she said.

"What does it mean?" Arthur asked impatiently.

Jimmie looked up, and for the first time all day, a relaxed smile spread over his face. Irene was grinning, too.

"It means 'Clover House,'" she said.

TWENTY-ONE

Domum Trifolium Incarnatum

THERE WAS NO SLEEP TO BE HAD WHEN Arthur and Jimmie returned to their room after dinner that night. They didn't even bother getting undressed. When, after some time, they heard a soft knock at the door, they opened it to find Irene. Her pocket watch read quarter till midnight.

Arthur stepped out, but Irene shook her head. "Toby sleeps downstairs," she whispered. "No way will we make it past him. We have to go the other way."

She grabbed the end of the rope anchored to the floor and gestured for Jimmie to open the window before casting the rope out. Then she disappeared behind it.

When it was his turn to climb, Arthur made sure his clover was still in his pocket and took a deep breath before lowering himself out.

So it was that the trio found themselves clinging to the rope as they shinnied their way down the tower wall, rustling through the ivy and past the windows of their sleeping classmates.

Once they reached the ground, they crept through the inky night. The sky was cloudy, and they hadn't dared bring candles, so they stumbled along using the looming shadows of the buildings to guide them. Once, Arthur was sure he heard the sound of footsteps behind them, but when he turned, he couldn't make out anyone in the dark.

Still, he had the prickling feeling of being followed.

Finally, they reached the northeastern corner of the grounds. Ahead, skeletal trees clawed at the sky. Arthur peered into the darkness, trying to make out the shape of a hut.

"What now?" Irene asked.

"Shhh," Jimmie hissed. "Listen."

The soft sound of chanting could almost have been mistaken for a breeze blowing through the tree boughs. But when Arthur listened closely, he could make out the edges of words.

"It's coming from over there," he whispered, pointing to what looked to be a densely thicketed part of the forest.

As they walked into the trees, damp leaves squashing under their feet, Irene bumped into something.

"Ow!" she cried. "What is that?"

There was just enough light that Arthur could make out the shapes of rounded objects shooting up from the ground at odd angles all around them.

"I think we're in a graveyard," he murmured.

Just who, he wondered with a shiver, was buried here?

"So is this the wrong place?" Jimmie asked.

"I don't think so," Arthur replied. "What better place to meet if you don't want to be seen or disturbed? And look!"

He was certain he had glimpsed a flicker of candlelight glowing from inside a looming shape ahead, which he had taken to be a large thicket. Dodging the tombstones, he led the others toward it.

As they drew near, the shape became quite solid. It was covered in ivy, but when he reached out a hand, he felt stone beneath the vines. His heart quickened when he caught sight of a dull glint from the corner of his eye. *A door handle.*

"This is it!" he said, striding to the door. "We made it!"

He grinned at the others.

"It could easily be mistaken for an old mausoleum," Irene murmured. "Grover would love this."

Arthur's smile faltered. He didn't like being reminded that not all his friends had received an invitation to this club.

"Well?" Jimmie said impatiently. "What are we waiting for then?"

Arthur took hold of the handle and pushed. The door gave way easily. He just had time to see the shapes of several people illuminated in the dim light. The next thing he knew, someone was dropping something over his head. Everything went pitch dark.

"Welcome," boomed a voice, "to Clover House."

"Hand over your clovers," said a girl. Arthur rummaged in his pocket and held his up, then felt someone pluck it away.

"Congratulations," came the first voice—a boy's—again. "You have each been found worthy of—"

He stopped short at the sound of the door creaking open behind them.

"Ah," said the boy. "I see we have one more visitor."

There was something familiar about the voice, but Arthur couldn't quite place it.

"Hello?" someone new called.

Arthur recognized *this* voice right away. He badly wished he didn't.

"Sebastian," Jimmie hissed to his left.

Was it a coincidence, Sebastian arriving only moments after they did? Or had he followed them? Perhaps he hadn't even bothered to look for the Clover House himself. This might have been his plan all along. As long as someone else found their way, his work would be done for him. Arthur's hands balled into fists. He couldn't stand a cheater.

"It's past midnight," came the first boy's voice again. "Lock the door."

There came the heavy sound of a dead bolt being drawn.

"Now," the boy went on. "You have each been found worthy of consideration for entry into the Clover. And you have each passed the first hurdle toward acceptance. Congratulations. Already, one of our invitees has failed to rise to the challenge."

Who? Arthur wondered. *And where do I know this voice from?*

"Some of you might never have heard of us before receiving your invitations. Others might have heard rumors. Some of you even have family members who were members before you. But I assure you, none of you know our true greatness. None of you can imagine the power and the influence we wield. Not until you are one of us. But to become a part of the Clover, you must prove yourself deserving."

Arthur thought he felt a flicker of flame pass by his face.

"We do not choose our members based on creed or class like other elite organizations," said the boy. "We select those with strength of character. That is why you will each undergo a series of three tests, one for each leaf of the clover. We will test your bravery, your honor, and your loyalty. If you fail any one of these tests, you will not be invited to join our number. And I assure you, we shall test you to your very limits. But if you pass, you will be initiated into the Clover. Here, with us, the spoils of your wildest dreams will be at your very fingertips. Without us, they will likely remain ever out of your reach."

Suddenly, Arthur wanted to be a member of the Clover so badly he could almost taste it. The thought was overwhelmingly sweet, like Mrs. Hudson's pineapple tart. For so many years, he had tried not to allow himself to dream. What use was it for a boy like him? But now, he had a chance to dream as big as he liked.

"I will pass our sacred chalice to each of you. If you accept the challenges that lie before you, then drink. Otherwise, you will leave this place tonight, never to return."

Arthur licked his lips. He waited a moment, then heard someone shuffle in front of him.

"Do you choose to drink?" whispered the voice.

"Yes," said Arthur.

As the cold chalice touched his lips, Arthur finally realized where he had heard the boy's voice before. It was the same one he had heard in the library earlier that day, speaking in hushed tones about the Green Knight!

He wasn't sure if it was this sudden surprise or the fact that the liquid in his mouth tasted suspiciously like vinegar, but either way, he began to cough. The sound echoed through the chamber.

Next to him, Jimmie elbowed his side, which only made him cough more.

"You have all chosen to accept our challenge," said the boy. "Now, you must await our summons to your first test. It may come at any time and in any form. Keep your eyes open and your ears to the ground. Be prepared."

Arthur waited for the boy to go on, to give more instructions. But everything was suddenly very silent and very still. He felt himself being led back outside and heard the shuffling sounds of other people moving around him. After a few minutes, the sounds turned to silence.

"Is anyone still there?" Arthur called.

There was no response.

Arthur lifted the hood from his face and found himself standing alone in the dark, empty night.

TWENTY-TWO

A Tale of Two Letters

Dear Mam,

I'm sorry it's taken me so long to write. Thank you for your letter, which I received on Friday. I can't believe I've been here nearly a month. It's good that everyone is doing well, and that Pa is making progress on his painting. Has Constance had her first tooth yet? If so, I hope she isn't a biter like Caroline.

As for me, Baskerville Hall suits just fine. I have many friends and get along well with everyone except

Arthur paused, his pen hovering over the paper on his desk. It was late, and Jimmie snored loudly in bed. Candlelight flickered over Arthur's words, which had gone slightly crooked on the page. He'd been about to write "except for a boy named Sebastian," but changed his mind. He didn't want to give his mother reason to worry. He certainly wasn't going to share what had happened at breakfast that Monday, when Sebastian had switched out the water in his cup for brine. Arthur had spat it all over Irene and Pocket, who were forced to go to Dr. Watson's class smelling like two of his pickled specimens. Arthur clutched the pen tighter as he thought about it.

> ***. . . except that my studies have been keeping me very busy. My roommate is a boy named Jimmie from England. His father sent him a chess set, and we like to play at the end of the day. Jimmie has had years of practice, so he usually beats me, but I am getting better all the time. I am also friends with Irene, a girl from America whose parents sing in operas, and Pocket . . .***

Here Arthur paused again. How, he wondered with amusement, to describe Pocket? He doubted his mother would approve of her habit of keeping small animals on her person, or for that matter, miniature sticks of dynamite. In fact, he had been seeing less of Pocket recently. She'd been spending more and more of her time assisting Professor Grey in her electrical experiments. When they did see her outside of class, she was usually bursting with excitement to tell them about their progress. She swore up and down that they would see an electrical flying machine in their lifetimes.

> *. . . Pocket, who is very passionate about her studies. Oh, and I nearly forgot Grover, who is a funny sort of boy, but nice all the same.*

Arthur smiled when he recalled what had happened the morning before, when Grover had sat down next to him at breakfast.

"I've got something for you," Grover had said, sliding a piece of paper over to Arthur. "Well, it's not *for* you. It's my newspaper audition, but I figured you might like to see it."

Arthur glanced down at the paper, then did a double take. He was looking at his own obituary.

> **"Yesterday morning, at the venerable Baskerville Hall school, Arthur Doyle was taken from this life. After choking on a lemon drop while laughing at one of his own jokes (it wasn't very funny), Doyle could not be resuscitated."**

Arthur read on in disbelief.

"But . . . I'm not dead!" he protested. "And a lot of this stuff isn't even true. I don't have an Aunt Gertrude or a pet badger, and I definitely don't feel passionately about chamber music."

Grover's forehead wrinkled. "Well, I needed to add *some* details. Otherwise it's not very interesting."

"I gave him the idea for the badger," Pocket chimed in. Irene and Jimmie had started reading the obituary, their shoulders shaking with silent laughter. "Frank was a wonderful pet. If only he hadn't been so fond of Da's ankles."

"It *is* quite entertaining," Irene said as she finished reading. "But I'm not sure if it's the right thing for your audition for the newspaper. You need an interesting subject."

"Thanks a lot!" Arthur said.

"You know what I mean," Irene continued. "Grover needs someone who he doesn't have to make things up about. Someone who's already had amazing experiences and achieved great things."

"Like Professor Grey!" Pocket exclaimed. "Most people couldn't do in ten lifetimes what she's done in hers so far. *And* she's leaving at the end of term, which is almost like dying. They might even publish it as a kind of tribute to her."

Grover's eyes lit up. "Of course!" he said. "It's perfect. I've got to ask her if I can do an interview. Right now! Is my breath okay?"

Grover took out the little tin from his pocket where he kept his lemon drops and popped one in his mouth. "There," he said. "That's better. Would anyone else like one?"

He had offered the tin to Arthur, who, remembering his obituary, politely declined.

Arthur yawned. It must have been getting very late, but he wanted to finish the letter to his mam, which was extremely overdue. He quickly dashed off a few more lines.

> ***I am learning lots in all my classes. I really like boxing, but my favorite class is Anatomy with Dr. Watson. He is a very kind man, and his lessons***

are never boring. Perhaps I will be a doctor one day, too. We are meant to apply for a field of study—they call them Circles here—by the time we're second years, but I have no idea which one to choose. They're just all so fascinating! But I'll figure it out one day, I'm sure. I am doing everything I can to make you proud.

Ever your loving son,
Arthur

He set aside the letter with a sigh and was about to fall into bed when he heard footsteps out in the stairway. A second later, a creamy envelope came sliding underneath his door.

Arthur's heart leapt. Finally, another letter from the Clover! It had already been nearly three weeks since the meeting in the Clover House. If not for the fact that Jimmie and Irene had also heard nothing, Arthur would have already decided the Clover had changed their minds about him.

He was across the room in two bounds and was about to call out to Jimmie when he saw the name on the envelope. He picked up the letter to examine it more closely.

It wasn't addressed to him. It was addressed to Irene and had been posted from France.

Arthur opened the door, but no one was there.

It didn't make any sense. Who had left him a letter obviously meant for Irene? And, perhaps more important, why?

Valencia Fernandez

ARTHUR TOLD JIMMIE ABOUT THE LETTER as they washed and dressed the next morning.

"Did you open it?" Jimmie asked.

"Of course not," Arthur said, offended by the very suggestion that he might violate a friend's privacy.

There was a chill in the air as they walked to the manor, and the sky was a heavy gray that heralded the nearing of November. Arthur was grateful for the rush of warmth that greeted them as they entered the hall.

As they passed the conservatory, Professor Loring bustled out to hold the door open for the woman who glided through next. She wore a khaki dress that had been lined in olive tweed and mud-splattered boots. On her head was a wide-brimmed hat adorned with peacock feathers. Her black hair was tied back from her tawny face in a simple knot.

"Who is that?" Jimmie asked, his eyes fixed on the woman.

Arthur couldn't help but stare at her, too. Partly because she was dressed so strangely and partly because she was so, well, beautiful.

"That," said a voice, "is Valencia Fernandez."

Reluctantly, they turned to see Professor Grey standing behind them, gazing from one to the other with her sharp blue eyes.

"The visiting explorer?" Arthur asked.

"The very one," Grey said. "Now, if you're done staring, might you move along? You're blocking the hallway, and I have a very sensitive experiment to tend to."

"Sorry, Professor," said the boys together, stepping aside to make room.

She gave them a knowing look. "It's all right. She cuts a dashing figure, doesn't she? I think you'll find, though, that her mind is even more striking than her appearance."

Jimmie and Arthur shared an embarrassed look.

Professor Grey turned toward the east wing while Jimmie and Arthur followed behind Professor Loring and Valencia Fernandez. The professor kept up an insistent prattle, while the explorer gazed with interest at the portraits and artifacts displayed along the hall. Arthur remembered that he still hadn't seen the mysterious falling portrait of Lord Baker that had nearly crushed two of Baskerville Hall's former residents.

Irene was already seated at their usual spot, blowing the steam away from her cup of tea, when Jimmie and Arthur arrived.

"Did you see?" she asked, nodding to the table where Valencia Fernandez was still being badgered by Professor Loring. "Isn't she fabulous?"

"She is," said Arthur. "But, Irene, I need to talk to you."

He slid her letter across the table. She frowned as she picked it up. "Why do you have this?"

"Someone slipped it under our door last night," Arthur explained. "Maybe they thought it was your room?"

"But our rooms all have nameplates," said Irene. "And mail gets delivered to the pigeonholes."

She nodded toward the doors of the buttery, outside of which stood a tall, rickety set of shelves that had been divided into a hundred or more cubbies. Each student had one, and it was indeed where their mail was usually delivered.

She took the letter from the envelope and began to read. When she was done, she looked up at Arthur and shrugged. "It's just a letter from my mother. Nothing out of the ordinary. Have a look for yourself."

Arthur gazed down at the letter. Irene's mother wrote that the Eagles were very well, but that their show in Paris had been canceled, and they would be traveling to Vienna soon to start rehearsals for a new show. They would write to her as soon as they arrived, so she would have the new address.

Just as he was about to hand the letter back to Irene, he noticed some faint indentations at the top.

He glanced up at her. She was laughing at Pocket, who had produced a small pot of rhubarb jam from one of her pockets and begun spreading it over her toast. He hunched over the letter and squinted at it, turning it this way and that to catch the light. The indentations were the outline of words that had been written on another piece of paper, which had probably been placed directly on top of Irene's letter.

Secretary of State for War,
War Office, Whitehall, London.

Arthur's brow furrowed. *Strange . . .* he thought. Why would a pair of opera singers be writing to the Secretary for War?

He lowered the letter so he could ask Irene, then nearly shot out of his seat. A narrow face was peering into his own where before there had only been an empty seat.

"Grover!" Arthur cried.

"Good morning, Arthur," said Grover. "Did you sleep well? No visitations from spirits in the night?"

Arthur shook his head.

"No," Grover replied glumly. "Me neither."

Arthur didn't have another chance to speak to Irene during their busy morning of lessons. Then that afternoon, something happened that made him forget about the letter altogether.

When they entered the conservatory, Valencia Fernandez was sitting next to Professor Loring under the great, gnarled tree, with several steamer trunks beside her. Everyone took their places on the assorted benches and rugs that had been set out under the enormous tree canopy.

Professor Loring began to introduce the explorer, but she waved him off. "They aren't here to talk about me, Loring," she said. Her voice was rougher than Arthur had expected, more like a sailor's than a lady's. Which, he supposed, she was. "They want to see my findings."

She began to produce artifact after artifact from her trunks.

There were ancient fossils trapped in rock, teeth the size of Arthur's fist, ancient jawbones and tiny skulls, and a finger bone that looked eerily similar to the ones belonging to Napoleon, Dr. Watson's skeleton.

Best and strangest of all, though, was the egg.

Dr. Fernandez pulled it from her trunk with great tenderness, as Arthur's mam had picked up Constance when she was still a newborn baby.

"Now this," she said, "is a treasure of invaluable worth. A perfectly preserved dinosaur egg."

Everyone gasped. The egg was inside a glass jar, atop a bed of soft cotton. If Dr. Fernandez hadn't told them it was a dinosaur egg, Arthur might have mistaken it for one of Cook's dinner rolls. They both had the same hard, mottled look of a rock that would hurt if someone were to throw it at you.

"But how is such a thing possible?" asked Sophia.

"I'm not certain yet," Dr. Fernandez admitted. "It was found deep in the ground, inside a pocket of blue clay that we're still working to identify. It is my theory that this clay had some kind of preservative properties, but the question requires further investigation."

Ahmad was so intent on getting a closer look at the egg that he tipped forward off his bench, causing Dr. Fernandez to leap backward. Professor Loring scolded Ahmad to be more careful and apologized profusely.

"What will you do with the egg now?" Irene asked, when order had been restored.

"Another good question," answered Dr. Fernandez. "It is my

hope that its contents have been preserved as well as the egg itself has been."

"You mean—" Arthur started.

"I hope to find a fossilized dinosaur embryo, yes," she said. "If I am successful, it will be the first of its kind ever discovered."

Professor Loring shot up from his seat and began to applaud.

It was only when Arthur's head hit his pillow that night that he remembered Irene's letter. But he was tired from the previous night's restless sleep, and before he could think much about it, he found himself drifting off . . .

. . . And then, in what seemed to be the very next moment, being shaken awake.

"Get up and get dressed," said a gruff voice. "It's time."

"Time for what?" Arthur said, sleep still fogging his mind. He blinked, waiting for his eyes to adjust so he could see who had woken him. But whoever was there was already melting away into the inky darkness.

"Your first test," the voice said, "starts now."

TWENTY-FOUR

A Leap of Logic

WHEN ARTHUR AND JIMMIE EMERGED FROM their room, they were blindfolded immediately, just as they had been on their first encounter with the Clover. They were led down the spiral steps of the tower in complete darkness. Arthur clutched the railing tightly, but his palms were hot and slippery despite the cold. Half of him couldn't wait to find out what the first challenge would be. The other half was sick with nerves.

Remember what Dr. Watson said, he told himself. *Mind over matter. Stay calm and observe.*

He wondered how the Clover members had snuck past Toby, and how they would now get past the wolf to go out. When they reached the ground floor, though, the smell of raw meat—familiar to Arthur from his many visits to Mr. Fraser's butcher shop—greeted his nostrils, and he could hear the sound of ferocious gnawing.

Apparently, Toby was a faithful watchdog, but only up to a point.

After being led from the tower and spun around several times, Jimmie was told to put his hands on Arthur's shoulders, and Arthur was made to place his hands on the shoulders of the person in front of him and start walking.

"Irene?" he whispered. "Is that you?"

"Yes," she hissed back. "What do you think we're in for?"

Someone nearby shushed them as they began to shuffle forward.

They walked for a long time, seeming to occasionally double back on their path so they couldn't keep track of where they were. Every few minutes, Arthur's heart gave a painful squeeze, as though it might burst from the anticipation. In the Clover House, they'd been told there would be three tests . . . one of bravery, one of honor, and one of loyalty. Which was this to be?

Eventually, the grass underfoot gave way to hard, knotty earth. Brambles caught the hem of Arthur's trousers. He heard an owl hooting overhead. *We must be in the forest.*

He thought with a jolt of the cloaked figure he'd seen in the trees. Was it possible that they were being taken to the man who called himself the Green Knight?

"Ouch!" gasped Irene, shaking Arthur from his thoughts.

"Oh yes," came another voice. "Watch your step. We're going up."

They shuffled forward again until Arthur felt something solid and flat underfoot. A second step told him it was stone.

"Not yet," said the voice. A hand pushed Arthur backward, breaking his hold on Irene. "One at a time. The rest of you wait here until you're summoned."

Good luck, Irene, Arthur wished silently as he heard her being led away.

"Where are we?" Jimmie whispered behind him.

But another member of the Clover must have been left to guard them, because Jimmie was immediately shushed.

The next few minutes seemed to stretch on and on. Arthur's stomach kept flipping, and his heart only pounded harder. Then, finally, he heard a set of footsteps coming back down the stairs. But only one.

"You're next," their guide said, taking Arthur by his arm and jerking him forward.

"Where's Irene?"

"That's none of your business."

"Is she all right? Did she pass the test?"

"Just walk."

They were going up some kind of staircase. The air had gone clammy, and it smelled damp. They were obviously in a building of some sort, probably an old one. *What kind of building would be all the way out here in the forest?*

Whatever it was, it must have another way out, otherwise where had Irene gone? Or was she still at the top?

It might simply have been his imagination, but the staircase felt very steep. He counted the steps as they climbed. *One, two, three . . .*

Ten . . .

Twenty . . .

Thirty . . .

When he had counted forty-seven steps, the air changed once more. The sharp, fresh smell of the forest rushed back in, along

with some other familiar scent. But Arthur was too nervous to place it. For some reason, it reminded him of his sister Mary.

"Initiate!" boomed a voice before he could think anymore about the smell. "You have accepted the challenge of the Clover. You will now be tested. If you fail, you will never be one of our number. But if you pass, you stand a chance to become another link in a great and powerful chain. Do you understand?"

Arthur's mouth had gone dry. He licked his lips. "I do."

The blindfold was ripped away. Arthur blinked. He couldn't see much at first, but after a moment, he began to make out shapes. He was on some kind of round roof, lit by a single candle. Its light flickered over the masked faces of two figures who stood together staring at Arthur.

"Good evening, Arthur," the taller figure said. Arthur was sure this was the same boy who he'd overheard in the library, and who had led their first Clover meeting. There was something slippery about his voice. It reminded him of a magician he and Catherine had once been to see, whose enchanting words had tried (and failed, in Arthur's opinion) to distract from the fact that his tricks were not very good.

"Tonight, we test your bravery," said the other figure, a girl. Arthur's heart gave another jolt. He recognized this voice, too. It was high and lilting, like a nightingale's. It was the girl who they had overheard in the library with the Magician.

She pointed to the edge of the platform, where the parapet had crumbled away. Arthur inched toward it and looked over. Squinting, he could just see the outline of what he thought was a log that stretched off into the distance like a makeshift bridge. Looking below it, he couldn't see a thing. But he knew exactly how high they were, having counted the steps. Forty-seven steps would be a long way to fall.

"On the middle of the log rests a wooden clover," the Nightingale continued. "You must walk across, collect the clover, and continue until you reach the end of the log at the other tower. But beware. Should you lose your balance and fall . . . well, it might be the last thing you do. If you choose to return before reaching the clover, or should you reach the other side without it, you will fail. Is this understood?"

Arthur nodded. He tightened his hands into fists to keep them from shaking.

It might be the last thing you do. Surely they couldn't mean that? Could they?

"Then take this," commanded the Nightingale, handing him a lit candle, "and begin."

Arthur turned to face the darkness. The candle provided enough light to see the log beneath him, but nothing more. He stepped on with one foot, then the other, lifting his free arm up for balance. When he was confident in his stance, he edged out a bit farther.

The log wobbled.

Arthur's legs wobbled in return.

He gritted his teeth and took a step, then another.

His pounding heart seemed to be tugging him back toward safety, but he forced himself onward. With each step, he thought of one of his sisters and what it would mean for them if he were accepted into the Clover.

Arthur kept his eyes focused on guiding his feet until finally he caught sight of a small object. A polished wooden clover, sitting

right in the middle of the log, so close in front of him he had nearly kicked it.

All he had to do was bend down and pick it up.

Slowly . . . slowly . . .

He felt a burst of triumph as his hand closed around the clover.

Yes!

That was the hard part done. Now he just had to stand up and make his way across the last half of the log.

But as he stood, the log seemed to wobble more than ever, and the more it wobbled the less steady Arthur became. Halfway back to standing, he felt himself teeter. He was going to fall, unless—

He shot out both hands to grip the log and steady himself. And in doing so, he threw both the candle and the clover out into the darkness.

"No!" he cried.

But it was too late. The clover was gone.

It was over. He had failed.

He thought again of his sisters as he stared down into the darkness.

Catherine, Anne, Charlotte, Mary—

Mary!

As a memory clicked into place, three things suddenly became clear.

"Doyle!" called the Magician. "The clover fell. You're finished."

"Not quite yet," Arthur replied.

Then he took a deep breath . . . and jumped.

TWENTY-FIVE

Arthur Makes a Splash

ARTHUR ONLY HAD A SPLIT SECOND, AS HE plummeted through the darkness, to question whether his three observations would prove correct.

First, the smell in the air had made him think of Mary because it reminded him of the pond in the park nearest to their home in Edinburgh, where Mary always liked him to take her to feed the ducks.

Second, he had heard a small tinny sound immediately after he dropped the clover—just the kind of sound a duck makes when it lands on water.

And third, the Magician had said Arthur had to return with the clover or he would fail the test. And he was planning to do that—just not the way they thought. That is . . . unless he was wrong and was currently plummeting toward the hard ground.

He had just enough time to wonder whether his sisters would rather have a brother who failed a test than a dead one before he hit the icy cold water and went under.

He emerged a second later, spluttering and gasping for air. *Yes!* Well, he wasn't dead, but he still needed to find the clover. Shivering with the cold, he skimmed the surface of the water, but found nothing. And then, miraculously, something small and solid swept into his hand. The clover. He had it!

He let out a whoop of joy and began to swim for shore.

He could make out a lantern burning at the bottom of the tower he was supposed to reach. Soaked through, freezing, and wary of the slimy things swimming around his ankles, he climbed onto the bank and ran up the tower stairs. He startled the two Clover members waiting at the top of the tower, one of whom had to stop the other from falling over the parapet.

"You're supposed to be on the log!" said a girl's voice through her mask. It was strong and indignant, and Arthur recognized it immediately. It was Afia, the reporter who had interviewed him for the paper.

"I was supposed to get across and bring you the clover," Arthur said, holding up the wooden token. "I did that, in a way of my choosing."

"But how did you know it was safe to jump?" the other figure asked.

"I could smell we were near a pond," Arthur explained. "And I heard a little splash when the clover fell in. It could have just been a puddle or a stream, but it suddenly occurred to me that a group like the Clover wouldn't want to draw attention to themselves by having first years breaking their necks during an initiation challenge. So . . . I jumped."

Afia shook her head, but when she spoke, Arthur could hear she was smiling. "Well, this is certainly a first. Congratulations on passing your first challenge, Doyle."

"You did *what*?!" Irene exclaimed on their way to breakfast the next morning.

Jimmie motioned for her to keep her voice down. Sophia, Harriet, and Ahmad were walking just behind them.

Arthur repeated the whole story for her.

"Well, how did you know you would find the clover once you dropped it into the pond?" Irene asked, when he was done. "How did you know it wouldn't sink?"

"They said it was made of wood," Arthur said. "And they needed to be able to retrieve it if it dropped. Otherwise, how would they test the others who came after?"

"They might have had one for each of us," Irene pointed out.

Arthur frowned. "I didn't think of that."

"And there might have been eels down there."

"Trust me," Arthur replied, "there were."

"What about you, Irene?" Jimmie asked. "Were you scared?"

Jimmie had moved so slowly he had taken nearly half an hour to cross the log, which had taken the place of a swinging rope bridge that had long since crumbled away. Apparently, the bridge over the pond had never served any real purpose but had been built to entertain Lord Baker's children.

"Let's just say . . . I had insurance," said Irene.

"What's that supposed to mean?" Arthur asked.

"Well, when the Clover came and told me to get dressed last

night, I did what they said. Only . . . I put on Pocket's uniform instead of my own. I thought she might have something in there that could come in useful. I was rummaging in the pockets as we walked over, and I found a length of rope. It was just long enough to loop around the log and then knot around my waist. If I fell, I knew the rope would catch me. But I didn't need it. Turns out it's quite easy to balance on a log as long as you know you aren't in danger."

"That was clever!" Arthur exclaimed.

"Yes. And it didn't involve any eels." Little furrows appeared between her brows. "But still . . . it seems like kind of a nasty trick to play."

"How could they test our bravery without scaring us a little?" Jimmie asked. "And besides, Arthur called their bluff. We were never in any real danger."

Irene still looked troubled. "And if someone had fallen who couldn't swim?"

"I'm sure they had somebody ready to swim to the rescue if they had to," Jimmie said.

"Perhaps," Irene replied. "I just hope they're honest in the next test."

"It's hard to be too honest when you're a *secret* society," Arthur pointed out.

"Yes, I suppose that's true. . . ." Irene said. Arthur had hoped his remark would put Irene's mind at ease, but she began fidgeting with her pocket watch, something he had noticed she did when she was feeling uneasy.

They were walking up the stairs to the manor hall now, and students were shoulder to shoulder all around them.

"Speaking of the next test, what do you think it will be?" Arthur whispered. "And when?"

Irene and Jimmie both turned and shushed him, putting an abrupt end to their conversation.

At breakfast, Arthur amused himself by looking around the buttery, searching for clues as to who among his fellow diners might be members of the Clover. As his gaze made its way around the room, looking for hooded eyes and stifled yawns—sure give-aways of a late night—he caught Afia's eye over his teacup. She turned quickly back to the conversation she had been having.

The problem was, beyond Afia, he didn't have much to go on. He didn't know many of the other older students besides Oscar from the *Bugle*, and Bruno, who had walked the first years to the tower on their first day. There was Sinead, who took care of Lucky. And Thomas and Ollie, the spiritualist pair who were currently huddled together on their own as usual. But Arthur didn't really know much else about any of the older students.

Anyone could have been a member of the Clover. Well, perhaps not the beetle-obsessed Bruno, but *almost* anyone.

Sebastian entered the buttery halfway through breakfast, looking a bit pale but with a swing to his step. Arthur heard him wish Harriet and Roland a cheerful good morning. Presumably, then, Sebastian had found his own way to pass the Clover's first test, too. That was a shame.

As Arthur finished his last bite of bacon, Mrs. Hudson stepped forward to remind them about the banquet and presentation by Valencia Fernandez that evening.

"If you have formal attire, you may wear it," she said. "Otherwise, your uniforms will suffice. Dinner will commence at half six sharp. Now let me see . . . was there anything else?"

A scowling Cook waved her arms at Mrs. Hudson from across the buttery, but Mrs. Hudson, who was consulting her notes, appeared not to notice.

"You told me half *seven*!" Cook finally bellowed. "Seven, not six! I can't be ready a moment before half seven."

Finally, Mrs. Hudson looked up and squinted across the room. "Did I? Well, then I suppose that's what I meant." She cleared her throat. "You will all be here at half seven and not a moment later. Or, apparently, earlier. I expect everyone in their seats when the clock strikes the half hour, which is to say half of—half past—"

"Half six?" someone called out. Arthur craned his neck to see Oscar staring with wide, innocent eyes at Mrs. Hudson. His mouth, however, twitched with barely controlled laughter.

"Exactly," said Mrs. Hudson. "Now it's time to—"

Not to be outdone, Toby tipped his head back into a howl, and chairs across the room scraped against the floor as students rose to their feet.

"Half *seven*!" Cook bellowed in vain. "Come at half *SEVEN*, else you'll all be eating air!"

Arthur stifled many a yawn that day, as the excitement began to wear off and the sleepless night took its toll. By the end of their lessons, he wanted nothing more than to return to the tower and fall into his bed for an hour or two before dinner. Instead, he forced himself back to the library and up the stairs to the history section. There were a couple of books on King Arthur's legends that he wanted to flip through.

The Magician and the Nightingale had been looking for

something at the request of someone who called himself the Green Knight, and that couldn't be a coincidence. Perhaps reading the legend about the original Green Knight would provide Arthur some clue as to who this mysterious figure was—and what he wanted.

Arthur was surprised to see Grover already there, stooped over a stack of books so high Arthur could only make out the top of his head.

"Doing a bit of light reading?" he called.

Grover peeked up above the stack of books. "Research," he said. "For the obituary. I asked Professor Grey for an interview, but she's so busy with her experiments, she keeps putting me off. I've got to start somewhere. Professor Grey is mentioned in all these books, can you believe it? She *wrote* three of them. How will I ever fit it all in?"

He didn't wait for Arthur's response before sinking back down below the dusty stack.

Arthur dragged out two heavy volumes of his own before flopping down in a threadbare armchair. He'd told Irene and Jimmie they could come, too, but neither of them seemed very interested nor at all certain why Arthur himself was so focused on the mysterious knight. Arthur couldn't quite explain it, either. He just had a feeling that the Green Knight's presence was important and that he had something to do with the break-ins. What was it he was looking for at Baskerville Hall, and who else wanted it??

Arthur knew from his mother's stories that the Green Knight of legend was a mysterious, almost supernatural figure who used devious tricks to put other knights' courage to the test.

In the most famous tale, he challenged Sir Gawain, one of King Arthur's Knights of the Round Table, to strike him with an

axe, and then receive a strike in return. But when Sir Gawain took off the Green Knight's head with his blow, the knight simply bent down, picked his head up off the ground, and placed it back on his neck. Then it had been the Green Knight's turn to strike. But the Green Knight spared his opponent for the time being, as Sir Gawain had proved his courage by keeping his promise.

Arthur studied the illustration that had been printed alongside the tale in the book in front of him, tracing the shape of the strange star that decorated Sir Gawain's shield.

So was the Green Knight in the legend a protector? Or a supernatural threat?

Professor Niles D. Nilrem, the author of *The Secrets of the Table: A Second Look at Arthurian Legend*, seemed just as confused about the original Green Knight as Arthur was about the one lurking around Baskerville Hall:

> **Perhaps the most mystifying character in all the legends remains the Green Knight. To some, he is a ferocious apparition, possessed of unnatural and ill-gotten powers. To others, he is the ultimate defender of virtue and chivalry. Even his appearance cannot be agreed upon, as in some tellings, there is nothing exceptional about the knight's appearance, while in others, his name is explained by the fact that his very skin is green, as if overgrown with moss. Is the knight associated with the color green because it is the color of nature and spring? Or because it is the color of poison, and even death?**

Arthur's mind was ill at ease when he left the library that evening. None of his questions had been answered. But he *did* know that the so-called Green Knight was connected to the Clover. The Magician and the Nightingale, at least, seemed to be working for him. And perhaps that meant he should be asking the same questions Professor Nilrem was asking about the Clover itself. Like the Green Knight, the society was possessed of great powers, and it claimed many virtues—bravery, honor, and loyalty. But also like the knight, it was shrouded in shadow.

Yet somehow, Arthur couldn't help but feel that he was the one still in the dark.

TWENTY-SIX

A Misunderstanding

ARTHUR'S MIND WAS STILL ON THE GREEN Knight and the Clover as he and Jimmie entered the hall later that evening, but one step into the buttery swept all his worries away and replaced them with . . . discomfort.

The long room was awash in silk, crepe, poplin, and velvet, and was ablaze in shades of emerald, tangerine, and scarlet. The girls were nearly all in evening gowns, with many of the boys in tailcoats.

Arthur glanced down awkwardly at his own uniform. Mrs. Hudson had said that formal attire was optional, but he suddenly wished very much that he had something better to wear than his shabby purple suit.

"I didn't know *everyone* was going to dress up," he murmured.

"Not everyone's dressed up," said Jimmie. "There are others in uniforms. Look, Bruno's wearing his. And Grover. Those Circle of the Spirit people are wearing the same strange white clothes as always. And Pocket's wearing—what *is* Pocket wearing?"

Pocket and Irene were just coming through the doors. Irene was striking in a deep blue gown. Pocket was striking, too, but for a completely different reason. She was dressed in a flouncing garment that seemed to have been stitched together from a hundred different dresses. Each patch was stitched to the next in a swooping pattern, like a garland. Arthur realized that each patch was in fact—what else?—a pocket.

He and Jimmie weren't the only ones staring. Harriet Russell, who was wearing a sweeping ruby gown that was quite fitting for a duchess's daughter, pointed at Pocket and giggled. Sophia De Leon, who was standing next to Ahmad, held a beautiful wooden fan and murmured something behind it about bizarre English fashion. If Pocket noticed the attention, she didn't seem to mind.

"Hell-ooo, gentlemen," she said in a nasally voice as she approached, dropping into a deep curtsy. A pair of small scissors fell from one of the pockets. "Oopsy-daisy!"

Arthur bent to pick them up for her. "M'lady," he said.

Irene watched their little play with an arched brow and a small shake of her head.

Better all eyes be on Pocket than on me, Arthur thought. "You look nice," he said to Irene. It was true. She looked extremely pretty in the blue dress, and she had curled her dark hair back into an intricate coif. "It's a beautiful dress."

She smiled. "Thank you," she said. "One of the perks of being an opera kid. I know lots of costume designers."

"I'm starving," Pocket said. "I thought dinner was being served

at half seven sharp. And I've got to get back to the lab soon."

The hall was peppered with little groups of students talking and laughing. A wonderful aroma wafted up from the kitchen, but there was no food to be seen yet on any of the tables. Arthur noticed that a banquet table had been placed at the head of the room. Valencia Fernandez sat at the center, with Headmaster Challenger on one side and Professor Loring on the other. It made Arthur feel a bit better that Challenger had stuffed himself into a shabby suit that was at least two sizes too small and looked like it was half a century old. Loring, meanwhile, had changed into a smartly cut three-piece suit but had forgotten to change out of his rubber work boots.

A series of booms echoed through the buttery, as Challenger banged the hilt of a large knife against the table.

"Sit!" he commanded, once the room had gone silent.

The first years slid into their places along the center table. Arthur was none too happy when Sebastian took the seat across from him.

"Good evening, students," Challenger called, once everyone was settled. "Tonight, we are here to honor the successful completion of a long and important mission undertaken by Valencia Fernandez. She is a true example of the Baskerville spirit. She will regale us with tales of her adventures in short order. But first . . . we eat."

Right on cue, Cook banged through the kitchen doors, followed by waiters holding trays of silver platters. She barked orders to them in a way that suggested she might once have had a successful military career. Brigadier Gerard must have thought so, too, since he watched her with admiration.

"Professor Grey isn't up there," Pocket said, scanning the head table. The rest of the teachers had taken their place. "She must still be in the lab. Maybe I should see if she needs any help."

Just then, a waiter set a steaming platter of roast beef down in front of them. Pocket licked her lips.

"Well, I suppose a little dinner first wouldn't hurt. Breakthroughs come much easier on a full stomach."

Boiled potatoes were next, then asparagus salad, and, of course, Cook's bread rolls. Pocket scooped a bit of everything onto her plate and began eating as though she were in a race. Jimmie and Irene had somehow become locked in a debate over who had eaten the least appetizing meal during the course of their travels (German tongue sausage for Jimmie, Danish cod pickled in lye for Irene).

So it was only Arthur who saw Sebastian glance at him before muttering to Roland, "Honestly, my mother would die of embarrassment if I showed up to a formal banquet without the proper attire."

Roland said something back that made Sebastian laugh. Arthur gripped his fork until his knuckles turned white.

"Oh, I know," Sebastian replied. "It's better than that girl's collection of rags. They look like they smell. You know her father's a sheep farmer? It's enough to put one off one's dinner."

Pocket stopped eating and looked up at Sebastian. Had he miscalculated how far his words would travel? Arthur thought he had probably *wanted* Pocket to hear his cruel words. She was staring at him with wide eyes.

Arthur shot up from his seat.

"You—you—absolute *knave*," he said. "Take it back. Say you're sorry."

Jimmie gripped his arm. "Arthur, what—"

Sebastian cocked his head. "I don't know what you're talking about, Arthur. I think you've misunderstood—"

"I haven't misunderstood anything," Arthur snapped. "If you won't apologize, then we'll have to settle this some other way."

People around the hall were starting to look up from their food.

"My grandfather used to say that Scotsmen could never hold their tempers," Sebastian said evenly. "So he would never invite one to dine. I suppose he was right."

Arthur slammed one hand down on the table and reached over to grab Sebastian's collar with the other. Suddenly, he was back on the street in Edinburgh, squaring off against the bullies who could only make themselves feel good by putting the poorer boys down.

"Arthur, don't!" Jimmie said. But Arthur barely heard him.

One punch in the nose. That's all he wanted to give Sebastian.

He had pulled Sebastian halfway across the table before he felt thick arms around his waist.

"Doyle!" Professor Stone barked. "Settle down, man! It ain't the time nor place!"

Arthur finally released Sebastian's collar and let Stone tug him back down to his seat.

"That's it, Doyle, steady yourself now," Stone counseled. "Your passion for the art of the fight is admirable, but you must remember yourself."

Arthur took a deep breath. People were staring at him, pointing and whispering. Headmaster Challenger and Dr. Watson were both eyeing him from their place at the high table, wearing matching frowns of disappointment. Arthur's rage drained at the sight of them, and he suddenly wished he could shrink away.

The seat next to him, he realized, was empty. Pocket had slipped off amid the commotion.

"I . . . I need to go," Arthur said haltingly. "For a walk."

"I was just about to say the same thing," Stone said. "Go pull yourself together, and I'll tell the headmaster that it was all a misunderstanding. Wasn't it, Moran?"

"I suppose it must have been, sir," Sebastian said, breathing heavily. A snarl curled at his lip.

"Good men," Stone said, clapping Arthur on the back. "Now, save it for the ring."

TWENTY-SEVEN

Daguerreotypes and Dynamite

JIMMIE OFFERED TO GO WITH ARTHUR, BUT he shrugged his friend off. He strode from the hall with as much dignity as he could muster under the eyes of all his classmates. How disappointed his mother would be if she had seen him. Only now that it was too late did Arthur realize he had played right into Sebastian's hands. The brute had probably meant for Arthur to hear everything, hoping to provoke him. And now Arthur was the one who looked like the fool, while Sebastian maintained the illusion of the perfect gentleman.

Arthur gritted his teeth as he wandered through the empty halls toward Professor Grey's classroom to find Pocket. He needed to make sure she was all right.

But when he reached the classroom, it too was empty. There was no sign of Pocket or Professor Grey. Perhaps they had gone to her office? He had a vague idea that it was on the second floor, so he plunged farther down the deserted corridor, toward the back staircase.

He walked slowly, reliving the last moments in a kind of horrible trance. Would Challenger punish him? Write home to his parents? Or worse?

It was with this grim thought that Arthur looked up to find himself face-to-face with the ugliest portrait he had ever seen. A sneering, jowly man stared down at him. At least, one eye did. The other seemed to be looking up at the ceiling. The golden plaque at the bottom of the portrait read: *Lord Hugh Baker.*

This, Arthur realized, was the portrait Oscar and Afia had told him about—the one that had fallen and nearly killed two people. Arthur, who still had half a mind to pick a fight, was debating whether to tempt his luck and tell the sneering man exactly what he thought of snobs like him when he heard a loud bang, a scream, and then footsteps from overhead.

Arthur ran to the steps and climbed them two at a time.

He had just reached the top when a tall, cloaked figure came barreling down the hall and nearly crashed into him. He was about to follow the runner when he smelled something burning.

Smoke rose through the air from the direction the figure had come. Arthur was torn. Follow the figure or the smoke? Then he remembered why he had been on his way upstairs in the first place. To look for Pocket. What if she had been the one screaming?

"Pocket!" he called out. "Pocket, are you all right?"

Turning away from the runner, Arthur sprinted around the corner in time to see two people stamping out a small fire that

was burning on the hall carpet. It was Pocket and Professor Grey. Pocket was supporting the older woman, who had gone completely white.

"What happened?" Arthur exclaimed. Together, he and Pocket led Grey to an armchair inside an open office door. The chair was one of the only things in the room that had not been overturned. A handsome desk lay on its side. Books and silver instruments littered the floor.

"We just came up to find a reference book," Pocket said. "But someone was already here. He did all this." She gestured around to the mess. "Professor Grey confronted him, but he pulled out a knife. So I lit a bit of dynamite and told him to run or he'd be toast."

"Good thinking. I saw him!" Arthur said. "Running away, just now."

Pocket stared at him for a second. Then, "Well, what are you waiting for?" she exclaimed. "Go after him!"

Arthur took off the way he had come, tearing down the corridor. He was nearly sent tumbling all the way down the stairs when a slinking shadow appeared from the gloom.

"Toby!" Arthur yelled, leaping in a most ungraceful manner to avoid treading on the wolf. The animal growled back, its fur bristling.

"It's not me you should be worried about," Arthur snapped. "There's an intruder! Help me—or at least get out of my way!"

The wolf gazed at Arthur for a moment before turning back down the stairs and trotting off toward the buttery.

"I've seen cats make better guard dogs," Arthur muttered, before continuing down himself.

When he arrived breathless at the entry hall, the front door was ajar. He stopped in the doorway, searching the darkness for any sign of the intruder, but all was still and quiet. He could be hiding in a thousand places by now. It would be like hunting a needle in a haystack. Arthur was considering whether to go out and keep searching anyway when he heard a gruff voice ring through the hall.

"What in the blazes is going on here?" Arthur spun around to see Headmaster Challenger scowling at him through the murky light. "First you try to start a fight at the banquet, and then I have Hudson in my ear—in the middle of Valencia's speech, mind you—telling me Toby is whining and scratching at her skirts."

"Because he was!" said Mrs. Hudson indignantly, shuffling up behind the headmaster, holding up fistfuls of her full yellow skirt. Toby appeared beside her, his eyes staring into Arthur's once more. "He was alerting me that something was wrong."

Perhaps Arthur had misjudged the animal. Apparently, he was smart enough to have gone for help.

"That's right," Arthur said. "Please, Headmaster. There was someone here—an intruder. He broke into Professor Grey's office and threatened her and Pocket. Whoever it was ran off and must have gone out the front door."

Challenger's scowl drew tighter. He glanced at Mrs. Hudson and nodded.

"Go, Toby," she said, motioning toward the door. "Follow the scent."

Obediently, the animal bolted out into the night.

Challenger was already heading up the main stairs. Arthur followed.

"Was anybody hurt?" Challenger called over his shoulder.

"I don't think so. Although Pocket did throw a stick of dynamite at the intruder. . . ."

If Challenger found this at all surprising, he didn't show it. He stalked down the hallway with a determined pace that Arthur could only match at a jog. When they reached Grey's office, the professor was still sitting in her chair, looking dazed and breathing hard. Pocket was organizing the strewn books into piles.

The headmaster took a long look around the office.

"Are you all right?" he asked, placing a steadying hand on Grey's shoulder.

The old woman nodded.

"Who was it? Could you see?"

"Whoever it was wore a cloak," Pocket said. "Black, with a black mask, too. We couldn't see anything else."

"Anything taken?"

"I don't know," Grey said. "I can't think . . . what would anyone want from here? All my experiments are in the lab. Up here it's just books and my—my personal effects."

She glanced down at a silver picture frame that had been thrown to the floor. It was a daguerreotype of a young woman with the same piercing eyes as Professor Grey's.

"Perhaps they weren't looking for anything at all," Challenger mumbled, to himself it seemed. "Perhaps they were sending a message."

"A threat?" Grey asked, sitting forward. "But why me? I'm retiring at the end of term. Going to live out the rest of my days in quiet study with my niece. Who would want to threaten me?"

"I don't know," Challenger said, though judging by his

furrowed brow he was thinking furiously.

"Headmaster?" Arthur said. "Could this have to do with the other break-in at the beginning of term? Nothing was stolen that time, either, right?"

"How do you know about that?" Challenger barked, glaring in Arthur's direction.

"I heard about it from someone on the student paper."

"Hmph," said Challenger. "More press. That's just what we need."

"Well, they don't need to know about this," said Professor Grey. She seemed to have recovered her nerve. Her voice no longer wavered. "I'm embarrassed enough as it is."

"You're right," Challenger said. "Doyle, Pocket, do you hear? Not a word to anyone about this. I won't have panic breaking out at my school. Not until I understand what's going on."

"Yes, sir," Arthur and Pocket said together.

"Good. Now, I need to return downstairs to see if Toby's come up with anything. You two stay with Professor Grey and help her clean up this mess. Go straight to the tower after. It will just draw more attention if you return to the buttery."

They nodded, and Challenger swept from the room.

Professor Grey was staring again at the picture on the floor, her bright eyes dulled by a fog of worry, or memory, or both. Arthur bent down for the picture and brought it to her.

"It hasn't been harmed," he said.

"Thank you," Grey replied. "I'm very glad. It's a likeness of my mother—the only one I have."

Arthur glanced at the picture again. The woman was younger than Professor Grey, with rounder cheeks, but she still bore an

unmistakable resemblance to her daughter, so much so that it took Arthur a few seconds to notice where the picture had been taken.

"This looks like Baskerville Hall!" he said, pointing to the manor house in the background.

"Actually, it was known as Baker Academy in those days," murmured the professor.

"Professor Grey is a third-generation teacher," Pocket said, peering over Arthur's shoulder. "Her mother worked here, and her grandmother before that."

"Without them, I wouldn't be here," said Grey, a little smile flickering across her face. "It's not easy, you know, to be a woman with dreams. At least ones that don't involve slaving away over a hot oven all day. They forged a path for me. Taught me everything they knew. They have been the inspiration for all my work."

She stroked the face in the photograph.

"That's enough now," she said suddenly, looking up. "I may be old, but I'm not infirm. I can clean up the rest of this mess. You've both done enough for me already this evening. I won't forget it."

Arthur and Pocket both protested, but Grey wouldn't hear another word. As she closed the door behind them, Arthur wondered if she wanted to be alone with her thoughts and the memory of her mother. He thought of his own mam, who had been "slaving away over a hot oven" nearly her whole life. What could she have been in the world, if given the chance?

She hadn't been given one, but Arthur had. It was a chance for his whole family to do something—to *be* something—more.

"So what were you doing lurking the halls?" Pocket asked, ripping Arthur from his thoughts.

"I came after you," he said. "To see if you were all right."

Pocket cocked her head. "Why wouldn't I be?"

"Well, because of what Sebastian said."

"Oh. Did he say something about me? Is that why you started yelling at him? I did wonder, but I had just had the most wonderful idea about Professor Grey's project, so I had to run to tell her."

Arthur groaned. He might have been expelled—squandered his chance—over coming to blows with Sebastian. And for what? Pocket hadn't run from the room in humiliation. She'd been too busy with her own dreams to even notice what anyone said about her.

Perhaps he needed to take a page from Pocket's book.

"Anyway," she said, poking Arthur gently in his ribs. "It's nice of you to stand up for me and all, but . . . I can take care of myself."

She produced another stick of dynamite from one of her many pockets and winked before skipping off down the hall.

TWENTY-EIGHT

The *Bugle* Disappoints

ARTHUR HATED TO BREAK HIS WORD TO THE headmaster, but he had to tell Jimmie what had happened.

"I think the intruder was looking for something," he said, once he had finished the tale later that night. "And I have a feeling it's the same something the Green Knight is trying to find."

Jimmie sat cross-legged on his bed. A deep divot appeared between his brows. "You think this Green Knight person did it? That he's who ran past you?"

"I don't know," Arthur said. "I've only ever seen him from far away—at least I think it was him—and I didn't get a good look. But the Magician and the Nightingale said something about keeping this thing safe. So maybe they're helping the knight protect it from someone else. That could have been who ransacked Grey's office, too."

"But what are they looking for? What would Grey have that they needed so badly?"

"I don't know," said Arthur again, distastefully. They were three of his least favorite words in the English language. "But we need to find out."

When Arthur and Jimmie entered the buttery that morning, Irene was hunched over the table, reading something. As they approached, she looked up and then smoothly tucked the paper into the pocket of her trousers.

"We need to talk," Arthur said. "Something happened last night."

"Pocket's already told me," Irene replied.

Pocket gave Arthur an apologetic shrug and a very *un*apologetic grin before slipping two pieces of toast into her pockets and announcing she needed to go and check on her mentor. Grover, meanwhile, was stooped over his black tea and grave rubbings, deep in thought. So Arthur was free to share his concerns about the Green Knight with Irene.

To his surprise, she didn't have much to say on the matter. She seemed preoccupied, chewing the corner of her lip and tapping her foot against the ground. She spat out her tea after accidentally putting in a spoonful of salt instead of sugar. She was really acting quite strange. "Is everything all right?" Arthur asked her.

"Yes, of course," Irene said quickly, pouring herself a fresh cup of tea.

Too quickly, Arthur mused. *What was she hiding?*

"*There* you are!" called a voice, making them both jump. They turned to find Afia standing behind them, holding a stack

of newspapers. She held one out to Arthur. "Thought you should be the first to get a copy," she said. "Since you're the lead story. You can share it with your friends."

She gestured to Irene and Jimmie.

"Oh, thanks," Arthur said. He looked down at the front page, where an artist had sketched a picture of Lucky the chimpanzee baring his teeth at a terrified boy who looked nothing like Grover.

"Sure thing. Happy reading. Oh, and . . . see you soon." Afia winked, then strode off to deliver the other papers.

Jimmie and Irene each leaned over one of Arthur's shoulders to get a better look at the paper.

"UNLIKELY HERO AVERTS MONKEY MAYHEM," read the headline.

"What does she mean 'see you soon'?" Irene asked.

Arthur cast a wary glance around. "She's one of them," he whispered to his friends. "A member of the Clover. I recognized her voice at the first challenge."

"Do you think she was talking about the second test?" Jimmie asked. "Have you gotten an invitation?"

"No," said Irene.

"Me neither," said Arthur. "Unless . . . what if *this* is the invitation?"

"She *did* tell you to share it with Jimmie and me," Irene said.

Arthur cast a glance down at the newspaper. Sebastian was peering at his own copy of the *Baskerville Bugle* with a sour expression that warmed Arthur's heart.

He opened the paper and they quickly scanned the pages, but nothing jumped out to any of them.

"Well, they wouldn't make it obvious," Jimmie said. "If there is a message in the paper, it'll be in code or something."

Arthur nodded, but he was distracted by an article on the inside fold of the paper.

MYSTERY BREAK-IN GOES UNSOLVED

"Look," he said, pointing to the headline. "It's about the break-in. The first one, that is."

Eager to see if Afia had uncovered any clues, Arthur read the article as fast as he could.

> **On the morning of October 10, residents of Baskerville Hall on their way to breakfast noted a broken window in the front entrance to the main hall. They may not have thought much of it. There are, after all, many innocent explanations for a shattered pane of glass. The *Bugle* has uncovered through confidential sources, however, that the window was broken in the course of a break-in attempt. According to staff members, nothing was taken during the incident.**
>
> **Professor Loring, who asked to remain anonymous, insists there is no cause for alarm. "It's not the first time something like this has happened, you know," he says. "To be honest, the villagers of Little Bigsby have never been particularly thrilled to be our neighbors. I don't suppose it helped that Headmaster Challenger once nearly burned down The Flying Pig—their public house—while**

conducting an alchemical experiment over one too many pints."

Loring believes that someone from Little Bigsby most likely broke into the school as a prank or on a dare. "It is cowardly behavior, of course," he says. "But ultimately harmless. Nonetheless, security measures have been increased, as I'm sure you'll have noticed. Bars across the windows, a night patrol. Now, if that's all, could you please stop blocking my way to the loo?"

Arthur reread the article. Was that all? It wasn't much of an investigation, in his opinion.

"I suppose Loring's theory does explain why the burglar broke in through the front door," said Irene. "Remember, Arthur, how you thought that was so strange? But if someone was playing a prank or trying to scare us, they'd *want* us to know they'd been here."

"But what about the break-in last night?" Arthur said. "*That* wasn't a prank."

Irene tapped her fingers on the table. "No," she admitted. "It wasn't. Perhaps they're unrelated?"

Jimmie suddenly snatched the paper from Arthur's hands.

"Hey! You could have asked."

Jimmie was holding the paper up, letting the light from the windows stream in. "I knew it," he murmured. "See? If you look close enough, there are little holes punched under some of the letters."

Arthur peered up at the paper, and sure enough, saw that Jimmie was right. Tiny pinpricks of light were shining through holes that had been made in the paper.

"Put it down," Irene instructed, "before you look suspicious."

Jimmie turned the paper back to the front page and set it on the table. "Hmmm, it begins with *T*," he said. *"O-N-I-G-H-T."*

"Tonight," breathed Irene. "You were right, Arthur. This is our invitation!"

Jimmie kept reading out the letters until the message was complete.

Tonight. Midnight. Bugle Office.

All will be revealed.

TWENTY-NINE

All Is Revealed

ARTHUR NEVER FOUND IT HARDER TO GET through his lessons than he did that day. His mind was like the vivarium where Professor Loring kept his flock of translucent butterflies. The Green Knight, the Clover, the break-ins . . . each of them fluttered through it, sometimes settling for just a moment and then flying off again in a different direction.

Arthur wasn't the only one who was distracted that morning. Rather than teach a lesson, Dr. Watson instructed them to spend the hour reading a chapter and copying an illustration from *Gray's Anatomy,* which Watson called "a doctor's bible and encyclopedia." Then he retreated to his desk and began writing something with urgency.

Professor Grey was not in class at all when they arrived at her lab. Headmaster Challenger was there substituting. He told them that Grey had been taken suddenly ill, flashing a warning glance in Arthur and Pocket's direction as he spoke.

By the time Arthur and Jimmie returned to their room that night, they were both jittery with anticipation. Arthur paced back and forth while Jimmie played game after game of chess against himself. And judging by his occasional grunts and sighs, neither side was doing very well.

It was a relief when they heard the soft knock at their door and opened it to see Irene.

"Here we go again," Jimmie said, breathing out a long stream of air.

"Ready?" Irene asked as Arthur pushed the window open.

"I think we have to be," Arthur said.

They slung the rope out of their window, climbed down the tower wall, and dropped to the ground. It was easy, now they'd had practice.

But they hadn't made it much farther before Irene gasped and whispered for them to duck down in the tall grass. Someone was walking along the path toward the tower, carrying a lantern. As the figure grew closer, Arthur saw it was Professor Loring. He was swinging his light back and forth, squinting into the darkness. When he reached the tower door, he turned back the way he came.

"What's he looking for?" Jimmie hissed.

"He's keeping watch," Arthur said. "Remember the article in the *Bugle*? It said that there was a new night patrol. I bet that's what he's doing."

"He's not who I would have chosen," Irene said. "Not exactly an intimidating presence, is he?"

They waited until Loring turned off the path that led to the manor and headed for the dwellings. Just as they stood, Arthur sensed someone approaching behind them.

"Hello," Sebastian said. "Mind if I join you?"

He addressed his question to Arthur with a calm, infuriating smile.

If Sebastian knew the meeting was tonight, that meant he had cracked the code in the *Bugle* and would also already know where it was to be held.

Arthur shrugged. "We're all going to the same place, aren't we?"

Sebastian fell into step with Jimmie, while Arthur sped up to walk next to Irene.

"Don't let him get to you," she advised. "You need to stay focused on the test."

"I know."

The four of them climbed the manor steps in a silence that only deepened as they made their way into the hall and up to the second story. Arthur, the only one who had been to the newspaper office, led the way. Just as he had been on his last visit there, he was startled nearly out of his skin by the clanging of a hundred clocks as they passed the horology clubroom.

"What in the—" Jimmie started.

"I'll explain later," Arthur said, speeding up. "They're chiming midnight. We'll be late if we don't hurry."

When they reached the *Bugle* office, the door was locked. Arthur gave a soft knock, and it swung open.

"Welcome," said a soft-spoken voice. A masked face loomed from the darkness. "We've been expecting you."

❧

Arthur was ushered into the room first, while the others remained in the hall with a guard.

The room was much as it was when he had seen it last, except that next to the printing press, there now crouched a monstrous metal chair that had unpromising straps and tangled wires sprouting from it in all directions.

"Hello, Arthur," said a figure, stepping forward. It was the Magician.

"Hello," he replied evenly.

"Do you know why you're here?"

"All will be revealed," Arthur said.

The boy chuckled.

"Indeed it will. Please, have a seat and our interview will begin."

He gestured to the strange chair.

"What is that?" he asked. "And what do you mean, an interview?"

"We'll be asking the questions," said another figure.

"But—"

Arthur closed his mouth, thinking better of protesting. How stupid he would sound if he admitted to thinking that the Clover would be revealing anything tonight. But if *they* weren't, that meant . . .

"It's a Deception Machine," answered the Magician. "It will test your loyalty and trustworthiness to us. You sit in the chair. We attach these wires to your arm and your chest. Then we ask you questions. The machine can tell us if you're lying or not. Depending on how you answer, you will reveal your true self to

us . . . or reveal yourself to be a liar. Now, sit."

His hands sweating, Arthur did as he was told. It sounded simple enough. Two members of the group stepped forward and attached cuffs to his wrists and around his chest. The chest cuff was strapped tight enough that Arthur had to take shallow breaths.

When they were done, someone flipped a switch, and something began to whir behind Arthur, making the chair vibrate. The Magician pulled up his own chair in front of Arthur's. The rest of the group sat at a table behind him. It was unsettling, all those masked faces staring at him. The room was dark except for a few candles. Enough to see by, but not enough to attract notice by the night patrol.

"Your name?" the Magician said.

"Arthur Conan Doyle."

He heard the chair make a ticking noise.

"Where are you from?"

"Edinburgh, Scotland."

The questions went on like this for a few minutes. How many siblings did Arthur have? Where did he attend school before coming to Baskerville Hall? They were harmless queries, and Arthur found himself beginning to relax.

"Now I'll open the floor," said the Magician. "Any questions for the initiate?"

There was a moment's silence. Then the Nightingale's voice piped up. "Do you have family in London?"

Arthur hesitated. What a strange question. "Yes," he answered. "My father's family live there."

"Do you see them often?"

"No."

"Write?"

"No."

Arthur didn't like where this line of questioning was heading.

"Why not?" asked the Nightingale, sitting forward.

"I . . ." Arthur started, then trailed off. "I think there was a disagreement between them and my father."

"Come now, Arthur," coaxed the Magician. "You can be more specific than that, can't you?"

Arthur felt his cheeks reddening, half in embarrassment and half in anger. It was almost as if the Clover already *knew* about his father. But that wasn't possible . . . was it?

"My father has—has fallen on hard times," he said. "He hasn't managed his finances well."

"Because he is a drunkard?" the Magician said softly.

A few of the masked figures behind him snickered.

Arthur straightened, straining against the cuffs. "He is *not* a—"

"Careful, Arthur. If you lie to us, you will fail."

Arthur took a steadying breath. He was only here, in this room, because he wanted to do what his father had not—to provide for his family. And if that meant he had to tell them the truth . . . well, so be it.

"He cannot control himself around drink," he said finally. "It is a sickness of the mind. There is no medicine or cure to treat it. Not yet, at least. But one day—"

"Are you a violent person?"

This question came from another member of the gallery of onlookers. It was unexpected, but Arthur was relieved to move on from talking about his father.

"If you're referring to what happened last night," Arthur said,

"I didn't hit Sebastian. But I suppose I would have if I'd been given the chance. He spoke in a brutish way about a friend of mine."

"Do you have a history of picking fights?" came Afia's voice. She was sitting to the left of the Nightingale.

Arthur thought of the tussles he'd been in back home. "Yes," he said. "But only to defend others."

"Loyalty is a virtue we prize above almost any other," said the Magician, his voice close to encouraging now. Arthur sat back an inch in his chair. "And I'm sorry to say it has come to our attention that one of our initiates is deceiving us."

"Sebastian?" Arthur asked.

"No, not him."

Arthur's brows pinched together. "Jimmie?"

"Not him, either."

"Irene?"

Arthur would have laughed, but for the fact that no one else in the room did. In fact, no one said a word.

"What would Irene be hiding that would matter to anyone here?"

Even as he spoke the words, though, the answer dawned on him. *The letter.*

"Do you have any reason to believe her parents are not, in fact, opera singers?"

Arthur's mind raced as he remembered, for the first time that day, the letter that had been slipped under his door, and the discovery he'd made about who else Irene's parents had been writing to. He knew very well that American opera singers in Paris would have no reason to write to the War Office. Which meant they could be . . . what? Secret government operatives? Spies?

Clearly, the Clover had reason to believe they were more than simply opera singers, and that Irene was in on their secret. *How did they know so much?* What would they do if Arthur confirmed their theory? Confront Irene? What if they went further, and their network outside the school somehow jeopardized the Eagles' safety?

It was one thing to share his own secrets. It was quite another to betray a friend by sharing hers. But if Arthur lied and pretended to know nothing, he would fail the test. Unless . . .

Unless he could outsmart the Deception Machine. He knew enough from Dr. Watson's class to realize that the cuffs on his arms would be taking his blood pressure, and the one around his chest would be measuring his heartbeat.

Mind over matter.

That's what Dr. Watson had said the day he had felt Arthur's pulse to deduce that he had been lying about the reason he, Jimmie, and Irene needed to locate a map of the school. This machine was just a more sophisticated version of Watson's trick.

"We're waiting, Doyle," said the Magician.

"I'm . . . I'm trying to think," Arthur stalled.

He closed his eyes. He imagined lying in bed with his sisters, telling them a story. That's all he had to do now. Not lie—just tell another story. Stories came naturally to him. It would be easy.

When Arthur opened his eyes, he felt much calmer. He looked straight at the boy sitting in front of him, but his mind's eye saw Caroline and Mary. He took a deep breath, then began to exhale very slowly.

"Irene's parents are in Paris," he said. "But they're moving to Vienna soon to start a new show. Irene herself is no opera singer,

but I have no reason to believe her parents are anything else."

He forced himself to take in another slow breath. "Is that all?" he asked.

The boy made a gesture, and two of the other Clover members stood. They walked behind Arthur to examine something behind him. One of them looked up and gave a sharp nod.

"Well done, Doyle," said the Magician. "You've passed our second test. But . . . perhaps not the way you thought."

Arthur slumped with relief as his cuffs were taken off. "What do you mean?"

"You were lying about the Eagles."

Arthur's heart lurched, and he was grateful the machine was no longer monitoring it. "I—you just said I passed."

"You did. The machine didn't pick up on your lie. This was not, as I said earlier, a test of loyalty. This was a test of honor. You answered all the questions about yourself truthfully. But when it came to your friend—and fellow initiate—you found a way to take control of yourself to protect her secrets. You showed great honor. Congratulations."

Arthur was speechless. His mind reeled.

"For your third and final test, you will report to Clover House at midnight in two weeks' time. You must bring with you a tribute. If we deem it worthy, then you will be initiated into our ranks."

"A . . . a tribute?"

"An object of great value. To prove your loyalty."

"But . . ."

Arthur had begun to say that he didn't own anything of great value, but he stopped himself.

"Don't worry," said the Magician, as though reading Arthur's mind. But surely *that* was a power even the members of the Clover did not possess, however much they seemed to know. "We don't want something of yours. We want something else. Something you must go to great pains to get."

Arthur could barely contain his shock. "You mean to *steal*?"

A few members of the gallery shifted in their seats or exchanged glances.

"Of course not," said the Magician sharply. "We are not a collection of street urchins. We have no need to steal. All we ask is that you *borrow* something. You have proven yourself trustworthy tonight, and now you must prove that you will trust *us.* We need to know you can follow our orders, even if you do not understand them. Will you try?"

Arthur's mouth was dry, but he managed to give a nod.

"Good. The more precious and rare the object, the higher we will hold you in our esteem. Then you will be free to return it to wherever you found it. No harm done. Now my colleague will show you out. Bring Moran in next."

A figure stepped forward and took a firm hold on Arthur's arm, then led him from the room. He could only shoot a stunned glance at the others before being hurried down the hall. Before he knew it, he was standing alone in the dark night. The sharp cold helped bring Arthur back to his senses, and he felt uneasy as he hurried alone back to the tower.

The Clover had known that *he* knew about Irene's parents corresponding with the War Office. That meant they must know he had received and read Irene's letter. And the only way they could know that was if they themselves had intercepted it and sent it to him.

It was dishonorable, but it *had* been a clever way to test Arthur's own honor. How else could the Clover ensure he would keep their secrets—including Irene's—in the future?

The idea of "borrowing" something wasn't an appealing one, but he supposed if he could return it later there would be no harm done. And surely the good that the Clover could bring to Arthur's life would outweigh his momentary discomfort? After all, he mused, officers sometimes gave orders that their soldiers didn't like. A foot soldier saw only the fight he was in, but a general saw the whole war.

Arthur desperately wanted to believe that the Clover was trustworthy enough to follow into battle.

THIRTY

Irene Takes a Stand

"DID YOU PASS?"

Jimmie couldn't even wait until he was all the way through the window of their room before asking. Arthur didn't need to return the question. Jimmie had a broad grin on his face, and even in the gloomy light, Arthur could see the flush of excitement on his cheeks.

Arthur nodded, returning Jimmie's smile.

"I knew you would!" Jimmie beamed even brighter. "I was surprised, actually. It wasn't a very difficult test, was it?"

"What did they ask you?"

Jimmie hesitated. "Actually . . . they asked me about you. About your family, and most particularly your father."

Arthur's stomach gave a sickening churn.

"Don't worry," said Jimmie. "I didn't tell them anything.

That was the point, right?"

But the Clover already knew about Arthur's family, and his father's drinking. They must have known it even before his interview, just as they had known the contents of Irene's letter.

"And you fooled the machine?" Arthur asked.

"Apparently so. But like I said, I didn't think it was very hard to do. I . . . I have to pretend to be something I'm not quite often, actually. Around my father. So I suppose it's become a bit like second nature."

Arthur looked at his friend with sympathy. Clearly, he wasn't the only one with a challenging father. He started at a rustling sound from the window. "Did you hear that?"

Arthur went to the window and, looking down, saw Irene climbing up through the ivy. *That was fast*, he thought, holding out a hand to help her through the window. He was surprised to feel hers was trembling.

"Irene? Are you all right?"

She jumped lightly to the floor, wiping stray bits of vine from her skirt.

"Me? *I'm* fine."

"What happened?" Jimmie asked.

Irene shot an uncomfortable glance in his direction. "What happened is . . . well . . . they wanted me to tell them all about *you*."

So Arthur had been interrogated about Irene's family, Jimmie had been interrogated about Arthur's, and Irene had been interrogated about Jimmie's.

Jimmie's smile slid from his face. "But you don't know anything about my family."

Irene's expression was pained. "Actually," she said, "I do. When I went to my pigeonhole this morning, I found a copy of a newspaper article. It was from a London paper from over a year ago. Just a few sentences, really. It said that a Sir James Moriarty had been acquitted on fraud charges after a key witness had disappeared."

Jimmie's expression went dark. "He was innocent," he snapped. "My father isn't a criminal."

Irene studied him for a long moment. "Of course not," she said finally. "As soon as they began asking me questions, I knew that they must have been the ones to put that paper in my pigeonhole. Scaring us in the first challenge was one thing, but digging up family secrets to hold over our heads is another. I didn't want any part of their little game. So I told them to unstrap me and let me go."

"You mean . . . you failed?" Jimmie asked, flabbergasted.

"I most certainly did not," Irene retorted. "I declined the invitation to be a part of their little group."

"Little group?" Jimmie repeated. "Irene, they're the most powerful group of people in the country. Probably the world!"

Irene lifted her chin, which wobbled slightly. Arthur had the feeling she knew exactly what she had walked away from, and that it hadn't been an easy choice.

"Well, maybe that's the problem," Irene said. "Power shouldn't just be for small groups of people who meet in secret."

Arthur could feel the truth of Irene's words. But *someone* had to fill the offices in Parliament and Downing Street. Someone had to publish the newspapers and fill the spots at the important universities. If the Clover wanted to help a poor Scottish boy like

him be one of those someones . . . wasn't that a good thing?

She and Jimmie stared at each other, neither willing to back down.

"So they asked each of us about each other," Arthur said, trying to cut through the tension. "It's quite clever, actually. In a devilish way. They try to turn us against one another. If they can't, then they know we'll always protect each other's secrets . . . and *theirs*."

"They must be the ones who sent you my letter," Irene said. "Did they ask you about my parents' show being canceled in Paris?"

"Actually . . ." Arthur mumbled, "there's something I need to tell you."

He explained what he had discovered in her letter, and how the Clover seemed to suspect that Irene's parents were working with the War Office.

She watched him intently as he spoke. When he was done, she hesitated for an instant, then burst into laughter.

"What?" Jimmie asked. "What's so funny?"

"The Clover aren't as smart as they think they are," she said. "My parents get a lot of fan mail, and they try to answer as much as they can. The current War Minister is a devoted opera fan. He came to every performance of *Carmen* my parents did in London. He still writes to them every few months, asking them to come back and perform here."

Arthur was speechless for a moment. "That . . . makes sense," he said finally.

"More sense than them being secret employees of the War Office!" Irene agreed. "Can you imagine?"

Arthur couldn't help but notice how quickly Irene had changed the subject. Her explanation made sense, certainly, yet something about the way she didn't meet his eyes gave Arthur pause. Again, with the strange behavior. He thought about pressing her on the subject, but decided he'd leave it, for now.

"But . . . how did the Clover know about your father, Arthur?" Irene went on. "Have you told anyone besides us?"

"I thought about that," Jimmie said. "And I'll bet someone was following us that morning when Arthur told us about his family."

"That's right," Irene said. "Arthur thought someone was watching us, but then we saw Didi and assumed that's all it was. I wonder who they asked Sebastian about?"

"If he passed, then it wasn't me," said Arthur. "He'd be more than happy to tell everyone my secrets."

"He knows a lot about my family without the Clover even interfering," Jimmie said. "It was probably me."

Irene shook her head. "I wonder what they've got in store for you next."

"Actually . . ." Arthur began.

Irene dropped to his bed in disbelief when he told her about the third and final challenge.

"You won't do it, though," she said, looking from him to Jimmie. "Right? You won't steal?"

Jimmie shrugged. "I don't have much of a choice. If I don't get in, my father will probably send me to rot in some school in Australia. Make me join the army, then marry me off to a rich old maid with gum disease. The Clover is the only path for me in his mind. Otherwise, I'm useless."

Irene turned her sharp gaze to Arthur. "What about you?"

"It's not stealing," Arthur said. "It's borrowing. We're going to put back what we take. It's just a test of loyalty."

"No harm will come to anyone from it," Jimmie added.

"Unless you get caught," Irene pointed out.

"I have to think of my family," Arthur mused aloud. "I have to think of what's best for them."

"Well, it's certainly not having you expelled for stealing," Irene argued.

Which was rather a good point.

"But if he joins, he can—"

Arthur put up a hand. His head had begun to ache, and he suddenly wanted very badly to blow out the candle and be alone with his thoughts.

Arthur lay awake for a long time that night, turning the evening's events over in his head. When Irene had realized the Clover had been snooping in all their families' secrets, she had refused to play along. Perhaps she really had been infuriated by their trickery. But was that all that had made her walk away from the Clover? What if she had another reason?

And what about him? What was the best way to protect his own family? To stay in the Clover with Jimmie, or to leave it like Irene?

The answer will come, Arthur told himself. *It always does.*

THIRTY-ONE

An Answer Arrives

THE ANSWER CAME FROM MARY.

Her letter was waiting in his pigeonhole the following week. It was such a relief to have a reminder of home that he clutched the envelope to his chest as he hurried into the buttery to read it.

But what he found inside brought him little comfort.

Dear Arthur,

Hello. How are you I am well. Mam said you went on an AIRSHIP. Could you please bring it back and pick me up? I want to come live with you and I promise I will be very quiet and tidy and I will not throw your things out the window or eat pages out of your books. Mam said to say everything is fine and not to write about Pa staying in bed all day and Baby Constance crying all night. It is very tyresome. Now I have to go help with supper. Please come get me soon.

Your very favorite sister,
Mary

Arthur read it twice, letting the words sink in. The letters at the end were so thick and blurry he could hardly discern them. They had obviously been written with the nub of a pencil. And the handwriting was unsteady, as though Mary had been shaking with cold when she had written it.

Pa staying in bed all day . . .

Baby Constance crying all night . . .

His pa had broken his promise to take care of their family while Arthur was away at school. Arthur couldn't simply wait and hope for his pa to become the man the Doyles needed him to be. The letter was a reminder that he had to do what his pa couldn't. He had to find a way to give his family a better life. And the fastest way to do that was to join the Clover.

So it was that Arthur spent his weekend trying to plan a theft.

How ironic, he thought, that only a few days before, he had been the one trying to *solve* an attempted burglary, and now he himself had become the burglar.

The only problem was that he couldn't think of anything to steal. He spent most of his time sitting in front of a crackling fire in the library, frowning at the flames and running through options in his mind. What was something rare and valuable enough to impress the Clover that Arthur could take without anyone noticing? He thought of the pillowcase Harriet claimed had come from Queen Victoria's bed. It would be easy enough to sneak into her room and take it. But the idea of showing up at the Clover's headquarters holding a pillowcase that may or may not have once belonged to the Queen wasn't very appealing. And besides, he hated the idea of stealing from one of his fellow classmates.

He thought of taking a glass-jarred specimen from Dr. Watson's shelves. But those were more grotesque than valuable, and he couldn't bear the idea of being caught by Dr. Watson, who had been nothing but kind to him, and whose lessons in "mind over matter" had helped him twice now—first to stop Lucky from attacking Grover, and then to defeat the Deception Machine. The glasshouses and vivariums were full of rare plants and creatures, but he didn't know how to hide or care for any of them.

Jimmie and Irene sat with Arthur in the library sometimes, Jimmie in the armchair beside Arthur and Irene sprawled out on the floor, warming her toes close to the fire. Jimmie alternated between reading and scribbling down ideas of his own. Irene had made it clear she wanted nothing further to do with the Clover, or with Arthur's and Jimmie's plans for the final test. But she had also seemed to accept Arthur's decision when he told her why he had to keep going. Truly, she seemed more interested in the new novel she was reading, *Little Women*.

Pocket was busier than ever with Professor Grey, barely surfacing from the laboratory for meals. And she wasn't the only one with Grey on the mind.

A cry interrupted Arthur's thoughts on Saturday afternoon. He had jumped from his armchair to see what the matter was, and had found Grover in the next section, clutching a tattered volume to his chest.

"Grover! What's wrong?"

Grover gestured for Arthur to follow him to the table where he'd been gathering his research on Professor Grey. "Look! Look what I found!" He raised up the ratty book as though it were the Holy Grail.

"What is it?"

"Elizabeth Grey's research journal!" Grover exclaimed. "She was the current Professor Grey's grandmother. There's a fount of knowledge to inform my obituary here. With an object of such personal significance, I might even be able to contact her spirit. Imagine, if I could interview her about Professor Grey. Now *that's* an obituary everyone will want to read."

"That sounds wonderful, Grover," said Arthur, trying to muster some enthusiasm for his friend. "Good luck with the interview."

The buttery was full of laughter and chatter on Sunday night as friends exchanged tales of their weekend adventures. Some had taken part in the chess tournament Mrs. Hudson had hosted in her parlor, while others had spent their afternoons on the muddy grounds playing cricket with Professor Stone or saddling up for a hack in the woods with the brigadier.

Arthur wasn't in the mood for merriment. He felt alone, singled out among the crowd by an invisible burden. So he stuck a few of Cook's bread rolls and some cheese into his pockets and headed for the library. If he was going to feel lonely, then he would rather actually be alone.

The hallways were nearly empty. He only passed the strange pair of psychical science students, dressed in their usual white, coming down the stairs. They halted their hushed conversation when they saw Arthur. Thomas, tall and stooping, glared at him from his hooded eyes as though he had been eavesdropping. Ollie blushed a deeper red than usual and scowled as he brushed past Arthur.

Maybe the rumors were true and those two had some kind of secret powers, but Arthur thought he would take Jimmie and Irene over them any day.

The library was mostly abandoned, too, when Arthur arrived. The only sound that interrupted his thoughts were the snores of Mr. Underhill.

Arthur was himself tired from several restless nights, and the warm flicker of the fire lulled him into a soft daze. It was nice, relaxing into the armchair and letting his thoughts drift along a gentle current. He let his eyes close, just for a moment.

When he opened them again, the library had gone dark. The fire in the grate in front of him was only smoldering embers. The air was cold.

Arthur shot up. He must have fallen asleep. How late was it? He needed to get back to his room before anyone caught him.

He took the stairs two at a time and broke into a run as he reached the main floor of the library. But as he stepped into the hall, he nearly ran into someone else passing by. Arthur skidded to a halt, noting that the person was carrying a lantern in one hand and something bulky in the other. A cloak billowed around the figure's legs.

The last time he had seen a cloaked, shadowy figure stalking the manor halls, it had been running away from Professor Grey's office.

"You!" he exclaimed.

The figure whipped around.

"Who's that?" came a voice. A woman's voice.

Then she held the lantern up to her face, and Arthur saw who it was.

Valencia Fernandez.

THIRTY-TWO

Into the Clock

"WH-WHAT ARE YOU DOING HERE?" ARTHUR sputtered.

Dr. Fernandez snorted. "I rather think I should be the one asking that question."

She didn't exactly sound like a criminal caught in the act. And she wasn't wearing a cloak at all, just a heavy skirt.

"I've half a mind to go see Eddie—that's Headmaster Challenger to you—first thing in the morning and tell him that one of his students is running through the halls at all hours of the night, accosting esteemed visitors."

"Please don't!" Arthur said. "I fell asleep in the library. When I woke up, it was dark. It was just an accident."

Dr. Fernandez's sharp features softened. "Lighten up, boy," she said. "I was only angry because you startled me. I won't tell

Eddie. I don't mind a child who bends the rules. I've spent my whole life trying to snap them in half. Anyway, as you're here, you might as well make yourself useful."

Arthur sighed in relief. "Of course. Anything you need."

She handed him the lantern.

"I'm moving the last of my artifacts back to my laboratory. They're very delicate, you know. That's why I waited until no one else was around. I didn't want to find myself in the midst of some silly game of horseplay and risk dropping them. Of course, I didn't realize there would be students lurking the halls at this hour. But perhaps it's a good thing you're here. In all my wisdom, I forgot that I would need one of my hands to hold the lantern."

Arthur obediently held the light aloft as she shifted a wooden crate to hold it with both arms. "Which way?"

"Upstairs." She glanced at him and then did a double take. "Say . . . I know you. You're the boy who tried to start a fight during my banquet."

"Yes, ma'am," Arthur admitted as they started up the stairs. "I'm very sorry."

"What was it about? A girl?"

"No," Arthur said quickly. "Well, not in the way you mean. The boy I wanted to fight is a bully. The kind who thinks he's better than everyone else."

"That's the worst kind," Dr. Fernandez replied. "Shame you didn't give him what was coming to him. But don't you worry. Bullies usually get what they deserve in the end."

Arthur flashed a timid smile.

"Do you like traveling around the world?" he asked.

"Very much. Out at sea, every day is a new adventure. And it's a thrill, going on a journey and never knowing what the destination will be like."

"I'd like to go on a ship one day," Arthur said. "I've never been on one before."

They reached the top of the steps, and Dr. Fernandez guided them down the east corridor. Near the end, she nodded to a door on the right. Arthur opened it and stepped in after her.

The room was mostly empty but for two long tables. On them sat an array of bones, crates, and silver instruments. Dr. Fernandez set her crate down among the others. She leaned over it and pulled out a jar.

"Hello, my little beauty," she said, holding up the jar to inspect it.

As he watched her, Arthur felt his heartbeat quicken. It was the jar containing the preserved dinosaur egg.

An idea struck him. A wild, impossible idea.

The egg was one of a kind. What more rare and valuable object could there be to present to the Clover?

But how could he take it without her knowing? Could he double back for it after Dr. Fernandez was gone? She would be sure to lock the door, though. And she would be certain to notice its absence. When she discovered it missing, her suspicions would fall on him.

Unless . . .

Arthur's hand slipped into his pocket. He still had a bread roll from dinner. A bread roll that bore an uncanny resemblance to the egg.

She never even knew it was gone.

"Come on, then," said Dr. Fernandez, turning for the door.

"High time you were in bed."

On one corner of the table, Arthur spotted a heavy brass key.

Before he could stop himself, he had darted out a hand for it and shoved the key in his pocket.

"Oh. I've forgotten the key," she said, glancing back at the table. Arthur stood frozen, sure she would realize that he had taken it only seconds before. But she patted her pockets, then gave a huff of irritation.

"Perhaps it fell out somewhere," she muttered. "I'll have to go back to my rooms for the spare. Will you be all right to get back to the front hall without a lantern? It's quickest for me to go out the back way."

"Oh yes," Arthur replied, his voice coming out too loud and sure of itself. "I'll be fine."

Dr. Fernandez cocked an eyebrow. "All right, then. Thank you for your help."

Arthur managed a nod before turning on his heel. He walked to the end of the corridor and waited, listening for any sound other than the roar of the blood as it pumped through his veins.

When he was quite certain Dr. Fernandez had gone, he crept back to the laboratory, opened the unlocked door, and slipped inside. Moonlight streamed in silver ribbons through the windows, illuminating the jar with the egg. Arthur drew closer.

Was he really going to do this? Steal such an invaluable treasure?

Borrow, he corrected himself.

He didn't know if he believed in fate, but if there was such a thing, it had led him straight here. To the perfect opportunity.

He fumbled in his pocket for the bread roll and bent down

to examine it side by side with the egg. They really did look very similar.

Dr. Fernandez would be back soon. There wasn't time to dither over his decision.

Arthur began to untwist the top of the jar. He plunged a hand inside and carefully wrapped his fingers around the egg. In a few more seconds, he had replaced it with the roll.

He had done it. There was no going back now.

There was only escaping without being caught.

He left the key in the shadow of some kind of weighing scale, where Dr. Fernandez could easily believe she had missed seeing it, then strode to the door and closed it behind him. Retracing his steps through the hall, he cradled the egg to his chest to ensure it wouldn't drop. He felt sick to his stomach.

When he heard the first creaking floorboard, he told himself he must be imagining it. But then the sound came again, louder this time.

Someone was coming up the stairs.

Panicking, he turned to the doorway to his left. Locked. He rushed back up the corridor, trying each door he came to. Finally, one opened, and he stumbled in, then closed it behind him.

If someone came looking for him here, he couldn't be caught red-handed with the egg. He'd be expelled for sure! Desperately, he scanned the cramped room. It was an office, but even in the dim light, he could tell it hadn't been occupied in some time. A layer of dust covered the desk. In one corner loomed the largest grandfather clock Arthur had ever seen. It stretched almost to the ceiling and was nearly twice as wide as most clocks of its kind.

Perfect.

Many such clocks had glass doors through which you could see the great pendulum counting off the seconds. But this one was solid wood. Still, there would be a door. Arthur felt around its ridges until his fingers landed on a little latch. He pushed, and the front of the clock swung open. As gingerly as he could, he placed the egg on a shelf in the compartment and swung the door closed. It made a firm clicking sound as it shut.

As soon as it did, suddenly, inexplicably, the clock began to whir.

Arthur had never heard a clock make such a noise before. To his dismay, the sound grew louder and more high-pitched with every second. He frantically tried to undo the latch again, but it would not give.

Then something even worse happened. The office doorknob began to rattle. The door swung open just as a flash of green light burst from the clock's compartment. Arthur winced as he waited to see who stood on the other side, but no one was there.

Then he looked down.

"Toby!" he whispered.

The wolf stared up at him with his moonish eyes. His ears were pinned back. He let out a low growl.

Another burst of light came from the clock, quickly followed by a loud *CRACK!*

Toby jumped into the air, gave a startled yelp, then shot off down the hall.

A moment later, the clock went quiet.

Arthur tried to steady himself. He was lucky that Toby had

been scared away, but he knew the wolf would run straight to its mistress. He had very little time to retrieve the egg and make his escape.

When he tried the latch again, the door opened easily. A plume of foul-smelling smoke spilled out. Arthur waved his hands to dispel it, trying not to cough. Before he could reach in for the egg, however, he heard someone else coming down the hall. This time, the footsteps were unmistakably human.

He picked up the egg—relieved to find it whole and seemingly undamaged—and squeezed himself into the cavity inside the clock, pulling the door nearly shut behind him.

Only a second later, he heard footsteps enter the room.

Through the crack in the clock's door, he saw a bobbing light, and two figures behind it. They paused in the doorway.

"The noise definitely came from this room," said a girl's voice. Arthur recognized it immediately. The Nightingale. "Smells strange in here, too."

"Check under the desk," ordered the second voice. The Magician.

A shuffling sound as the Nightingale followed the command.

"Nothing here. But I'm sure this is where we heard it."

"Perhaps. But this office is the last place the machine would be hidden."

Arthur couldn't believe his ears. The Clover was looking for a machine? His first thought was of the Deception Machine, but that made no sense. They obviously knew where to find that. So what kind of machine were they looking for?

Arthur heard another noise, a soft tapping. He leaned his ear closer to the crack. The tapping came again.

He had the sudden, dreadful realization that the noise was coming from *inside* the clock.

Was there something in here with him?

He forced himself to stay still, hoping the two intruders wouldn't hear.

"We've run out of places to look," said the Nightingale. "And it's becoming more dangerous now that all the professors are on high alert. Which is *your* doing, by the way."

Tap tap.

"I know. But we had to send a message. It was just bad luck, that strange girl being in the office with Grey, and then Doyle blundering along."

"Well, hopefully we've done enough to throw everyone else off the scent," said the Nightingale.

"It was a good idea you had," replied the Magician. "Staging a break-in through the front door. But you're right. All our searching hasn't gotten us anywhere, and we don't want to take any more risks than we have to. It might be time to move on to more—*forceful* methods."

Tap tap tap.

The Nightingale sighed. "I was afraid you'd say that. You're sure it's worth it?"

"Finding that machine is the knight's highest priority. Given the choice, I'd rather risk Challenger's wrath than his."

TAP!

Arthur's whole body clenched, as though it had turned to stone.

"What was that?" asked the Nightingale.

"Maybe someone's coming," said the Magician. "Let's go."

More shuffling footsteps, and the click of the office door being closed. Then . . . silence.

Arthur drooped in relief. He scrambled from the clock. What had he just overheard?

It had certainly sounded a lot like the Clover plotting to steal an important machine from under Headmaster Challenger's nose—by any means necessary.

But he couldn't think about that now. He needed to make a hasty retreat back to the tower with the egg before something happened to it.

When he held the egg up to the moonlight to inspect it, however, he saw that something had *already* happened to it. Just moments before, the egg had looked fine, but when Arthur examined it now, he saw a large crack running through it. His heart sank.

What was he going to do?

As he stared miserably at the egg, something rather impossible happened.

TAP! TAP TAP!

Arthur's heart leapt. The noise hadn't just been coming from inside the clock! The noise was coming from *the egg itself.*

Indeed, as he watched, the crack was growing larger, splintering into *many* cracks. But surely it couldn't . . .

Too stunned to breathe, Arthur leaned in even closer just as something inside the egg let out a mewling sound.

Arthur couldn't believe what he was seeing.

The egg hadn't broken.

It had hatched.

THIRTY-THREE

A Baby Finds Its Mother

"*THERE* YOU ARE!" IRENE EXCLAIMED AS Arthur climbed into his room through the window.

Jimmie, Irene, and Pocket all sat on the floor around a single candle. They scrambled to their feet at the sight of Arthur.

"What are you all doing here?" Arthur asked. He had not expected to have an audience, and it wasn't a welcome sight.

"Trying to decide if we should go searching for you," said Jimmie. "When you didn't come back after dinner, I was worried. So I went upstairs to ask Irene if she'd seen you."

"Are you sick?" Irene asked. "You look like you've eaten some bad prawns."

Arthur didn't know how to answer that. "I fell asleep in the library," he said.

"Is that all?" Pocket looked disappointed. "I was hoping it might be something exciting."

Just then, a mewling sound came from inside Arthur's jacket.

"Um, what was that?" Irene asked.

Arthur reached a trembling hand under his jacket. "Be careful what you wish for, Pocket."

He scooped up a gray, rather slimy, little creature and set it on the table.

For a minute, no one said anything. They all stood, staring at the long blue beak, the ridged head and narrow eyes, the rubbery wings that tapered into sharp claws.

"Is it . . . a bat?" Irene asked finally.

"It doesn't look much like any bat I've ever seen," Jimmie replied.

"More like a baby dragon," said Pocket. "Please say it's a dragon, Arthur!"

"I think . . . I think it's a dinosaur," Arthur said.

Jimmie shot him a befuddled look. "Arthur . . . dinosaurs have been extinct for ages and ages. How could there be one in our bedroom?"

Arthur gulped. He would have to explain himself. And maybe it was for the best. If he was going to get himself out of this mess, he wasn't going to be able to do it alone.

"After I woke up in the library, I ran into Valencia Fernandez," he said. "She asked me to help carry some things to her laboratory. One of them was her dinosaur egg. I—um—got a little lost, and I set the egg down somewhere I thought it would be safe. Inside a clock, actually. But when I closed its door, this noise started up, and then lights started flashing and there was

all this strange smoke. When it cleared, I opened the door and there was the egg. And it was hatching."

"You got *lost*?" Irene repeated. "And just happened to set the egg down in a *clock*?" She obviously knew Arthur was lying, and he'd wager she knew why, too.

"Let's stay focused on the real issue," Jimmie said quickly. "Which is what we're going to do with the *baby dinosaur*."

Arthur let out a moan.

"I'm going to be expelled," he said. "I am most definitely going to be expelled."

The little animal let out a chirp that sounded a bit like a hiccup. It took two clumsy hops toward its onlookers and peered up at Arthur.

Irene flinched. "Is it dangerous?"

"It's only a baby," Pocket said. She reached out a cautious hand. Quick as a flash, the creature snapped its long jaws at her, only just missing her finger.

Jimmie shook his head. "I suppose a baby dinosaur is still a dinosaur."

The creature hadn't stopped staring at Arthur. It stretched out its little wings, gave another hop, and flapped up from the table. Everyone jumped back as it soared in a bobbling circle around the room. Jimmie leapt to the window to pull it closed before the dinosaur could fly out. But it seemed not to have any intention of flying away. Instead, it fluttered down onto Arthur's shoulder. He froze. He could feel the thing breathing on his neck, its nose prodding at his earlobe.

He steeled himself. If he had to lose a body part to those jaws, he supposed an earlobe wouldn't be the worst thing to go.

But instead of the sharp pain of a bite, Arthur felt a gentle nudge. The dinosaur was *nuzzling* him. It folded its wings, settled down, then gave a contented sigh.

"Oh dear," Pocket said.

Arthur glanced at her but didn't dare turn his head in case it startled the dinosaur. "What? Oh dear, what?"

"I know what it's doing," she replied. "We see it on the farm all the time."

"See *what*, Pocket?"

"It's imprinted on you. It thinks . . . it thinks you're its mother!"

THIRTY-FOUR

Kipper

IF ARTHUR HAD EVER SPENT A STRANGER, more restless night than that one, he certainly couldn't recall it. All night, the little dinosaur slept in the crook of his arm, now and then snuffling like a piglet.

Meanwhile, Arthur had lain stiff as a board, trying to make sense of the evening's events. After bidding good night to Irene and Pocket, Arthur hadn't had the energy to tell Jimmie about overhearing the Magician and the Nightingale. He knew he would only have to repeat the story to Irene the next day anyhow, and this way he had time to think about what he had heard.

While Arthur couldn't fathom how a clock had apparently transformed an ancient egg into a living dinosaur, certain other things were starting to become clear. The Clover had been behind both the break-in that occurred just before Arthur's arrival and the sacking of Professor Grey's office.

It made so much sense that Arthur felt ashamed he hadn't put it together before. The reason nothing had been taken in either break-in was that the Clover had been looking for something specific: a machine. And the reason they had broken in through the front door in the first instance was to make it look like the burglary had been committed by outsiders. After all, why would students who already had access to the hall have a need to break into it? Afia had even written an article in the *Bugle* to support the story, writing that the crime had been committed by disgruntled villagers.

And . . . that clock *must* be what the Clover was searching for. Or rather, the machine inside it was.

It felt as though Arthur had just managed to slip into a restless sleep when Brigadier Gerard's French horn awoke him with a start. The small dinosaur was staring at Arthur with wide, unblinking eyes. When it saw him waking, its wings gave a pleased little flutter, much like a dog thumping its tail.

From his own bed, Jimmie gave a groan. "I was hoping it had all been a dream."

"Worst luck," Arthur grumbled.

The dinosaur refused to be parted from Arthur as he got dressed. Wherever he walked, it hopped or flew to reach him, and when Jimmie came near, it let out a shriek of protest.

When it was time to go to breakfast, Arthur did what he had done many times for his sisters when they were babies. He tucked the small dinosaur into his bed and pulled the sheets tight.

"You're going to leave it here?" Jimmie asked.

"If baby dinosaurs are anything like baby humans, it'll sleep most of the day," said Arthur, striding swiftly for the door as the creature struggled against the grip of the sheets. "I'll come check on it betw—"

The moment Arthur closed the door behind them, the shriek became a scream.

CAAAAAA-AAA-AAAA-WAAAA-AAA-WAAAA!

Then something crashed into the door, causing the boys to jump.

CRASH!

CAAAA—

CRASH!

CAAA-WAAA—

The creature was throwing itself against the door.

Arthur flung it open just in time for the dinosaur to hurtle straight into his nose, where it clung with its sharp claws while it used its wings to cover his face in what could only be described as a loving embrace.

It whimpered as he peeled off one wing, then another. Then it scampered up and burrowed into his hair.

He threw a desperate look at Jimmie, who was shaking his head in disbelief.

"What do I do?"

"I think you've got to take it with you," Jimmie said.

"Good morning, Arthur," said someone else.

They spun around to see another boy standing behind them.

"Did you know," said Grover, "that there appears to be a pterodactyl stuck to your head?"

After swearing an amazingly serene Grover to secrecy ("How can I be surprised when I have long suspected that death is not the end for any of us?" he asked), Jimmie waited on the landing for Pocket and Irene to come down, then swept them inside the room.

"Oh, good!" Pocket said. "Grover's here, too. I was going to tell him about our little friend at breakfast."

"The dinosaur is a *secret*," Irene scolded.

"Pocket, Arthur needs, well, a pocket," Jimmie explained. "On the inside of his coat, where no one will see it. Can you stitch one now?"

She could, of course. The fivesome made it to breakfast just in time to grab the last of the kippers and toast. At the smell of food, the pterodactyl began to squirm against Arthur's chest. He stuffed a bite of kipper underneath his coat, and felt it instantly disappear. He fed the creature another bite and then another, until it gave a tremendously loud burp—which attracted a few disapproving glances from down the table—and then settled into stillness.

"What are you going to do about that . . . thing?" Irene asked, leaning in.

"We should give her a name," Pocket said. "So we can talk about her without anyone understanding what we're talking about."

"What makes you think it's a her?" Jimmie asked.

"I grew up on a farm," Pocket said. "Do you want to hear more?"

Jimmie blushed and looked away.

"How about Kipper?" Irene suggested. "Since that seems to be her favorite food."

"I like it," Arthur said. "And, Irene, to answer your question, I

have no idea what I'm going to do. I can't tell any of the teachers, because they'd only ask where, er, *Kipper* came from."

Irene dabbed at her mouth with her napkin. "We also need to figure out how this happened," she said. "I mean, how is Kipper *here*? After being a fossil for who knows how many years?"

"That was no ordinary clock I hid—I mean—put the egg down in," Arthur said. "I think there's some other kind of machine inside of it. But I have no idea how it could possibly work."

"I can help you there," said Pocket.

Everyone turned to her expectantly.

"Well, not *now*," she said. "But if you take me to it, I might be able to figure it out."

A machine that could take something old and make it young again . . . that could even rekindle a spark of life in an ancient egg . . . It was unnatural.

Whoever owned it would be powerful beyond measure.

And just what, Arthur wondered, did the Clover intend to do with all that power?

THIRTY-FIVE

Kipper's Close Calls

THEY CAME UP WITH A PLAN.

During their study hour that afternoon, Arthur would show Pocket to the office where he'd found the clock, while the others stood guard.

First, though, they had classes to get through. Dr. Watson's class was easy enough, since once again he asked them to read from *Gray's Anatomy* while he wrote at his desk. He only looked up from his work to dismiss Roland from class after he began flashing drawings of the more shocking organs around to the others.

Halfway through Professor Grey's class, Kipper began to stir against Arthur's chest. She snapped her jaws, pinching his skin and causing him to shoot up from his seat.

"Yes, Doyle?" Grey said, raising her eyebrows at him.

"I—need to use the washroom—quite badly."

"We don't need all the details," she said. "You may—"

She hesitated, her sharp gaze suddenly flashing to the lapel of his coat. Then she blinked and shook her head. "I really must stop drinking so much coffee with breakfast," she murmured to herself. "It's no substitute for sleep. Go on, Doyle."

He fled from the class, not caring about the laughter that followed him into the hallway. Kipper must have peeked out over the collar of his jacket. Thank goodness Professor Grey didn't seem to have believed her own eyes.

"We got lucky there, Kipper," he muttered, once he had reached the privacy of the washroom. "But you have to stay put from now on when we're around other people."

In response, the little dinosaur emerged from her pocket and stared up at him with her big, questioning eyes.

"I know," Arthur said, softening. "You didn't ask for this either, eh?"

He gave her a pat on her head. For something so scaly, she was rather cute.

Kipper licked his hand in response, then nibbled his finger again.

"Don't worry. It's almost lunchtime."

While Arthur fed Kipper bites of liver, he told Irene and Jimmie what he had heard the night before. Jimmie's eyes grew wider with every word, while Irene's grew narrower. He told them everything: his certainty that the Clover had been behind the break-ins; that they were looking for the machine that seemed to be able to grant life; that they seemed to be willing to do anything to get it.

Irene shook her head. Her lips were pressed into a knot. She glanced at Grover, who was reorganizing his grave rubbings. Pocket was once again with Professor Grey.

"I knew it," she said. "I knew that group was no good. But who is their leader? Who is this so-called 'Green Knight' person they're working for?"

"Someone who wants that machine very badly," Arthur replied.

"We don't know why he wants it, though," Jimmie said. "Irene's assuming the worst. What if the knight wants it so he can protect it from someone else? Someone who wants to misuse it? Or maybe to heal someone who's sick?"

"That's what I was wondering, too," Arthur said. "After all, when we heard them in the library, the Clover leaders did say they wanted to find the machine to keep it safe."

Irene opened her mouth, as though to continue arguing, but settled for a single shake of her head.

Arthur was grateful when Mrs. Hudson clapped her hands together to get the first years' attention, then announced that they would be having their first lesson in Equestrian Arts that afternoon.

Not wanting a repeat of what had happened with Professor Grey, Arthur wrapped up a parcel of liver bites to keep Kipper content if she woke up during Professor Loring's class. But the creature didn't stir during their hour in the conservatory, or during the first half of their lesson in the stables.

"You will each take turns riding in the ring, so I can observe your skill level, or lack thereof," Brigadier Gerard explained when they arrived.

Worry and excitement braided together in Arthur's stomach as Jimmie gave him a leg up into the saddle. He had always wanted to learn to ride a horse, but he'd never done it before.

"Heels down, Doyle!" the brigadier commanded as Arthur entered the ring on a chestnut-brown mare named Minnie. "Chin up! Elbows to your sides! Now, trot. Trot, I say!"

Arthur squeezed his knees and clucked as he'd heard the other riders do, but Minnie maintained a sluggish pace as she hugged the edge of the ring.

"You've got to ask like you mean it! Here!"

The brigadier gave the mare a swat on her backside, and she suddenly sped forward, sending Arthur bouncing in his saddle.

Arthur knew he didn't look anywhere near as graceful as Irene or Jimmie had, but he savored the feel of the wind in his face. He grinned as he bounced up and down, left and right. For the first time in days, he felt light and free.

"Goodness, is that how they ride in Scotland?" came a smooth voice from behind. "How very unusual."

Sebastian had ridden up behind Arthur, so close that his horse was nose to tail with Arthur's. Arthur felt Minnie tense beneath him as she pinned back her ears.

"You're too close," Arthur snapped. "Back up, or you'll get us both thrown off."

"I haven't been thrown from a horse since I was six," Sebastian answered. "But if you're so worried, why don't you pick up the pace? My grandmother rides faster."

Arthur didn't have much of a choice. He gave the mare a little kick. But as she trotted faster, so did Sebastian's horse. Minnie was growing more and more agitated, bucking her head and snorting.

He twisted around in the saddle. "Look, why don't you just—"

But before he could finish, Sebastian's eyes went wide. Not nearly as wide as his horse's, just before she reared up onto her hind legs with a loud bray of fear. Sebastian's feet slipped straight out of the stirrups, and he landed on his backside in the mud as his horse took off, galloping for the gate as though she meant to break through it.

As Arthur slowed Minnie to a stop, wondering what on earth had just happened, he heard a very un-horselike mewling noise. He looked down, and suddenly understood three things.

First, Kipper had climbed halfway out of her hidden pocket and was now staring up at him with hungry eyes.

Second, the sight of her was what had spooked Sebastian's horse.

And third, Sebastian's eyes had widened *before* his horse had reared. He had seen Kipper, too.

THIRTY-SIX

A Most Remarkable Clock

"YOU CAN'T BE SURE HE SAW ANYTHING," Irene said as they trudged back to the manor.

"And even if he did," said Pocket, "I doubt his mind went straight to *pterodactyl.* He probably thought you were keeping a pet lizard in your pocket or some other perfectly normal thing."

After Sebastian had been thrown, Brigadier Gerard had taken his horse in hand, then led a limping Sebastian from the ring to see Dr. Watson.

"But if he did . . . if he tells . . ."

"You'll certainly be expelled," Grover droned. "Perhaps even criminally prosecuted."

Jimmie fell into step beside Arthur. "You won't. If Sebastian *did* somehow recognize Kipper as a dinosaur and decided to tell on you, he would have done it already. He wouldn't want to give you the chance to hide Kipper somewhere and make him look like a raving lunatic."

Arthur tried to take comfort in the logic of these words.

"Jimmie's right," Irene said. "But . . . I don't know how much longer you can keep Kipper hidden. We have to come up with a plan."

"First things first," Pocket said, rubbing her hands together, her eyes alight. "We have a clock to examine."

Irene and Jimmie stationed themselves at either end of the corridor, while Grover was positioned directly outside the office where Arthur had seen the clock. If Irene or Jimmie saw anyone coming, they would signal to Grover, who would knock on the door to alert Arthur and Pocket.

The first trouble came when Arthur tried to open the door. The handle wouldn't turn.

"It's locked," he said.

"Was it locked last night?" Pocket asked.

Arthur shook his head. "Someone must have been here since then."

"Well, it doesn't matter."

She began opening the various pockets on her skirt, scrounging around inside until she found what she was looking for. "Lock-picking kit!" she said, holding up a set of various wires and hooks.

Arthur had never been more grateful for Pocket's many eccentricities. She fiddled with the doorknob for just a moment before it swung open. "After you," she said, with a bow and a grin.

She closed the door gently behind them, then let out a low whistle.

She was staring at the enormous clock. Now that it was daytime, Arthur could see it was quite striking, and not only for its size. The chestnut wood was streaked with gold, and its sides had been carved with ornate flourishes. The hands on its face stood still, as though time had come to a halt in the dusty little room.

He suddenly remembered the large gap along the wall of the horology clubroom, where hundreds of other clocks of every shape and size were kept. Someone must have moved this clock from there to this office. But why here?

This office is the last place the machine would be hidden, he remembered the Magician muttering.

Pocket opened the clock's front panel and gasped.

"See this?" she said, pointing to a compartment on the clock's side wall, which held something that looked like a spice rack. Except instead of glass, the two dozen or so small jars were made of some kind of metal, and each had a wire connecting it to a copper bracket.

"It's a lead-acid battery," Pocket explained. "All these little jars store electrical charge. But they should be connected to something up here."

She pointed to the top of the rack, above the copper brackets, which were clearly designed to attach to something. "This is where a conductor should go. A copper rod, or a silver one, maybe. To take the charge from the battery."

Pocket followed a path of singed wood that led to a second compartment, this one on the clock's back wall. It contained a jagged gray rock the size of Arthur's fist that had been split into several pieces. Arthur stepped forward and picked up one piece.

"Whoa," he breathed. "Look at this."

The inside of the rock was a glittering maze of gold, purple, and green. Pocket took the other half to study it.

"It's pretty, isn't it? I wish I knew what it was." She frowned. "Ahmad might, though! He knows everything there is to know about rocks."

She tucked her part of the rock into a chest pocket. "It looks like the current goes through whatever this rock is, and then over to the other wall."

She pointed to burn marks in the wood that led from the second compartment to a third, which was strewn with shards of something Arthur took at first to be glass. Careful not to puncture his finger, he reached in and picked up a larger shard.

"It looks like some kind of shattered crystal," Pocket said. "Almost like the current that ran through it was so strong it cracked the first rock and then shattered the crystal."

"So . . . what does that mean?" Arthur asked. "How does it work?"

Pocket, deep in thought, rubbed her temples. "I don't understand it all," she said, "but this is definitely some kind of electric circuit. It might even create an electromagnetic field."

Arthur blinked. "A what?"

"It's when an electrical current creates a magnetic force," Pocket said. "And I think that's what the inside of this clock is. When it's turned on, anyway. The rock and the crystal . . . they must do something to the electrical current. Something that was able to . . . to . . ."

"To bring Kipper to life?" Arthur finished.

Pocket stared at him with wide eyes and nodded. "I don't know how, but yes. We need to find out more about the rock and

the crystal." She looked around, taking in their surroundings for the first time. "What is this place, anyway?"

"That's what I've been wondering," said Arthur.

On one wall, there was a tapestry of a sprawling park. Arthur recognized Big Ben in the background, so it must have been a park in London. On another wall hung a violin. There was a bare desk, covered in scratch marks and what looked to be several bullet holes. *No... Bullet holes?* Surely, that was Arthur's imagination running wild.

Pocket picked up something silver from the shelf behind the desk.

"A letter opener," she said. "With the initials *S. H.* Ring any bells?"

Arthur racked his brain but couldn't think of anyone he knew. He shook his head.

Maaaw! came a sleepy call from his pocket. Kipper was stirring.

"She's hungry," Arthur said. "We'd better go. If we're first into the buttery for dinner, I can feed her without anyone seeing."

Pocket cast a final glance around the office. "At least we have some clues to go on now." Then she cocked her head.

"Arthur?"

"Yes?"

"You said you went into the clock to get the egg," she said. "But . . . where is it?"

Arthur stared at her. "What do you mean?"

"Well, you brought Kipper back to your room last night. But you didn't have the egg with you. Or rather the egg*shell*."

Arthur felt his heart stop for a moment before it lurched

forward. How could he have been so neglectful? In his shock and his rush to get away before anyone found him . . . he hadn't thought about the egg at all.

"I must have left it here," he said. "And someone's taken it."

It had to be the Clover. The Magician and the Nightingale must have returned the night before to double check the room, found the machine, and then locked the door to keep it safe until they figured out what to do with it.

What would they make of the broken eggshell inside the clock's hidden compartment? Would they realize what it was? What the machine had done to it? If so, then they would know there was a baby dinosaur somewhere on the grounds of Baskerville Hall.

And now Sebastian knew exactly where to find her.

THIRTY-SEVEN

The Nighttime Visitor

ARTHUR SUSPECTED HE HAD A LONG NIGHT of tossing and turning ahead of him. He had enough worries to keep him awake for a month. But his exhaustion got the better of him, and the next thing he knew, he was being awoken by a loud shriek.

In the haze between sleep and waking, he thought it must be Brigadier Gerard's French horn. But when he cracked an eye open, the room was still pitch black. And the noise wasn't the kind to come from an instrument. It was—

"Kipper!" Arthur cried, jolting straight up in bed.

By the dappled moonlight coming through the ivy strands, he could make out someone standing near the door. Whoever it was seemed to be locked in a struggle.

"Jimmie? Is that you?"

"What's going on?" came the sleepy reply from Jimmie's bed.

Arthur threw back the covers. Kipper wasn't on the pillow next to him. He could hear the little dinosaur's jaws snapping at air. Someone was trying to take her!

"Let go of her!" he growled, bolting toward the figure. He raised his fists, but before he could get close enough to land a blow, he heard a gasp and then a grunting sound. Kipper came spiraling through the air, colliding with his forehead and folding her trembling wings tightly over his eyes.

"Kipper, no—get off—"

Before he'd even managed to peel her wings away from his face, he heard the door slam. The attacker had fled.

"I'll go after him!" Jimmie said, brushing past Arthur.

As soon as Arthur was able to pry Kipper off his head and bundle her under one arm, he raced out after Jimmie. His friend stood on their shared landing, shaking his head. The tower was silent.

"Whoever it was is gone now," said Jimmie.

"Oh, I know exactly who it was," Arthur growled. "Someone who knows about Kipper. Someone who's had it out for me from the beginning." He started for the stairs.

Jimmie grabbed the collar of Arthur's nightshirt. "Wait. Where are you going?"

"That had to be Sebastian! And he's gone too far this time."

"No, Arthur," Jimmie muttered, pulling him back onto the landing. "We need to think this through. Kipper's all right, isn't she?"

"Yes," Arthur conceded. "But only because she bit him, so he let her go."

"Right. So we don't need to do anything rash. We can't even be sure it was him."

"It *was* him. I know it."

"Well, let's find a way to prove it. So we can use it against him if he tries to go to a teacher. He's got something over your head, so we need something to hold over his."

As Arthur's pulse steadied, he allowed Jimmie to herd him back into their room. He locked the door behind them, but then again, he'd locked it before going to bed, too. He remembered how easily Pocket had been able to pick the office lock earlier that day. For good measure, he carried his desk chair across the room and jammed it beneath the doorknob.

Even so, he couldn't sleep. Instead, he sat staring out the window, stroking Kipper's surprisingly soft back. Every now and again, she gave a soft sigh and smacked her gums together before nestling deeper into his chest. Arthur was surprised at the strength of his feelings for the little creature. Apparently, Kipper wasn't the only one who had become attached—he had, too. He couldn't—*wouldn't*—ever let Sebastian get his hands on her.

It wasn't long before dawn light started to trickle through the window. In another half hour, the first proper rays of sunlight pierced through the ivy curtain. When Arthur looked back at the room, he saw that the morning light had illuminated a zigzagging trail of boot prints on the floor.

"Jimmie!" Arthur called. It would only be a few more minutes until the brigadier's morning serenade woke him anyway. "Jimmie, look."

Jimmie screwed up his eyes against the light. "What? What is it now?"

Arthur pointed to the faint outline of muddy prints that led from the door to his bed and back again. "Boot prints," he said.

When Jimmie merely blinked, Arthur went on. "Don't you see? They belong to the attacker. All we have to do is match them to Sebastian's!"

"Well done," Jimmie croaked. "Knew you had it in you."

Then he rolled over and went back to sleep.

THIRTY-EIGHT

Lord Baker's Portrait

BY THE TIME BREAKFAST WAS SERVED THAT morning, Arthur had already been to Grover's room to borrow his grave rubbing supplies, then used them to make a charcoal rubbing of the clearest print the attacker had left in their room. He had hoped he might be able to follow the trail all the way back to Sebastian's room, but the staircase was too crowded with the dusty prints of many other feet.

He wasn't sure how he would get a rubbing of one of Sebastian's boots, but he was certain an idea would come to him. When Arthur and Jimmie reached the manor, Arthur hurried in, eager to get a glimpse of Sebastian at breakfast. He half expected the boy to be sporting a bandage around one hand, trying to conceal a bite wound.

But before he funneled through the doors to the buttery, he

caught sight of his pigeonhole, where a small envelope was waiting. He cut across the crowd of students and plucked the letter out, keen to see his mam's familiar hand.

When Arthur turned the letter over, he blinked in surprise. It wasn't from his mam nor anyone else in his family. It hadn't even come through the post. It was merely addressed to "Mr. Arthur Doyle."

Mr. Doyle,

Please join me in my office for breakfast this morning. It's at the end of the east wing, first floor.

Yours sincerely,
Dr. J. Watson

"What's that?" Jimmie asked, peering over Arthur's shoulder.

Arthur frowned. "It's a note from Dr. Watson. He wants to meet with me."

"Is that what it says? I don't know how you can tell. He's got terrible penmanship."

Jimmie wasn't wrong. Watson had a narrow, vertical hand that staggered across the page.

"Don't all doctors?" Arthur replied. But the little joke did nothing to help his nerves.

"What do you think he wants?" Jimmie asked.

"I wish I knew. Could he have found out about Kipper?"

"I'm not sure he would be inviting you to breakfast if he had," Jimmie said. "Maybe he wants to make you his assistant or something . . . like Pocket and Professor Grey."

"Maybe," Arthur said, brightening slightly at the idea. "I suppose I'd better go. Can you smuggle some food for Kipper? I'm almost out."

Jimmie nodded, then headed into the buttery while Arthur turned down the east corridor. It was deserted except for him. Everyone was at breakfast. As he rounded a corner and the noise of the diners faded away, the only sounds were Arthur's padding footsteps and his thudding heart. Kipper slept in his pocket without stirring. He patted his trouser pocket to make sure he still had a few bites of chicken left from the night before, ready in case Kipper did wake up. If he had to, he could pretend to duck into the hall to sneeze and sneak the creature a bite or two to settle her again.

Arthur passed by Grey's empty classroom, then Dr. Watson's. He had never been to Dr. Watson's office before, and the only time he had been so far back in this wing of the school was the night of Dr. Fernandez's banquet, when he had taken the back stairs to get to Pocket.

Crrrrreak.

Arthur's head shot up. The noise had come from overhead.

He looked up to see a stern, ugly man staring down at him.

They had faced off once before. . . .

An image flashed into Arthur's mind. The board in the back of the *Baskerville Bugle* office, where articles from old issues had been pasted under a sign that read UNSOLVED MYSTERIES.

Crrrrreak.

"Uh-oh," Arthur said, realization dawning on him.

He dove out of the way just as the portrait of Lord Baker came hurtling from the wall. Instead of landing on his head, it fell to the floor with an enormous crash.

For a moment, he stared in stunned silence at the portrait, which had just narrowly missed claiming its third victim.

Breathing hard, he got back to his feet, wiping down his trousers. Then he peeked inside his pocket to make sure Kipper was all right. She looked up at him with one half-open eye, made a huffing noise, turned her head, and went back to sleep.

His heart hammered and he felt the gears in his mind spinning faster as he pieced together what had just happened.

"Who's there?" he called.

It couldn't be a coincidence that Lord Baker's portrait—the same one that had almost killed two others—had nearly fallen on him. Nor that this "accident" had happened mere hours after someone tried to kidnap Kipper. Arthur might have already made several enemies during his time at Baskerville Hall, but he didn't believe Lord Baker's portrait was one of them.

The corridor was still empty. No one all the way in the buttery would have heard the crash above the clang of cutlery and the buzz of conversation.

Arthur leaned cautiously over the fallen picture, examining its back. There was nothing remarkable about it. He turned in a slow circle, taking in the floor, the ceiling, the walls. Nothing out of the ordinary but a small hole in the plaster where the portrait had been hung.

He bent down and tapped at the wainscoting. The first two wall panels he tried felt solid beneath his knuckles, but the third

rang hollow. Arthur knelt to study the frame around the panel. As he ran his fingers over one of its sides, he felt a slight bulge. Like a very tiny knob. The kind meant to be undetectable unless you knew where to look. He pulled it.

The panel swung open.

Arthur stared into an opening that was just big enough for a grown man to crawl through. Three extremely dusty steps led up to a little room, no more than a few feet wide and long.

He suddenly remembered the priest hole he, Irene, and Jimmie had seen on the old map of the school in the library. *Of course.* It had been right here behind the portrait all this time.

Arthur stuck his head through the opening and tried not to cough. The air was very damp and carried the overwhelming smell of a freshly dug grave. Someone had obviously just been in the tiny room. They might have easily used a narrow rod to poke through the hole in the wall, pushing the portrait until it fell.

"I know you're in there!" he said.

But as Arthur's eyes adjusted to the darkness, he saw the room was empty. And there was another doorway leading from its opposite corner. He picked up a pebble and chucked it through the opening. It bounced five times before coming to a stop, each bounce sounding more and more distant. There was some kind of corridor that must lead to another exit.

Arthur's first instinct was to follow. Perhaps he could still catch whoever had been hiding here just moments ago. But he had no light, and the doorway looked pitch black. For all he knew, his attacker might trap him inside it.

After scanning the priest hole one last time to make sure it was most definitely empty, Arthur backed out into the hall and shut the wooden panel behind him. Someone else would have to deal with putting the portrait back up. Or, even better, finding a large bin to throw it in.

He jogged the rest of the way to Dr. Watson's office. When he arrived, the doctor was sitting behind a neat desk, lost in the stack of papers in front of him. Arthur knocked on the door. Dr. Watson looked up and gestured for him to come in.

"Arthur, my boy," he said. "To what do I owe the pleasure?"

"I got your note," Arthur replied. "About wanting to meet."

As he spoke, he observed the bewildered expression on Dr. Watson's face and the absence of any breakfast foods or tea laid out. So he knew what Watson's next words would be, even before they were out of his mouth.

"But, Arthur," the kindly doctor said, "I haven't written you any note."

A Consultation with Dr. Watson

"MY MISTAKE, SIR," SAID ARTHUR.

"It appears someone is playing a prank on you," said Dr. Watson. "Though I'm not sure it was a very entertaining one."

Arthur thought of the painting that had just nearly crushed him. "No, it wasn't. I'm sorry to have interrupted your work."

Someone else must have written that note so they could get him alone in the corridor. Then they had sat in that dark chamber and waited for the right moment. Someone had been willing to maim—or even *kill*—him, in order to . . . do what? Take Kipper for themselves? But she could have been crushed, too!

Dr. Watson glanced down at what he was writing. The words were still glistening and wet. Arthur chanced a look, which was enough to see that the doctor's penmanship—neat, tiny lettering—bore no resemblance at all to the handwriting on the note he had received. "Oh, this? Just a letter to an old friend who gives excellent advice."

He carefully placed the pages to one side and gestured for Arthur to sit in the chair facing his desk. "I'm glad you're here, in any case," he said. "I've been meaning to check in with you. See how things are going for you here."

"Oh?" Arthur tried to hide his surprise as he took his seat. "Why's that, sir?"

Watson shot a knowing look across the desk. "Places like this . . . aren't always easy for children like you. Children who don't come from means, if you don't mind my saying so."

Arthur felt a blush rising to his cheeks but ignored it and sat up straighter. "Why should I mind when it's the truth? I'm not ashamed of my family."

"As well you shouldn't be," Watson replied. "Look what an intelligent boy they've raised."

Arthur felt a swell of homesickness that stopped him from speaking for a moment. How lovely it would be to sit by the fire with his sisters for an hour, or to share a cup of tea in the kitchen with his mam.

"I'm doing fine, sir," Arthur lied, as images of a baby dinosaur and impending doom filled his head. "Truly, you've no need to worry about me."

Watson nodded. "I'm glad to hear it. Now, you'd better get back to the buttery if you have any hope of catching some breakfast before my class."

As Arthur reached the doorway, something stopped him. His hands had gone reflexively to his trouser pockets. Inside, he felt the forged note and something else, too. Something small and sharp—the crystal shard he had taken from the clock.

He remembered that it was Dr. Watson who had directed him, Jimmie, and Irene to the map section of the library, where they had found a map of the school that showed the location of the priest hole and of the Clover House.

They had found another map that day, too.

On a hunch, Arthur turned around. "Dr. Watson?"

Watson looked up from his letter, which he had resumed writing. "Yes?"

"I wanted to ask . . . When Irene, Jimmie, and I were looking through the maps in the library, we found one that showed what looked like a mine below the school."

For a moment, Watson seemed frozen. Then he blinked and cleared his throat. "That is a peculiar discovery," he said. "I knew there were once plans for a mine here, long before it was turned into a school. I did not know any of those plans still existed."

"So the mine doesn't exist?"

"No. There was an underground cavern of sorts, as I understand, but the entrance collapsed just as the operation began, sealing it off entirely. It was deemed too dangerous and expensive to try to open it again."

Arthur nodded. "What kind of a mine was it to be?"

A frown settled across Watson's face. "There were rumors about there being a rare type of crystal with powerful healing properties being found in the cavern," he said. "But that's all hogwash, of course. Why do you ask?"

"Just curious," Arthur said, doing his best to keep his voice level as he gripped the crystal in his pocket more tightly.

"You do have quite the inquisitive mind," Watson mused.

Arthur nodded and was about to step into the corridor when Watson's voice called out behind him.

"Arthur," he said.

Arthur turned. Watson seemed to be considering him carefully. "Yes, sir?"

"You're a sharp lad, so I don't think you will be surprised when I tell you that there have been some strange things happening at this school of late. Troubling things."

"No, sir," he said. "I was there when Pocket and Professor Grey were attacked."

Dr. Watson nodded. "Baskerville Hall is a dangerous place at the best of times," he said. "It is a place of many secrets. You would be wise to be careful which of its secrets you stumble across."

FORTY

Lightning Strikes Again

NO SOONER HAD ARTHUR SAT DOWN TO breakfast than Toby let out his customary howl, and the meal was over.

He didn't dare try to whisper the story of what had happened to his friends during class, particularly not in front of Dr. Watson. When he could, he snuck glances at Sebastian, trying to read the guilt on his face. But Sebastian seemed subdued all morning, rubbing his right knee and wincing when he stood up. When they were dismissed from Dr. Watson's class, Sebastian stayed behind so the doctor could examine the injured leg. He came limping into Professor Grey's classroom a few moments later, shooting daggers at Arthur. Arthur glared back. Falling off a horse and twisting his knee was the least Sebastian deserved after all he'd done.

Halfway through Grey's class, there was a flash of lightning and a distant rumble of thunder. The elderly woman, who had been unusually jittery, sprang from her seat in apparent anticipation, thrust open a window, and shouted for the class to climb through it.

Arthur, along with everyone else, was thoroughly confused until he heard Grey call out, "Pocket, the kites!" and remembered she had promised they would re-create Benjamin Franklin's famous experiment when the weather was right.

The kites that Pocket hoisted from the window had strings of hemp and silk at the bottom, and a wire at the top. A key had been tied to each hemp string, while Grey instructed the students to keep the silk string dry by stuffing it in their fist.

"Professor," called Ahmad, "is this quite safe?"

"Is Ben Franklin still alive?" she called back.

"I don't think he is, no!" Ahmad shouted over the rain, which had begun falling in a curtain around them.

Pocket started to yell something, but her reply was snatched by the next gust of wind. So, too, was the kite Arthur was holding, and he, Jimmie, and Irene watched as it soared into the sky just as lighting flashed again.

"Look!" Irene shouted. "Look at the string!"

She was pointing at the strands of hemp, which stood on end, full of electric charge.

Arthur spent a memorable half hour running across the grounds with Irene and Jimmie, taking turns holding the kite and daring one another to touch the key, which transmitted a little spark each time.

After a while, though, they were very wet and cold, and the storm seemed only to be growing darker and wilder. Irene pointed to the manor, and Arthur and Jimmie started after her. The grounds were slick with mud, and it was as Arthur nearly slipped and landed on his backside that he realized this would be the perfect opportunity to compare his rubbing of the boot print from his room to the tread of Sebastian's boots. He just needed to find him and follow close enough behind, so he would be able to decipher Sebastian's muddy prints from the others.

He squinted through the rain, searching for Sebastian's figure. Then a flash of lightning lit up the dark corners of the grounds and he saw, quite distinctly, a figure peering out from the woods. The figure sat atop a dark horse, wearing a heavy green cloak. It was staring straight in Arthur's direction.

The Green Knight!

Thunder shook the sky, and the horse reared up onto its hind legs. The rider sat firmly in the saddle, then pulled hard on the horse's reins to lead it back into the forest. They were gone in an instant.

Arthur hurried to catch up with his classmates. But again, there was no time to fill them in on what he had seen. Sebastian was limping into the manor as Arthur started up the front stairs.

"Arthur, what are you—" Irene called as he brushed past her.

He shouldered his way through the crowd until he was directly behind Sebastian. Then, ignoring the grumbles of the students coursing by, Arthur dropped to his knees and pulled out the rubbing he had made that morning. He unrolled it next to the print he had just seen Sebastian make. His eyes darted back and forth between the two, comparing.

Neither print was perfect, so they weren't an exact match. Still, there were similarities in the sizes and the treads. They *might* be a match.

Except . . .

There was no difference in the appearance of the right and left prints Arthur had seen in his room. He'd made sure of that before deciding which print to make a rubbing of.

But there *was* a difference between the right and left prints Sebastian had just made. The print made by his left shoe was distinctly bolder than the one made by his right.

"Because he's got a limp," Arthur muttered to himself, his heart sinking with disappointment. "He's not putting much weight on his right foot."

Which meant, for all he was guilty of, Sebastian was innocent of one thing. He hadn't broken into Arthur's room that night.

So who had?

FORTY-ONE

Suspicions and Silver

ONCE IRENE, JIMMIE, POCKET, AND GROVER had taken their seats in the buttery, Arthur finally recounted the morning's events in hushed tones. They all listened, slack-jawed, except for Grover, who was staring at the ceiling, seemingly preoccupied by more interesting thoughts.

"So someone deliberately tried to crush you with . . . a portrait?" Irene asked, when he was done.

"I know it sounds crackers," Arthur replied. "But it's true, I swear. You can see the secret room for yourself if you don't believe me."

"I believe you," said Irene. "I just wonder if it might be time to tell someone. Dr. Watson or the headmaster?"

Arthur shook his head. "How could I explain about the portrait without explaining everything else?"

"But if Sebastian wasn't the one to try and clobber you or take Kipper," Jimmie asked, "then who was it?"

"I've been wondering that myself," Arthur replied. He thought of the rider in the forest. His instinct told him that this man had to be the Green Knight. It couldn't be a coincidence that he had returned now. Had the Clover summoned him to come, after they had discovered the machine he'd been looking for?

"I think it's too soon to rule out Lord Baker's spirit," Grover said sagely. He had, apparently, been listening the whole time.

Their conversation was interrupted then by Mrs. Hudson, who announced there was to be a special treat that evening. "A magic lantern show," she said, "which will take place here after dinner. Therefore, you will skip your study hour and come to dinner after your lessons, so we can have the show afterward and still get you to bed at a decent hour."

Down the table, people were grinning and exchanging excited whispers. Were he not so distracted, Arthur would have been doing the same thing. He'd only been to a magic lantern show—in which an operator used a lantern and glass slides with images on them to project illusions onto a screen—once, when he was six or so. But at that moment, he just wished he had some time alone to think.

Alas, it was not to be.

"Don't be forgetting about my silver!" called Cook from the back of the buttery.

"Ah yes, of course," said Mrs. Hudson. "Cook believes that someone may have taken some of our finer silver pieces."

"I don't *believe* it. I know it!"

"Well, if you happened to come into possession of them,

please drop them off in my parlor by dinner."

"Otherwise, the lantern show is canceled!" Cook shouted.

"The lantern show will *not* be canceled, because the man has already been paid. But return the silver if you have it, and no questions will be asked."

Cook stormed off in a huff as they were dismissed for afternoon classes.

"Was it you?" Arthur muttered to Jimmie as they stood. "Did you take the silver?"

Jimmie shook his head. "I've got something else for tonight."

"Tonight?" Arthur asked. "The next Clover meeting is *tonight*?"

With everything else going on, Arthur had completely forgotten.

"At midnight. So technically, it's tomorrow morning."

"But we can't still go," Arthur said. "I couldn't tell you before, but I saw the Green Knight again. Just now, during Professor Grey's class. He's back, Jimmie. And it must be because the Clover have found the machine."

"Well, we suspected that they were looking for the machine," Jimmie replied. "So . . . now they've found it."

"Yes, but don't you see?" Arthur said, too loudly. He dropped his voice again. "That's not all they found. They found Kipper's eggshell, too. And who else knows about her besides Sebastian? Even if he wasn't the one who tried to kidnap her, he must have told them straightaway what he saw yesterday. They put two and two together, and now they want her. They love 'rare and precious' things, remember?" He snapped his fingers as another piece of the puzzle fell into place. "And Afia knows that portrait has fallen twice before! She's in the Clover—she might have told them about it, and they realized it was an opportunity to get me out of the way."

Jimmie's face darkened as Arthur spoke.

"Of course, I won't go if they're really behind all this," he replied in a hushed voice. "But . . . we don't know that yet. We've still got until tonight to figure out what's going on."

Arthur wanted to believe Jimmie was right. That the Clover had nothing to do with the attempt to kidnap Kipper. That he and Jimmie could still join and have a sure path to success. He *needed* to walk that path for his family.

Then he remembered the Magician's words inside the Clover House.

None of you can imagine the power and the influence we wield.

Despite his hopes, he was beginning to feel like Irene had been right all along. That that much power in the hands of so few could be a dangerous thing indeed.

FORTY-TWO

The Magic Lantern Show

WHEN THEY REACHED THE BUTTERY THAT evening after their class with the brigadier, the seats at the end of the first-years' table had already been taken, and there wasn't room anywhere for all five of them to sit together.

"I need to talk to you," Pocket murmured as Arthur sat down beside Sophia. "I found out something about that rock that was inside the clock."

"And I know where that crystal came from," Arthur replied. He hadn't had enough time at lunch to recount his conversation with Dr. Watson. "Let's talk after the show."

Pocket nodded before taking her own seat several places down the table.

A screen had already been set up in the front of the room, and once the sun had set outside, Mrs. Hudson and Professor Stone went around the room extinguishing all the wall sconces. Soon a veil of darkness fell over them. The only light came from the white screen, where a bright spotlight shone.

After a moment, the image of a ship appeared inside the spotlight. It bobbed along the ocean waves for a moment before the image changed again. Now it was a horse and rider galloping over the moors. Then dancers spinning in a ballroom.

With each new image, there were scattered gasps and applause. Jimmie stifled a yawn—he would have had the chance to see many such shows before—but Arthur found himself relaxing for the first time all day as the images washed over him. It was like flipping through the pages of a book, except every page was from a different story. And the pictures *moved*. He wished his sisters could have been there. He could imagine their expressions of delight and awe as they watched the flickering images.

After a picture of children sledding down a hill, the circle of light on the projection screen shrunk into a pinprick. Then a very small train appeared. As the circle grew bigger again, so did the train. It seemed to be coming closer and closer, as if it might rip straight through the screen and crash through the buttery. Someone gave a little scream.

Then there *was* a crash. From behind the screen, a cry rang out, then a loud clatter of something heavy falling to the ground. The screen went dark, plunging the room into inky blackness.

Arthur jumped to his feet. A few more people screamed. All around him came the sound of rustling and murmuring as people stood to get a better look or clutch the person sitting beside them.

"Everyone stay where you are," came Headmaster Challenger's

voice. "There's no need to panic."

Arthur felt someone push in beside him in the chaotic din.

"I'm worried about . . . our little friend," a girl whispered in a lilting, Irish voice.

"Pocket?" It was hard to hear her in all the noise. Arthur remembered their arrangement to meet after the show. Clearly, Pocket was too concerned to wait.

"Who else?"

Our little friend. Arthur gave his coat a little pat. He could feel Kipper's outline there, curled up in sleep.

"She's fine. She's sleeping."

Then there came a second commotion, this time at their own table. The sound of breaking glass and dishes rang out.

"Someone's coming this way," Pocket said. She sounded breathless and frightened, not at all like her usual self. "Arthur—what if they're trying to take her again?"

Arthur felt a twinge of panic as he imagined Clover members surrounding him in the total darkness.

"Give her to me," Pocket went on. "They won't find her if you don't have her. I'll keep her safe."

Another clang. Someone cried out nearby.

Pocket was right. No matter how much he had learned about boxing from Professor Stone, Arthur couldn't keep Kipper safe if he was outnumbered in the dark. The only way to keep her safe was to hide her. And what better place than in one of Pocket's endless pockets?

He gently pulled out the sleeping creature, then felt Pocket's hands close around her.

"I've got her," she said. "Don't worry. She's safe with me."

Arthur knew she was right. Pocket was clever and tough, and she would do anything to protect Kipper. He heard the rustle of skirts as Pocket turned away. He steeled himself, waiting for an attack to come.

But the next moment, several of the wall sconces flamed back to life as matches were lit and fumbling hands finally found the wicks.

Everyone was still in their seats, except Harriet, who seemed to have had a goblet of water spilled on her and was grabbing all the napkins she could find. No one had surrounded Arthur. No greedy hands were waiting to snatch Kipper.

And Pocket . . . Pocket was sitting where she had been before the lights went out. How had she gotten back to her seat so quickly?

"Pocket," Arthur called. "Were you there the whole time?"

She exchanged a look with Irene. "Where else would I have been?"

He waited for a sly wink or a knowing smile, but Pocket simply looked confused.

Something wasn't right.

"Not to worry, everyone," Mrs. Hudson called. "The lantern operator just stumbled over his equipment and had a little fall."

"I did not!" the man cried, indignant. "I was pushed!"

"I highly doubt any of our students would do such a thing. . . ."

"And why not?" Cook exclaimed. "If they're willing to steal my best silver!"

"Bedtime!" roared Professor Challenger.

As chairs and benches were pushed away from tables, Arthur sat quite still, afraid to confirm what he already knew in his heart.

Pocket scooted across the now empty bench to sit next to him. "Arthur, what's wrong?"

"Do you have Kipper?" he asked.

Pocket's eyes widened. "No," she said. "I thought you had her."

So it was true.

He had been tricked. Kipper was gone.

FORTY-THREE

An Anonymous Tip

BEFORE ARTHUR COULD COMPOSE HIMSELF enough to speak, he felt a hand on his shoulder. He whirled around to find Headmaster Challenger standing behind him.

"Doyle. I need you to come with me," he said.

There was something strange about the headmaster's tone. His voice was gruff, as always, but there was something else there, too. Something almost sorrowful. And he wouldn't meet Arthur's eyes.

Arthur struggled to piece his thoughts together. Kipper was gone. Stolen by someone who had been impersonating Pocket. And now here was the headmaster, looking like a man with bad news to deliver.

"What . . . what about?" Arthur managed. His throat was suddenly very dry.

"Just get up," Challenger said.

Numbly, Arthur did as he was told. He could feel his friends' gazes upon him as he followed the headmaster out of the buttery. His hand kept returning to his jacket, feeling the spot where Kipper should have been. Who had her? Was she safe?

The headmaster didn't so much as glance over his shoulder as he marched Arthur up the stairs and through the corridors. Arthur was still too stunned to pay much attention to where they were going. So it wasn't until they reached the laboratory door that he realized where they were.

Valencia Fernandez sat in the center of her lab, lit by the glow of a gas lamp. Her hands were folded in front of her. As Arthur was led in, she looked up and her lips twitched.

The sight of her shook Arthur from his daze. He gasped.

What if he *had* been wrong about Sebastian and the Clover all along?

It had been a girl—or woman—who had taken Kipper. Someone impersonating Pocket's voice—quite well, too. If Dr. Fernandez had realized that Arthur had replaced the egg with a bread roll . . . if she had gone looking for it and found the broken eggshell in the clock . . . she would know that a freshly hatched dinosaur was out there somewhere. And she would want it back.

"Was it *you*?" he asked.

She frowned, shooting a look at Challenger, who was now pacing back and forth in front of the window.

"If you mean was it me who caught on to your trick," she said, "then I must disappoint you. In fact, I had an anonymous tip."

Arthur squeezed his eyes shut and opened them again. "What? What are you talking about?"

"Don't play the fool, Doyle," snapped Challenger. "The game is up. We know you stole the dinosaur egg."

"Someone wrote to me," said Dr. Fernandez, "telling me that my egg had been swapped for a fake. Imagine my horror when I realized it was true. I also realized, of course, that *you* were the only person who could have taken it. You helped me bring it up here, and then I couldn't find the key. I returned less than half an hour later with another key and locked this room. You were the only one who knew the egg was there and that the room was unlocked."

Challenger had stopped pacing. He stared at Arthur with a look of bitter disappointment that made him want to wither from the shame. "Well, boy?" he said. "Do you deny it?"

Arthur shook his head. "No, sir. But—"

"Where is it?" Dr. Fernandez said. "Where is the egg now?"

Arthur frowned. If she had been the one to take Kipper, she would know that there was no more egg. And surely she would be scolding him over having kept Kipper a secret from her and asking him how on earth the egg had come to hatch.

"Doyle," said Challenger, "a man is only defined by his mistakes if he chooses not to correct them. This is your chance to put things right. Where is that egg?"

Arthur opened his mouth, but no words came out.

"You aren't going to tell us?" Dr. Fernandez asked, her voice sharper with every word.

"I—I can't," Arthur said finally. "Because—because it's gone."

"Gone?" Dr. Fernandez shouted, banging her fist on the table. "You mean to tell me that you stole a priceless artifact—the most important I have ever discovered—only to lose it?"

Should he tell them? About the machine, and Kipper, and the Clover? About all of it? The whole story rested on the tip of his tongue. But he would sound mad without proof to back it up.

The clock!

If he showed them the strange machine inside it, perhaps they would believe him.

"It . . . it might be easier if I showed you," Arthur said.

"Showed us *what*, precisely?" Dr. Fernandez snapped.

"Please, just come," he replied. "It's down the hall."

Dr. Fernandez and Challenger exchanged a look. Challenger sighed. "This had better be good."

They marched him through the hallway like a prisoner. Challenger went first, and Dr. Fernandez came behind. Arthur stopped outside the door to the office that held the clock.

"It's in there," Arthur said.

"In *here*?" Challenger grumbled. "What in the name of Newton's apple could we need to see in here?"

But as he spoke, he put a key into the lock and swung open the door.

Arthur looked inside, and the blood drained from his face.

There, where the great clock had stood, was a blank wall.

It was gone. His only proof. His only *chance*.

"The clock . . ." he muttered. "It was here. . . ."

"Yes," Challenger growled. "Lord Baker's prized grandfather clock was brought here for repairs by the only person able to handle them. It's probably been transported to one of the labs for further work. I'm sure it's safe. What exactly does that have to do with—"

He stopped suddenly, then strode across the small room and

swiped something up from the floor. "My bismuth!" he said. "I should have guessed you stole that, too."

"Your—your what?" Arthur sputtered.

"I told you not to play the fool," Challenger said. "Someone broke into my office last night and stole a large piece of bismuth from my mineral collection. Now I find you've smashed it!"

He held out his hand to show Arthur what he had picked up. It was a piece of the strange rock they had found cracked open inside the machine.

"I didn't break into your office," Arthur protested. "And that rock was here before last night. I found it when—"

"Does it matter?" Dr. Fernandez cut in. "You have already admitted to stealing the dinosaur egg. What excuse can you give—what story can you possibly tell—to redeem yourself?"

Arthur opened his mouth to speak but realized there was no point. The machine was gone. Kipper was gone. He would only sound like a desperate liar if he told them the truth now.

"You have nothing to say for yourself?" Challenger asked. "Can you explain why my bismuth is here, or what you have done with the egg?"

"I'm very sorry," Arthur croaked. "I never meant to cause any harm."

Challenger sighed deeply. "Dr. Fernandez," he said, "might you leave us?"

The famous scientist glared at Arthur for another long, boiling moment before sweeping from the room.

"I must say, I am very surprised," said Challenger. Arthur had never heard him speak so softly, and he wished the headmaster would growl and roar like he usually did. "I had hoped—but

never mind. What's done is done. You know, of course, what must happen?"

Arthur had been expecting this, but still, his heart plunged like an anchor in his chest. He nodded. "I'm to be expelled."

"You've left me no choice," Challenger said. "If you had returned the egg, then perhaps I might have been able to let you stay. You are absolutely sure you cannot return it?"

"Yes, sir," Arthur said, his voice little more than a whisper. "I'm sure."

"Then it is decided. I will arrange transportation home."

"When, sir?"

Challenger looked at him, and Arthur was sure he saw pity flash across the headmaster's beady eyes. "Tomorrow," he said. "First thing in the morning."

FORTY-FOUR

Grey the Elder

CHALLENGER WALKED ARTHUR ALL THE WAY back to the tower. Their destination might as well have been the Tower of London. Everything he had ever dreamed of for himself and for his family had been within reach, and now it was gone. How had he bungled it all so badly? What would they think of him when he returned? Not a boy destined for greatness, as his mother had believed, but one who had already made himself a failure.

He felt shame burning his cheeks as he looked up to see Thomas and Ollie, the somber spiritualist pair, headed down the path toward them. They both stared at Arthur, their expressions hard to read.

"Hood," Challenger barked, "Griffin. I hope you're on the way to your lodgings?"

They nodded, eyes still boring into Arthur. He was relieved when the sound of their footsteps receded into the night.

"I will come for you in the morning," Challenger said when they reached the tower door. "Go and pack your things. You're not to leave your room until I arrive."

"Yes, sir," Arthur mumbled.

Challenger's beard twitched, as though there were something else he wanted to say. But he only made a low grunting noise deep in his throat before he turned and was swallowed by darkness.

Arthur trudged up the stairs, dragging his feet on every step.

When he finally opened his door, he groaned. Inside, Jimmie was huddled in a circle with Irene, Pocket, and Grover.

"About time!" Pocket said.

"You've really got to stop making a habit of disappearing like this," Irene said.

Jimmie was pale and seemed the most agitated of them all. His foot tapped rapidly against the floorboards.

"Where have you been?" he asked.

Arthur opened his mouth, but he seemed to have misplaced his knowledge of the English language. He couldn't find a single word to say. Shaking his head, he turned toward the wardrobe, where he pulled out his tattered carpetbag and began stuffing things inside.

"Packing for a trip?" Grover asked. "I do hope you're going somewhere pleasant."

"What's going on, Arthur? Where's Kipper?" Pocket asked.

Arthur stiffened when he felt a gentle hand on his shoulder. Irene stood behind him. Her eyes were alight with concern. "Stop that and tell us what's happened."

This time, he managed to get a few words out.

"I'm . . . I've been . . . expelled."

"Expelled?" cried three voices together. Even Grover summoned a blink of surprise.

"But why?" Jimmie asked, shooting to his feet. "On what grounds?"

"On the grounds that Valencia Fernandez knows I stole the dinosaur egg. Someone sent her an anonymous tip."

Had *that* been from Sebastian? Arthur found he couldn't even summon the energy to be angry. For perhaps the first time in his life, all he felt was defeat.

"When I said I couldn't return it, Challenger said he had no choice," Arthur finished.

"Why didn't you show them Kipper?" Irene asked. "And the clock? I bet Dr. Fernandez would be so thrilled to see an actual dinosaur she wouldn't even care that you'd taken its egg."

Arthur put his head in his hands. He couldn't look any of them in the eye. "I tried to take them to the clock, but it was gone. Challenger said he thought it had been taken for repairs, but he doesn't know what it really is. And Kipper—she's gone, too. Someone took her during the magic lantern show. When all the lights went out. I thought it was Pocket next to me, and she offered to take Kipper to protect her, but it was someone else. I don't know who."

Pocket and Irene gasped.

"We've got to find her!" Pocket exclaimed.

"We *will* find her," Irene corrected. "And we're going to clear Arthur's name."

Arthur shook his head. The only bright side of this terrible day was that none of his friends had been dragged into the trouble he had caused. "I won't let you all risk your places here, too," he said. "And besides, there's no time. Challenger is going to collect me first thing in the morning."

"Say we did have time," said Jimmie, who had been pacing back and forth by the windows. "What's your plan, Irene?"

"Oh. Well . . ."

She trailed off, giving Arthur the strong impression that the plan was still very much in progress.

"I suppose we'd have to find Kipper and the clock. Surely they were stolen by the same person. If we had the evidence, Challenger would have to believe us. He wouldn't care much about expelling you if he had an actual criminal on his hands."

"Irene's right," Pocket said. "Someone took that machine, and there's only one reason anyone would do that. They want to use it for themselves."

"They probably took Kipper hoping she would give them some clue as to how it works," Irene mused.

Arthur remembered his conversation with Dr. Watson.

"I think *I* might have an idea of how it works," he said. "Dr. Watson told me that there's a cave below the school that's supposed to be filled with crystals with some kind of healing properties. He didn't believe it, but it must be true. Pocket and I found shards of crystal when we went to examine the machine."

"And that's not all we found," Pocket replied. "I tried to tell you earlier, Arthur, but there wasn't time before the show. I asked Ahmad about the other rock we found, and he told me it was—"

"Bismuth," Arthur finished. "I know. There was a piece of it left behind. Challenger said someone had stolen some from his office last night."

He glanced at Jimmie, who gave a small shake of his head to tell Arthur that he hadn't taken the bismuth for tonight's Clover initiation. "I've got Ahmad's loupe," he whispered so only Arthur could hear. "It's a special magnifying lens geologists use. His dad gave it to him, and he used it to look at the bismuth. The frame is made of solid gold and rubies. He told me I could borrow it."

Pocket was too busy thinking to notice their whispers. "Ahmad told me that there's all kinds of stories and legends associated with bismuth. He says there are people who think it's the longest lasting element in the world. They say it's so strong, it will outlast the universe."

"How is that possible?" Arthur asked. The idea made his head hurt.

"You'd have to ask Ahmad about that," Pocket said. "But now we know what the machine does! It runs an electrical current through an element that basically lasts forever, and then through a crystal with healing properties. Together, those two rocks create an electromagnetic field that somehow makes it possible to—"

"Bring a dinosaur to life," Irene breathed.

"Yes," Pocket finished. "One that's been preserved well enough. The machine created a field that restored it to its original state. A dinosaur that was just about to hatch before it got dropped in that strange blue clay Dr. Fernandez found it in."

"If someone is trying to use the machine," Jimmie murmured, "what else could they want to do with it?"

"To become immortal?" Grover suggested.

They all stared at one another in the flickering light.

"Think about it," Grover continued. "You could just reset yourself forever and ever."

Could it be true? Did someone want the machine because they wanted to defeat death—forever?

"Who . . . who at this school would actually want such a thing?" Irene said, rubbing her arms as if suddenly chilled. "It's unnatural."

Jimmie shrugged. "I wouldn't mind a turn. Not at immortality," he clarified, when Irene sent him a hard look. "But surely most people would jump at the chance to live a little longer?"

Arthur was only half listening now. Who would want immortality? Perhaps someone who had named himself for a knight who escaped death? A knight who, legend had it, had lost his head, then simply picked it up and walked away unscathed?

"The Green Knight," he murmured.

Whoever was after the machine hadn't named himself after the legendary knight because he was honorable and brave. He had chosen that name because the Green Knight represented *eternal life.*

Pocket cocked her head. "Come again?"

Irene and Jimmie both stared at him, wide-eyed. They knew exactly who he meant. He knew he would have to tell Pocket and Grover everything, but time was running short. Besides, Grover had inexplicably pulled out a tattered book and begun to *read.*

"Pocket, what else would someone need to make the machine work?" Jimmie asked, before Arthur could decide what to say next.

"The battery inside is rechargeable," Pocket replied. "So it just needs the bismuth and the crystal. And a conductor, of course."

"Like silver!" Arthur exclaimed. "You said silver was a good conductor, right?"

Irene gasped. She had clearly made the same connection Arthur just had. "Cook said someone had stolen her best silver!"

"Which could easily be melted down into a rod to conduct the electricity," Pocket said.

Arthur nodded. "And someone stole the bismuth from Challenger's office. Someone *is* trying to use the machine."

An image came to his mind of the clock looming against the brick wall of the Clover House. Hooded figures everywhere. A man in a green cloak stepping forward . . .

"So the only thing they might not have yet is the crystal," Jimmie said.

"Speaking of crystals, I'm sure Grey the Elder writes about them somewhere in here."

It was Grover. Everyone turned to stare at him as he finally looked up from his book. Arthur saw now that it was the old journal Grover had found, belonging to Professor Grey's grandmother. It was small, the pages yellow and brittle.

"It's taken me ages to decipher the handwriting, you know. It's mostly notes on her experiments. Quite disappointing, actually. I was hoping for more in the way of explosive family secrets. Ah, yes, here we go. She mentions them toward the end. At least, it's the end of what I have. The last few pages have been torn out."

"Grover?" Arthur said. "Do you mind getting to the point?"

Grover squinted at the page in front of him. "Ah, yes. Here it is. '*I am making great progress in my efforts to utilize this particular crystal to stabilize frequency. It can take on enormous charge levels—higher than any I have yet seen. However, I haven't yet been able to find the optimal frequency for my purposes.'"*

"Can I see the book, Grover?" Pocket asked.

"If you're careful," he said.

"That's odd," Pocket said. "The handwriting looks so much like *our* Professor Grey's. She was left-handed as a child but was forced to write with her right hand. She said she never really got the trick of it . . . that's why it's so messy. Usually, she just dictates to one of her assistants, and we write her notes for her."

Arthur sidestepped Irene so he could look over Pocket's shoulder.

The writing was extremely hard to read.

It was also extremely familiar.

Staring down at Grey's journal, Arthur's heart skipped a beat.

He suddenly understood three things.

First, the handwriting in the journal was the very same as the handwriting on the note sent from "Dr. Watson" that led him into the trap of the falling portrait.

Second, Professor Grey had been the one to write the note, just as she had written this journal.

And third, the machine in the clock was not a recent invention. In fact, it had been used several times already by its inventor.

FORTY-FIVE

Arthur's Last Chance

"PROFESSOR GREY'S GRANDMOTHER DIDN'T write this," Arthur said. "Professor Grey did."

Irene scrunched up her nose. "But, Arthur, look how old the diary is. There's no way—"

Then she stopped short. "Oh," she breathed. "I see."

Jimmie's eyes widened. *"Oh,"* he said. "But it does make sense. . . . Who else could build such a thing?"

"And Challenger said it had been moved for repairs by the only person able to fix it," Arthur added. "Who would he trust to do that more than Professor Grey?"

"Wait, wait, wait," Pocket interjected, holding up a hand. "What exactly are you saying, Arthur?"

Arthur cleared his throat. "I'm saying that Professor Grey is the *only* Grey who has ever taught at Baskerville Hall," he explained.

"She and her mother and her grandmother—they're all one and the same. She invented this machine back when she was first here and has used it to make herself younger several times. That clock belonged to Lord Baker, the school's original owner. And he only sold this place under the condition that the future owners would keep it safe, with all the rest of his collection. So Grey knew it would always be here, waiting for her to come back. And even if anyone opened it, no one would ever suspect what it was—especially not without the crystal and bismuth inside. I bet her notes on how she built it are on the missing pages of this diary."

Pocket's cheeks were pinched. She was shaking her head. "No. You're wrong."

A flash of memory came to Arthur. "You saw the daguerreotype in her office," he said. "The one of her mother. They could be twins."

"So first she used the machine to make herself younger," Irene reasoned, "then she left Baskerville for a number of years. She would have to, so no one would suspect anything. Then she came back and claimed to be the original Professor Grey's long-lost daughter. Who would doubt her, when she was the spitting image of her mother?"

Arthur felt breathless as he rushed to get the words out. Finally, *finally*, everything was coming together. "But we aren't the first ones to figure out her secret. We're just the first to *survive.* Because she found a way to get rid of the others, twice. Once to a student and once to a professor. And yesterday . . . she tried to do it to me."

"Do what, exactly?" Grover asked, looking at Arthur with polite interest.

"That portrait that fell on me yesterday morning? It's fallen and hit someone twice before—decades ago. Both times, the injuries were so bad that the victims had to leave the school. Grey must have realized I was getting close to the truth, so she sent the note pretending to be from Watson, then hid behind the picture and waited for her chance to clobber me."

"I can't believe you all," Pocket said. She was shaking now. "Professor Grey is a world-renowned scientist. And an amazing teacher. She . . . she wants to do *good* in the world. To forward humanity. She would never put anyone in danger."

Arthur fumbled in his pocket. The note was still there. With a heavy heart, he held it out to Pocket. He knew all too well what it was like to be disappointed by a grown-up you wanted to believe in.

"Look at the handwriting," he said gently. "I'm sorry."

Her face fell as she studied the note. Without a word, she handed it back to Arthur and put her head in her hands. She began to mutter under her breath, words too soft for the rest of them to hear.

"Well," Grover said, "I suppose I'm going to have to start all over on my obituary."

To everyone's surprise, Jimmie let out a snort of laughter.

"What's funny?" Irene asked.

"Professor Grey was going to retire at the end of term. To go spend time with her niece, wasn't it?"

"Oh, but she can't have a niece," Grover replied. "She was an only child."

"I'm sure that's who she was going to come back as in ten years," Arthur said. "It would be less suspicious than pretending to be a daughter no one has ever heard of."

"She had everything ready," Jimmie continued. "The machine. The crystal, the silver, all of it. Imagine how furious she must have been when she found that someone had beaten her to it! Imagine how furious she would be if she knew it was a *baby dinosaur*!"

Another piece fell into place in Arthur's mind. "I left Kipper's eggshell behind. Professor Grey must have found it and suspected what it was. So she examined the fake egg, realized it was just a bread roll, and then told Dr. Fernandez that it had been swapped."

"How did she know it was you who had Kipper, though?" Irene asked.

Arthur thought for a moment. Then it came to him. "She saw Kipper!" he exclaimed. "In class the day after she hatched. Grey got a glimpse when Kipper peeked out of my pocket, but she made it seem like she didn't believe her own eyes. She's a very good actress."

"She's had lots of practice," Irene pointed out.

Pocket straightened again. Her eyes were ruby rimmed. "What—what would Grey want with Kipper?" she asked in a trembling voice.

Arthur felt his stomach flip.

"She's kept her machine a secret for this long," said Jimmie, as though reading Arthur's mind. "She won't want word getting out now. If people found out about Kipper, they would have questions. Eventually, Arthur would have to answer them. She has to get rid of Kipper before that can happen."

"Not if I have anything to say about it," Pocket growled. Her sadness seemed to have hardened into anger, like a soft dough left in the oven too long. She stood up, fists clenched, and made for the window.

"Where are you going?" Irene asked, just as Pocket shoved one leg through.

Pocket paused, then turned back around. "Good point," she huffed.

"Her plan to get me out of the way didn't work," Arthur said. "And there are others breathing down her neck. That must be why they sacked her office. It was a threat. I don't know how, but the Green—I mean, *someone*—knows about the machine, and he was trying to get her to give it up. She must be spooked. She'll want to use it again and get out of here as quickly as possible."

"But she can't," Pocket said. "Not unless she has another one of those crystals. If she does, then . . . she could already be long gone."

"So we need to figure out how to get to that crystal cave," Irene said, "and hope we aren't too late."

"I have a good idea of how we might get there," Arthur replied. "We need to get to the manor."

"Then let's go!" Pocket said. "What are we waiting for?"

Jimmie consulted Irene's pocket watch with a sideways glance. It was eleven thirty.

"Jimmie?" Arthur asked. "Are you with us?"

Everyone in the room was looking at Jimmie, but he was staring straight at Arthur. His eyes flashed with something white hot—or had it been just a trick of the light? A spasm crossed his face.

Arthur understood how he was feeling. Part of him wished he'd never taken the dinosaur egg or stumbled upon the machine.

Then they wouldn't have had to ask so many questions about the Clover. They could be on their way to the initiation—to a future of power, money, and success—right now.

A few days ago, Arthur would have said there was nothing more important than that future. But he was beginning to see that life's questions for him were much harder to answer than a teacher's in a classroom. For one thing, sometimes an answer that had once been right didn't always stay that way.

Finally, Jimmie sighed.

"Of course I'm with you," he said. "I'm certainly not going to stand by while an innocent pterodactyl is killed by some . . . walking mummy."

"Actually," Grover said, "mummies are—"

"Later, Grover," Pocket said, grabbing him by the hand and pulling him to the window. "Time is of the essence."

Arthur didn't need to be told twice. He scrambled out of the window after the others, the five of them disappearing into the dark Baskerville night.

He prayed it wouldn't be his last.

FORTY-SIX

The Clover Catches Up

"WHERE EXACTLY ARE WE GOING, ARTHUR?" Irene hissed behind him.

He led the group at a brisk pace. A chill wind whistled through the bare trees. Arthur's eyes darted back and forth for any sign of the night watch. So far, though, only Didi the not-quite-dodo had crossed their path, stopping to squawk at them before Jimmie shooed her back toward the forest.

"If I'm right," Arthur replied, "there's an entrance to the cave inside the school."

"How are we going to get in?" Jimmie asked, nodding to the front doors as they approached the manor. "I'm sure it's locked."

"Well, I was hoping Pocket could help us with that," Arthur said. They all turned to look at her. She began to pat the pockets of her dress.

"I'm sure I've got something here that will—oh yes, that should do it."

She stepped up to the door and fiddled with the lock for a moment.

"There we are!" Pocket said as the door swung open.

Just as they were about to step inside, a voice rang out.

"Stop right there."

Arthur whipped around to see three figures standing behind him. Two were masked. Between them stood Sebastian Moran. All three were out of breath.

"Ah," said the taller of the masked figures. The Magician. "Doyle. We've been looking for you."

"Who is that, Arthur?" Pocket asked.

Arthur tensed.

"Wouldn't you like to know?" asked the Nightingale.

"What—what are you doing here?" Arthur spluttered.

"The same as you, I expect," said the Magician. "We're looking for Grey's machine. And Moran here tells us you have an inkling of where to find it."

Jimmie stepped forward. "What exactly did you tell him, Sebastian?"

"Just what I overheard your little gang talking about a few minutes ago," Sebastian said.

"You were listening at the door?" Jimmie asked.

"I looked out my window and saw Doyle being escorted to the tower by the headmaster," Sebastian said. "They didn't look very happy. I wanted to know why. I thought it might have something to do with that ugly thing you had in your pocket that spooked my horse. I didn't think it could get much better after I heard he'd been expelled. But I kept listening."

"And when he had heard enough, he came to us," said the Nightingale. "He proved his loyalty."

"Yes," the Magician continued, "and now it's your turn to do the same. Get rid of the others and take us to the machine, Doyle."

"Arthur, what's going on?" Pocket demanded.

"Not a word to her," the Magician snapped. "Tell them to go."

But it wasn't Arthur he should have been worried about.

"I believe the masked figures are members of a secret society called the Clover," Grover said. "They've been operating at Baskerville Hall for generations. Their alumni go on to seek power in positions of government, law, and business. Irene, Arthur, and Jimmie were all invited to apply for admission. They've been participating in initiation challenges since we arrived. As best I can tell, Arthur believes they're working for someone called the Green Knight to find the same machine that we are currently—"

"Enough!" snapped the Magician.

Irene's jaw had fallen open. Jimmie's face was frozen in shock. *How had Grover known?*

Pocket was looking at Arthur with a pained expression that fell upon him like a dagger to his heart.

"I'm sorry," he said. "We should have told you."

"I said *enough*," the Magician snarled. "Take us to the machine, Doyle, or we'll have to do this the hard way."

He reached into his pocket, and Arthur saw the glint of a blade winking from it. His heart leapt to his throat.

"Oh dear," whispered Grover.

Fingers squeezed Arthur's arm.

It was Pocket. She was still looking at him, but this time with a defiant expression. She gave the smallest nod of her head toward the manor doors.

The Magician took a menacing step forward. "I'm running out of patience."

"I know you," Pocket said to him. Her voice quivered with anger. "You're the one who ransacked Grey's office. You tried to scare me off once before."

As she spoke, Arthur saw her reach into one of her own pockets and pull out a glass vial.

"Pocket . . ." he murmured.

Something inside the vial was moving.

"You should already know," she said, ignoring him, "that I don't scare easily."

The Magician sighed. "I suppose we really will have to do this the hard way."

In an instant, Pocket had opened the vial and flung the contents at their three unsuspecting pursuers.

"What the—?!"

"Grover and I will hold them off," Pocket whispered. "You three go. Save Kipper."

Sebastian yelped. Arthur saw something small and dark crawling up his neck. The Nightingale let out a shriek and dropped the lantern she had been holding.

"Go!" Pocket shouted again. She was reaching into her pockets for more ammunition. "I told you before, I can take care of myself!"

With a grunt of pain, the Magician slapped something from

his ear. A large ant. Pocket had rained ants over them. And judging from the way the Clover members were now thrashing and flailing, Arthur figured they were the biting kind.

Pocket was right. She didn't need Arthur and the others. But Kipper did, and she needed them *now*.

FORTY-SEVEN

Into the Darkness

ARTHUR, JIMMIE, AND IRENE FLEW THROUGH the door and sprinted into the manor, not stopping for breath until Arthur skidded to a halt by the empty space on the wall where Lord Baker's portrait used to be. It had been removed from the hallway but not yet hung back up.

"Arthur," Irene panted, "can you tell us where we're going now?"

Arthur was already bent down, feeling around the wainscoting for the knot that would release the secret door. Ah, yes, there it was. The door sprang open.

"Quick," he said, "before someone comes."

He gestured to the gaping hole. Irene and Jimmie exchanged a questioning glance before scrambling into the dark compartment. Arthur took out the candle and matchbook he had brought from his room and lit the wick. Yellow light illuminated Irene's and Jimmie's twin expressions of fear.

"This is where Grey hid to drop the portrait on me," Arthur explained. "But it's not just this room. See? There's a tunnel that leads this way. Do you smell that?"

Arthur ducked into the tunnel. It was just tall enough for him to walk in a crouch.

"It smells of damp," Irene said.

"Not just damp," came Jimmie's voice. "It smells like . . . earth. Like mud and clay."

"Exactly."

Irene let out a shriek of alarm. "What was that? Something was crawling up my leg!"

"Probably a rat," said Arthur and Jimmie at the same time.

Irene groaned. "You'd better be right about this, Arthur. If I catch the bubonic plague . . ."

He didn't need Irene to tell him this. If he was wrong—if this tunnel *didn't* lead to the crystal cave—it would be the last wrong decision he would ever make at Baskerville Hall.

"Stop!" said Jimmie. "Look—point the light this way."

Arthur swung around and followed Jimmie's gaze.

He had been so worried about what would happen if they were caught that he had completely missed the rickety door in the wall behind them.

Jimmie tugged the iron ring that served as a handle, and it gave an enormous *CRRRREEEEAAAK* of protest as it opened. Arthur was about to walk inside when Irene gasped and shot out her hand, grabbing his wrist.

"Arthur, no! Look down!"

There was, Arthur saw, no ground beyond the door. He had nearly walked out into thin air.

He gulped.

"What is this?" Jimmie asked.

Arthur carefully held the candle out over the precipice. The dim light revealed a square space no bigger than the size the priest hole had been. In each corner, ropes the size of sapling tree trunks hung from some point above, and were pulled taut to some point below.

"I think it's the way down," he said. "There must be some kind of pulley system."

"Like an elevator, you mean?" Irene asked. "The kind they've begun installing in New York?"

"Exactly like that," he said. "When I realized Grey knew about the tunnel to the priest hole, I wondered how she discovered it . . . and what else she might be using this place for. This must be how she moved the clock. I'll bet there's another secret door somewhere in that office she was keeping it in that leads straight to this shaft."

"You're saying she took the clock down to the cave?" Irene asked. "I suppose it makes sense. It was already discovered once. She had to take it somewhere no one else would stumble across it."

"And she needed to go down there for the crystal anyway," Jimmie added. "The question is . . . is she still down there? I can't tell if the elevator car is above us or below."

"There's only one way to find out," Arthur said. He pointed to the thick ropes, then looked at Jimmie and Irene, who were staring back at him as though he were mad.

But perhaps there wasn't anything wrong with a little madness, every now and again. Perhaps when one had been drawn into a mad problem, the solution was *bound* to be equally so.

A few minutes later, Arthur, Irene, and Jimmie were each wrapped tightly around the rope in utter darkness. Arthur needed both hands to climb down, so he had left the candle on the edge of the tunnel. For the first bit of their descent, it had given them enough light to see by. Now, though, it might as well have been a single star on a moonless night.

"It can't be much farther," Arthur said, gritting his teeth.

He had no idea if this was true, of course. But it seemed like the right thing to say, given that Jimmie's breathing was becoming more and more shallow, while Irene had just reminded them that if they all died here, no one would ever find their bodies.

"I don't know how much longer I can hold on," Jimmie said between gasps.

"Just pretend we're climbing down the side of the tower," Arthur said, trying to sound calm.

When he was nearly about to give in to his own rising panic, his heel juddered into something hard.

"What?" Irene asked. "What is it?"

"I think we found the elevator car," Arthur said.

And not a moment too soon, because the next thing he knew, there was a loud thump, and Jimmie was lying in a heap beside him.

"Never . . . again . . ." he muttered.

Irene landed so softly that Arthur didn't realize she was next to him until she spoke.

"I think there's a door here," she said. "I landed on some kind of hinge."

Arthur knelt and fumbled his way around the top of the elevator car. Almost straightaway he saw—or felt, rather—that Irene was right. There was a seam with a hinge on either side.

"Jimmie, do you feel any kind of latch or handle or—"

"I've got it," said Jimmie. "Stand back."

As he pulled the door open, a square of dim light appeared below. Arthur drew a finger to his mouth.

Light could only mean one thing.

They were not alone.

FORTY-EIGHT

The Girl in the Machine

SINCE HE WAS TALLEST, ARTHUR LOWERED himself into the elevator car first. Then he helped Jimmie and Irene down. They were careful not to make a sound, though it was hard to keep from gasping at the sight that greeted them.

The door had been left open to reveal an enormous cavern. Stalactites hung from its roof like enormous fangs, and it was cut in half by a swift, churning river. Many lanterns had been placed in a circle in the middle of the cave, and their light reflected off the rough walls, which glittered and glowed a light purple.

Crystals, Arthur realized. The walls were made entirely from crystals.

Jimmie pulled out a small magnifying lens and held it to his eye, studying the walls of the cave. *That must be Ahmad's loupe,*

Arthur thought. "This is definitely the right place," Jimmie whispered quietly.

In the middle of the circle of lanterns was a dark silhouette. As Arthur studied it, another shadow appeared. Irene squeezed his arm.

It was Professor Grey's clock and the professor herself.

They crept from the elevator out onto the rocky floor. Arthur wasn't worried about being spotted. From within her lighted circle, Grey wouldn't be able to see them coming, so they could take her by surprise as long as they stayed quiet.

Drawing nearer, Arthur saw that she was holding a lumpy object in one hand. And the lumpy object was . . . *moving.* Just then, the object let out a tiny cry. *"CAAAA-WAAAA!"*

Kipper!

Before he knew what he was doing, he was running. He tried to keep his footsteps quiet, but he accidentally kicked a pebble with his left foot, and it bounced off, sending echoes shooting through the cavern.

Grey's head whipped toward him.

"You," she growled.

Grey scrambled out between two lanterns and down to the river's edge. She held the bag with Kipper inside over the water.

"Don't come any closer," she said coldly.

"Give her to me," Arthur shouted. "Please don't hurt her!"

"You would have only yourself to blame if I did," said Grey. "You're the one who created this mess in the first place! Which is why I made sure you would be expelled tonight. I had hoped Challenger would keep you under lock and key until he could throw you out tomorrow, but he's always been too soft for his own good."

She glared at him with bright blue eyes, and though her words were clipped with disdain rather than fear, her shoulders were twitching. The hand holding the squirming bag trembled slightly.

"You mean because he doesn't just drop portraits on people when they become inconvenient to him?"

Grey's eyes narrowed. She edged closer to the river.

"Let me try," Jimmie murmured, stepping forward.

"Professor," he said evenly, "clearly we all find ourselves in a situation that is . . . less than ideal. But perhaps we can come to an arrangement. All we want is the dinosaur. If you give her to us, we will leave and never tell anyone what we know about you and your machine."

"Oh, but you see, that won't do at all," said Grey. "Because as you well know, this little beast could ruin everything. People will ask questions. Questions lead to suspicions. And I can't have those suspicions lead back to me. You have to understand. It's not a selfish pursuit. I'm doing this for the betterment of humanity."

While Grey spoke, Arthur took several tiny steps forward.

"And how is that?" Irene said, her tone just as icy as Grey's.

Arthur took another small step closer to Grey, whose eyes were now locked on Irene.

Grey scoffed. "Look at what I have accomplished in three lifetimes!" she cried, gesturing wildly at the clock. "Imagine what I could do in ten! My work is not finished yet. We are only at the dawn of the electric age. We have just begun unlocking the power of the unseen forces at work around us all the time."

"And who would get all that power?" Jimmie asked. "It seems

to me the only person your machine has helped is you."

She gave him a pitying look, as though he had just come up with an embarrassingly wrong answer in class. "You should have brought your friend Pocket with you. She would understand."

"She knows everything," Irene said, "and if she were here, you would be covered in fire ants right now."

A flicker of surprise crossed Grey's face before it hardened into a scowl. "I am sorry it has to end this way. Truly. For all of you."

Arthur saw the curl of her wrist before she threw the bag. In the instant between the two motions, he leapt and lunged over the river. He grasped in the air until he felt a corner of fabric and clenched his fist around it.

"Yes!" he exclaimed as his toes landed on the rim of the rocky riverbank.

But the next instant, his feet were slipping. He was on the very edge of the cave floor, which cut a steep path straight down to the river. His arms windmilled, and just as he was about to tip over, he felt Irene pulling him backward by the hem of his shirt.

It was at that exact moment that Professor Grey lunged toward them both. She barreled into Irene, who nearly let go of Arthur, who nearly slid into the river.

"Jimmie!" Irene cried. "Get to the machine! Go now. Destroy it so she can't use it again!"

Arthur couldn't see Jimmie, but he heard his friend's footsteps clattering against the rocks.

A second later, Grey gave a cry of anger and set off after him. Irene and Arthur tumbled back from the edge of the river and scrambled to get up again.

Arthur began to untie the bag. He needed to make sure Kipper was all right. But Irene grabbed his hand and tugged him forward. "There's no time, Arthur!" she said. "We have to stop her!"

Jimmie was smashing a rock into the side of the clock when Grey reached him. She grabbed him by his collar and flung him away from the machine. Then, before Arthur and Irene could reach her, she slipped inside and slammed the door closed behind her.

Almost immediately, the clock began to hum and vibrate. Light flashed from within. Arthur tried to tug the door open, but it wouldn't budge. It began to shake more violently now, as all three of them tried anything they could think of to disable it. Jimmie kicked one side while Irene pushed on another. Arthur kept trying the door, watching as the clock hands began to spin faster and faster. They were spinning backward.

"Look!" Irene cried.

Fire licked within the machinery of the whirring clock, which Jimmie had damaged with the rock. When it caught the varnish on the wood, it roared into a column of flame.

"We need to go," Jimmie said. "Before the whole thing combusts."

"But Grey is still inside! We can't just leave her to burn alive," Arthur replied.

A scream came from inside the clock.

"She doesn't need us to get her out," Irene said. "Remember, she built this thing! She must know how to open it. She can come out whenever she—"

Just then, Arthur had to jump back as the door sprang open.

This time, it was Irene who screamed.

The woman who emerged from the clock wasn't a woman at all.

She was a girl.

Her red hair frizzed out in all directions from her head. She was swamped by the black-buttoned lab coat that had fit Professor Grey—that is, the *older* Professor Grey—so well.

"Look what you've done!" she shrieked. "The current! It was too strong! I needed more time to calibrate—"

"There's no time to fight! We have to go, now!" Jimmie yelled. The flames were growing quickly, and sparks were now flying from the top of the clock.

The young Grey turned her head to look, then screamed again. "*No!* My machine!"

"Leave it!" Arthur shouted, tugging at her arm. But she shook free of his grasp.

"Are you mad? This is the work of three lifetimes!" she cried. "I need water! I'll put the fire out!"

She ran down to where a little pool had collected in a deep divot in the cave floor, gathered water in her palms, and threw it at the clock. The water hissed and spit, and the flames burned on.

Jimmie turned to Arthur. "We have to leave her," he said. "She won't listen to reason. We've no choice."

Arthur spared the flailing girl one last glance—she would have looked at home among his own sisters if not for the furious flames reflected in her eyes. Jimmie was right; there was no saving her if they were to save themselves. He ran, clutching Kipper to his chest. Irene and Jimmie were just ahead of him.

They were nearly back to the elevator car when they heard a great *CRACK!* sing through the cave. For a moment, everything was a bright white. Then the cave took on an eerie orange glow. Arthur looked back to see fire licking the ceiling of the cavern.

The clock, and everything around it, had been swallowed by flames. There was no sign of Grey.

Then the earth beneath their feet began to tremble.

"Oh no," Arthur said.

From somewhere deep in the cavern, there was another booming noise as something smashed onto the floor.

"The explosion," he said as they reached the elevator. "It's causing a rockslide!"

"How do we get this thing to take us up?" Jimmie asked.

"Let's hope it's by doing this," Irene said. She grabbed hold of a lever beside the door and pulled with all her might.

"Get in!" she cried.

They tumbled one after another into the elevator car as it gave a groan and then began to lurch up, just as the cave began to thunder down on itself, swallowing everything inside.

FORTY-NINE

The Professor Returns

A FEW MOMENTS LATER, THE TRIO EMERGED into a dark passageway. Though really, they were a foursome, as Kipper was now nestled in the crook of Arthur's neck, her claws dug in tightly, making mewling sounds in his ear.

They had risen past the tunnel from which they had climbed into the elevator shaft, which meant they must be on the second floor of the manor. At least Jimmie had thought to bring one of the lanterns, and they easily found themselves at a door, which spit them out behind the tapestry of London in the office where Grey had, until recently, kept her machine.

If his mind had not been swirling with a thousand more important observations, Arthur might have noticed that the office had changed since he had last been in. Gone was the musty smell of a sealed, forgotten room. In its place was the rather more pleasant scent of pipe smoke. He might also have noticed the gleaming wooden cane leaning against the desk and topped with a silver raven's head.

But they didn't stop to rest in the office. There were sounds of shouting coming from outside, and a glance out of the small window showed that groups of people were clustered on the lawn.

"I think we're going to have some explaining to do," Arthur said.

Arthur scanned the predawn grounds as they barreled down the manor steps. Their classmates—all still in their nightclothes—were clustered around Mrs. Hudson by the chain of glasshouses. Toby circled them anxiously, his ears pinned back and his nose aloft, alert.

"There's Pocket and Grover!" Irene said, pointing to two figures who stood a few feet apart from the rest of the first years.

It was a relief to know they hadn't come to any harm at the hands of the Clover.

"Arthur, my boy!"

Arthur turned the other direction to see Dr. Watson approaching. His hands moved quickly on the wheels of his chair, and his face was drawn with worry.

"We've been looking for you three," he said. He took in the sight of them. Jimmie's trousers were singed in several places. Irene had a large scratch on her face. Arthur chose not to imagine what observations the doctor might make about *him.* At least he had coaxed Kipper into his pocket before they'd emerged from the school.

Dr. Watson dropped his voice. "Where have you been? Are you all right?"

"Doyle!"

Arthur didn't need to look to know that Professor Challenger was standing at the top of the stairs, glaring down at him. The excited conversations happening all around them were snuffed out in an instant. Everyone turned to look.

Arthur climbed slowly back up the steps, aware of the many sets of eyes upon him.

"Did you have something to do with this?" Challenger growled, sweeping one arm out toward the people assembled on the lawn.

Arthur took a deep breath. "Yes, sir," he said. "But I can explain. Truly explain, this time."

Challenger raised his bushy brows. "Well, it had better at least be a damned good story, for all the trouble you've put me to tonight. Let's go."

"Wait," Arthur called. "I need to bring Jimmie and Irene, too. And also . . . Dr. Fernandez."

Challenger looked at him with a stony expression. "You think yourself in a position to make demands?"

"Not exactly. But Jimmie and Irene can help me to explain. And I have something I think Dr. Fernandez will want to see."

He reached into his jacket and scooped Kipper out from her secret pocket. He held her close to his chest, so Challenger could see her but no one behind them would be able to.

Kipper blinked at Challenger. Challenger blinked back. Then he cleared his throat.

"Valencia!" he shouted.

❦

If Valencia Fernandez had been a lady in a novel, she would have swooned when she first set eyes on the pterodactyl. Instead, she merely stared at Kipper for a long moment before she was overcome with giddy laughter.

"Incredible," she murmured. "Magnificent. Absolutely—"

She had reached out a finger to stroke Kipper, who gave a firm snap of her jaws.

"Right you are," said Dr. Fernandez, pulling her hand back in surrender. But she continued to stare at Kipper the whole way to Challenger's office.

An hour later, Arthur, Irene, and Jimmie sat in silence across from Headmaster Challenger, Valencia Fernandez, and Dr. Watson—who had insisted on coming to ensure they didn't need treatment for their wounds. Kipper was once again perched on Arthur's shoulder, which was throbbing with the strength of her grip.

They had just finished relaying the whole story, from Arthur's sighting of the Green Knight on his very first day at Baskerville Hall to the unfortunate—but not exactly untimely—death of the late Professor Grey. Now the adults in the room sat in silence, their mouths ajar.

"So . . . that's all," Arthur said, with a nervous glance at his two friends.

"You are sure this . . . machine is destroyed?" Challenger said. "And that Professor Grey is dead?"

Arthur, Irene, and Jimmie nodded.

"And you definitely heard the Clover speak of the Green Knight? You are quite certain?"

"Yes, sir," Arthur said. "And I saw him twice with my own eyes."

Challenger leaned back in his enormous seat, crossed his arms over his chest, and frowned at the ceiling for a long time. Arthur wanted to ask what he was thinking but didn't dare.

"And what are we to do with little Kipper here?" Dr. Watson asked, to break the silence.

"She's rather attached to Arthur," Irene said.

"Yes, of course," Dr. Fernandez replied. "She must have imprinted on him."

"That's what our friend Pocket said," Arthur agreed.

"Well, how do we *un*-imprint it?" Challenger demanded. "I can't have it following him all over school."

"Or home to Edinburgh," Dr. Watson added, looking amused.

Arthur fought off a smile as he imagined what his mam would do if he brought home a *dinosaur.*

Dr. Fernandez tapped her lip. "We'll have to find a suitable maternal figure to replace Arthur," she said.

Jimmy threw a teasing look at his friend. "Hear that, Arthur? You're a maternal figure."

Dr. Fernandez didn't seem to have heard. "But I'm afraid another human is probably out of the question," she said, "now that she's been taught to fear us."

She couldn't have looked more disappointed if she had just been told her ship was being boarded by pirates. Then her face cleared. "Although . . . perhaps there is something we could try, as long as you still have what I brought back from my last expedition, Eddie?"

Challenger nodded.

"Well, then—it could be perfect. In fact, it might lead to an important discovery. The first of many, I should hope. Despite your thievery, I do owe you a debt of gratitude, Mr. Doyle."

She smiled brightly at him, and he commanded himself not to blush.

It didn't work.

"Does—does this mean I'm not expelled anymore?" he asked.

Dr. Fernandez looked to Challenger.

"Kipper might need him here," she said.

He sighed. "You may stay, Doyle. You have made mistakes, but I see now you have done your best to right them. And I must admit you've made things very . . . interesting . . . this term."

"And we thought the place was interesting before!" exclaimed Dr. Watson. "What innocents we were."

"Were you, though?" Irene asked, leaning forward. "I mean, did anyone suspect Professor Grey?"

Now it was Watson and Challenger who exchanged a glance.

"In fact, some of us *did* suspect her," a voice replied from the doorway.

Everyone's gaze turned to see who had spoken.

There stood a tall man in a tweed suit and top hat, with a thin beaky nose, a sharply jutting jaw, and a distinct gray gaze.

Arthur couldn't believe his eyes. The man looked different, much younger, than he had the first time Arthur had met him on a cobbled street in Edinburgh. Gone were his beard and his cane. But those gray eyes and that rich, arch voice were impossible to mistake.

"You're the old man!" he said. "The one I threw the rock at. Who saved the pram!"

"I had quite a painful lump there for over a week," the man said dryly. "Not that you asked."

Arthur gaped. He didn't know what to say. He was thoroughly confused. It was a rare sensation, and not one he enjoyed.

The man's mouth twitched. He held out a hand to Arthur.

"Professor Sherlock Holmes," he said. "Hello, young man. I am pleased to make your acquaintance. Again."

FIFTY

The Investigations of Sherlock Holmes

"BUT, MY DEAR HOLMES!" CRIED DR. WATSON. "What are you doing here?"

The professor laughed. "Where else would I be?"

"Investigating the haunting of an isolated Scottish manor belonging to the Widow MacDougal, I would have thought," said Watson.

"It's true," said Holmes, throwing himself into an empty armchair, "that I was initially tempted away from Baskerville Hall by a strange and intriguing letter begging for my help. Mrs. MacDougal presented me with a mysterious—even supernatural!—set of circumstances and asked me to come uncover the truth. Which I did, in the space of an afternoon."

"But you've been gone for weeks!" Watson argued. "I've been writing to you there—and you've been writing back!"

"I sent a trusted friend to intercept the letters in Little Bigsby," Holmes replied. "He made sure I have received them all."

"Where have you been if you solved her case so quickly?" Challenger asked.

"And *how* did you solve it?" Arthur asked.

Holmes gave Arthur an approving look. "Indeed, the answer to the first question lies in the answer to the second," he said. "During my tour of the house, I noted there was a broom closet that was locked. Naturally, I wondered why anyone would feel the need to lock a broom closet, so I broke in. Inside, I found the widow's stash of supplies. Costumes, lighting tricks, even a set of chains to rattle! She was prepared to put on quite a show in order to draw out my investigation and keep me there as long as possible."

"But why?" Jimmie asked. He was studying the professor with narrowed eyes.

"Well, precisely," Holmes replied, nodding. "Why create a fake mystery for me to solve?"

"To distract you from a real one," Arthur answered, without thinking. Holmes's thought process was so similar to Arthur's, that Arthur had almost forgotten he wasn't following one of his own trains of thought.

Holmes arched his eyebrow. "Very good, Doyle. Mrs. MacDougal, who had fallen on hard times since the death of her husband, confessed to me that she was in desperate need of money, and in no position to turn down the offer she received to put on this little show for me in return for a great sum. The offer was made anonymously, so she was unable to tell me who had put her up to it. However, I had my own suspicions on that score. So I set out on an investigation of my own, while Watson kept me well informed on the strange events unfolding here. I began to form conclusions, but I needed to be sure."

"Grey sent you away," Arthur said eagerly. "Isn't that right? She was worried that you would figure everything out and expose her before she had the chance to use the machine and escape."

"Indeed," Holmes agreed. "Which is exactly what I was on my way to do tonight, but I see I have been beaten to the punch."

He shot Arthur, Jimmie, and Irene a conspiratorial grin.

Arthur felt himself swelling with pride.

"At least I can say that I have been some help," Holmes continued. "When I felt the earth tremble, I guessed that it might have been the cavern caving in, and I knew Grey would be involved. I checked the only remaining external entrance that leads to the cavern in case she might try to escape."

"There's another entrance?" Irene asked.

"There was," Holmes corrected. "But only the smallest opening is left now. Certainly too small for Grey to have escaped through."

"Bed!" barked Challenger, banging a fist against his desk and making them all jump. "Tomorrow is another day, and one we can all use to clear up the rest of this outrageous mess. You three need to get back to bed. I suppose someone will have to escort you, as I can't trust you to walk from here to the tower without exploding half my school. Thank goodness the builders planned for the possibility that that cave might fall in on itself. You'll find no sturdier building in all of England."

Arthur, Irene, and Jimmie were too exhausted to argue. Dawn was already creeping into the sky like a purple thief.

"I'll go," said Dr. Fernandez. "We'll need to make a detour on the way."

They all three stood and followed her to the door. But there was one last thing that was bothering Arthur. He stopped next to Holmes.

"Professor," he said in a low voice. Irene and Jimmie had been through enough that night, and he didn't want to worry them unnecessarily. "You said the gap left in the tunnel wasn't big enough for Professor Grey to get through."

"That's right," said Holmes.

Arthur bit his lip. "But would it have been big enough for a child?"

FIFTY-ONE

Just the Beginning

CLASSES WERE CANCELED THAT MORNING, allowing everyone to sleep in after their wakeful night. Breakfast was still being served when Arthur, Irene, and Jimmie walked into the buttery around ten o'clock. A few groups of students lingered over their morning meal, while others had wandered out onto the grounds or gone to the library to catch up on their studies.

"Good morning!" Pocket called as they entered. "We've been waiting for you!" She waved them over as though they might not have seen her and Grover sitting in their usual spot.

They joined their friends and, over cups of strong, sweet tea, filled each other in on the events of the previous night. Pocket explained how she had been growing her supply of fire ants ever since she had been surprised by the attacker in Professor Grey's office. She wanted to be ready for him the next time, and so she was.

"But weren't you frightened?" Irene asked. "He had a knife!"

"Oh, it was only a letter opener," Pocket replied. "He had it with him in Grey's office, too. That's how I recognized him. He just wanted us to think it was a knife."

"You told *me* the attacker had a knife!" Arthur protested.

Pocket shrugged. "It made for a better story. But speaking of Professor Grey . . . What happened to the machine? Where is she now?"

Irene bit her lip. "Pocket . . . I'm so sorry. Professor Grey is dead."

Arthur said nothing.

Tears welled in Pocket's eyes, as though Irene had pinched her. "She was . . . I know she was awful . . . but she was a great scientist. And teacher. Tell me what happened."

So they recounted for the second time what had gone on in the cave. Pocket listened with wide, glistening eyes, while Grover struggled to hide his pleasure.

"I've got her obituary ready to go!" he whispered to Arthur. "What are the chances? The *Bugle* will have to print it now!"

"We owe you both our thanks," Arthur said, when they had told the others everything. "Without you to waylay the Clover, we would never have gotten to the cave in time. We should never have hidden anything from you."

"It's all right, Arthur," Pocket said. "We understand why you did."

"It's never too late to right a wrong," Grover agreed. "Unless you're dead. Then it's too late."

They burst into laughter. Their show of mirth was the last straw for Cook, who was not accustomed to breakfast stretching nearly to lunchtime. She shooed them out and slammed the doors behind them.

"But, Grover, how did you know all that about the Clover?" Irene asked as they made their way toward the front doors.

"Was it supposed to be a secret? You're always talking about it in the library and in the buttery."

"When we thought no one else was listening," Jimmie said shortly.

"Mother always said I have excellent hearing," Grover replied contentedly.

"Arthur, you didn't tell us what happened to Kipper!" Pocket said as they spilled out into the blustery blue day.

"Come and see for yourselves," Arthur replied.

He missed having Kipper snuggled close to him. He did not, however, miss her talons. And she was much happier where she was now.

Just then, Irene stopped in her tracks. "Oh no," she groaned. "What now?"

Sebastian was waiting for them at the bottom of the stairs, just as he had been the night before. He had deep circles under his eyes, his usually perfectly coiffed hair was sticking up in the back, and his face was covered in angry red blotches from where Pocket's ants had done their worst.

He stared at Arthur with undisguised hatred.

"I knew you were a common fool from the moment I set eyes on you," he said, when Arthur was level with him. "But you have no idea what a stupid decision you made last night." He turned his gaze to Jimmie. "I expected better of *you*, Moriarty."

Jimmie's jaw tensed. Some of the color drained from his face.

"We didn't name any Clover members to the headmaster," he muttered. "Not even you."

This hadn't been Arthur's choice. Jimmie had cut in just before he had been about to tell the headmaster about Sebastian listening in on their conversation the night before. But Arthur saw the wisdom in Jimmie's choice. They had walked away from their chance to be a part of the Clover, and now they had become the group's enemies. Jimmie was trying to control the damage they had done, and perhaps spare them some retribution.

"We don't want any more trouble, Sebastian," Jimmie added.

Sebastian sneered. "Perhaps you should have thought of that sooner," he said. Then he pushed roughly past Arthur and started to climb the stairs.

Two figures in white waited for him at the top.

Thomas Hood and Ollie Griffin.

They had matching spiteful stares and red bites dotting their faces.

"You'd better be careful, Doyle," said Thomas. Though Arthur didn't think he had ever heard him speak, he recognized his voice immediately. *The Magician!* "From this day forward."

"Very careful," agreed Ollie. "Especially if your darling mother wants you home in one piece."

As he heard her high, lilting voice for the first time, Arthur realized he had assumed she was a boy because of her name and short hair. But Ollie was a girl. *The Nightingale.*

"Thanks," he said, "but we can take care of ourselves." He glanced at Pocket and smiled. Then he squared his shoulders and turned his back on the lot of them. His friends followed suit.

When he glanced behind him a few moments later, the ghostly figures were gone.

Kipper was getting on famously in her new home in the forest, squawking happily in a large nest as Didi the not-quite-dodo fussed over her new chick.

"Poor Didi has been all alone here for so long," Irene said. "Dr. Fernandez had a hunch that she would adopt Kipper as her own chick if given the chance. She was very excited about it. She said it's evidence that dinosaurs might be more closely related to birds than to reptiles."

Spotting them below, Kipper flew down from the nest, swooping in and out of their little group. She landed on Arthur's shoulders and bit him on the neck.

"Ow!" he cried.

But he knew from having been bitten by Caroline so many times that it was a bite meant to communicate love.

"I'm glad she gets to stay here," Pocket said. "We can come visit her whenever we want!"

"I still don't know what Challenger is going to tell the rest of the school when she gets bigger," Jimmie said. He had brought some kippers from the buttery and began to throw them to her.

"A problem for another day," Irene replied.

They watched Kipper catch kipper after kipper, laughing at her midair acrobatics.

But Arthur was distracted by something he had spotted from the corner of his eye.

His friends deserved a carefree day. So he did not draw their attention to the long black horse hair he pulled from a nearby

bramble. And he did not tell them what had happened earlier that morning.

When Dr. Fernandez had led Arthur, Jimmie, and Irene to Didi's nest in the wee hours, Kipper had not been ready to leave Arthur's side. He and Dr. Fernandez had stayed behind in the forest as dawn broke, sending Irene and Jimmie to bed. She, too, had leaned against a tree and nodded off eventually.

So it was only Arthur who had heard the horse's low snort.

The Green Knight had ridden up so silently that Arthur hadn't sensed his approach. He was staring at Arthur across the mossy clearing.

Arthur jolted upright and clenched his fists for a fight, but the man who called himself a knight came no closer. In the gray light, and beneath the knight's hood, Arthur could only make out a sallow complexion.

"I fear you will come to regret what you have done tonight," said the Green Knight in a soft voice.

"I don't think so," Arthur replied.

He thought he could make out the curl of a hollow smile. It chilled him.

"You do not know what you have set in motion," the Green Knight said.

"Maybe not," Arthur agreed. "But I know I made the right choice not to help *you*."

Arthur hadn't known what he had set in motion the afternoon back in Edinburgh, either, when he saved the baby's pram from being trampled. That action had led him here, to Baskerville Hall. One never knew where one's choices might lead. All one could do was make the right choice in the moment.

"We will meet again, Arthur. Sooner than you think."

With that, the Green Knight had clicked his tongue and guided his horse away.

"What's that, Arthur?" Pocket asked.

"Nothing," Arthur said, suppressing a shiver as he let the horse hair float away on the breeze.

He would tell them all about meeting the Green Knight, but not today. Irene was right. It was a problem that could wait for tomorrow.

He watched her closely as she glanced down to check the time on her father's pocket watch, and thought of how quick-witted and fearless she had been the night before. She had caught Arthur from falling into the river, and it had been her idea to tell Jimmie to destroy the machine, which kept Grey from pushing them both into the churning water. Perhaps wit and bravery came naturally to her? Or perhaps, Arthur thought, someone had taught her those things. . . .

But that discussion, too, could wait for another day.

He joined in the fun until everyone's fingers were growing numb with cold, and they agreed to go warm them by one of the fireplaces in the library.

"Goodbye, Kipper!" Arthur said, giving the dinosaur an affectionate pat on the head. "We'll come see you again soon."

Kipper was too busy chomping on her fish to take much notice of their departure.

As they reached the edge of the forest, Arthur was startled by the sound of a stick snapping close behind them. He whirled

around to see Professor Holmes tromping through the forest a few feet away.

"Doyle," he said. "I need a word."

Arthur glanced at his friends. "I'll catch up with you later."

"You've had quite the first term at Baskerville Hall," Holmes said. "I knew I was right to recommend you. It was Grey who sent me on a wild goose chase to Scotland, but if I were a different kind of man, I might believe it was fate that put me in your path that day. I hope you aren't regretting your decision to come?"

Arthur thought back to the boy who had stood on Arthur's Seat, watching in awe as Challenger's airship made its descent. So much had happened since then. More than that boy could ever have dreamed of.

"Not at all, sir," he said.

"Good. Because we have more work to do yet."

"What do you mean?" Arthur asked.

Holmes stopped and pulled something from his pocket. A fragment of white fabric with a single black button still attached.

"Does this look familiar?"

Arthur stared at the fabric. It looked very familiar indeed. "It's from Professor Grey's lab coat," he said.

"I found it a few moments ago," Holmes said. "Snagged on a branch by the mouth of the tunnel."

Arthur's heart lurched. "You mean . . ."

"You were right. An adult never could have fit through the opening that was left after the rockslide," Holmes said grimly. "But apparently it was just big enough for a child."

Arthur swallowed. "So Grey is still alive?"

"Biding her time, I should think," Holmes said. "Most likely plotting her revenge."

"I need to tell you something, too," Arthur replied. He told the professor about his encounter with the Green Knight.

Holmes stared at Arthur for a long moment when he was done. Arthur could still hear the sounds of the others laughing as they walked toward the manor. He longed to rejoin them, to make the most out of the sunny day with nothing to do but enjoy the company of his friends.

"He was telling the truth, wasn't he?" Arthur asked. "This isn't over at all, is it?"

"I'm afraid not," Holmes said. "In fact, I suspect this is just the beginning. And my suspicions are nearly always correct."

Arthur shivered.

We will meet again, Arthur. Sooner than you think.

But Professor Holmes didn't look afraid. He clapped Arthur on the shoulder. "Prepare yourself, my boy," he said. His gray eyes brightened with a curious light, and a smile played at his lips. "The game is afoot."

Acknowledgments

My deepest gratitude to all those who helped this story into the world, including:

First and foremost, my wonderful family, who have supported me through this grand adventure. You are the reason that I can write, and the reason I ***do*** write. As Arthur says of his own family, you are the greatest thing of all.

My talented friends and colleagues at Working Partners, particularly the brilliant Michelle Corpora, without whom there would be no Baskerville Hall, and Chris Snowdon, who decided to take a chance on me way back when. And to the rest of the team for book one who helped shape the story: Karen Ball, Elizabeth Galloway, Stephanie Lane Elliott, Dan Jolley, James Noble, Sam Noonan, and Crystal Velasquez.

The Conan Doyle estate for trusting me with Arthur's story, and particularly to Richard Doyle and Richard Pooley, whose rich and colorful insights into his life and legacy proved wonderfully helpful along the way.

My former agent, Sarah Davies, who just squeaked in this deal before sailing off into a well-earned retirement, and my current agent, Chelsea Eberly, who has exceeded my every expectation and been an amazing advocate for Arthur's story.

The dedicated team at HarperCollins, including Eva Lynch-Comer, Karina Williams, Emily Mannon, Abby Dommert, Laura Mock, Amy Ryan, Jon Howard, Gwen Morton, and particularly my incredible editor, Alyson Day, who has always believed in me and been my champion. I don't know how I got lucky enough to have worked with her for so long, and to get to continue working together on this series is a dream.

Rights People, for their dedication in making sure readers around the world will be able to come on this adventure with Arthur.

Michael Dee, Theresa Reed, Dan Jolley, and James Noble for their hard work in bringing Baskerville Hall to the screen, and particularly to the late Michelle Forde, whose warmth, wit, and passion are dearly missed.

The marvelous Iacopo Bruno, whose fantastic and meticulous cover artwork has brought Baskerville Hall to life.

Daniel Stashower, whose works on Arthur Conan Doyle were indispensable in researching this book, and who was generous enough to answer my many questions.

Those who provided early feedback or reviews on this novel, including Anne Ursu, Kathryn Lasky, and Scott Reintgen.

Finally, and perhaps most important, to Arthur Conan Doyle himself, to whom every living reader and storyteller surely owes a great debt, and who prized fairness, progress, innovation, and integrity. And to his mam, Mary Doyle, who told him stories first.

Photos and Drawings from Arthur Conan Doyle's World

Portrait of Arthur Conan Doyle at age five by his uncle, Richard Doyle

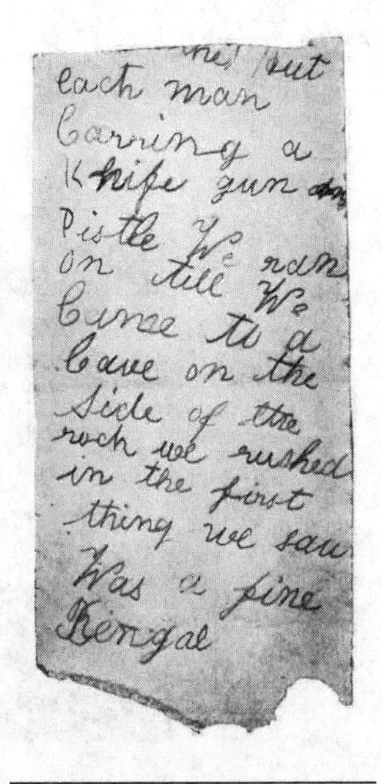

but
each man
carring a
knife gun
Pistle we ran
on till we
came to a
cave on the
Side of the
rock we rushed
in the first
thing we saw
was a fine
Bengal

Arthur Conan Doyle's childhood writing, age six

Young Arthur Conan Doyle

Arthur Conan Doyle and sisters

Sketch of Arthur Conan Doyle
at age twelve by his uncle,
Richard Doyle

Stonyhurst School

Arthur Conan Doyle in his cricket uniform, age fourteen

Arthur Conan Doyle with his children

Arthur Conan Doyle and his children

All About Arthur Conan Doyle

The real Arthur Conan Doyle was born in 1859 in Edinburgh, Scotland, and grew up in poverty surrounded by siblings, his adored mam, and his alcoholic father. In 1868, he was sent to a boarding school in Lancashire, England. He wrote comparatively little about it afterward, and rarely mentioned any friendships made during his time there. (Although it was recently discovered that there was a fellow pupil called Moriarty!) What strange and improbable things might have happened during his years wandering its grounds?

Doyle went on to attend medical school at the University of Edinburgh and become a doctor. He set up his own practice in Southsea, hoping to make enough money to help support his family, but found himself with very few patients. Sitting alone in his office, he began to write stories featuring a detective named Sherlock Holmes. When he sent the first Holmes story off for publication, he could not have imagined how many millions of readers would come to know and love the surly detective; his loyal friend, Dr. Watson; and the colorful cast of supporting characters, including James Moriarty, Mrs. Hudson, Irene Adler, and Mary Morstan.

Doyle also introduced the world to Professor Challenger in one of the first true science-fiction novels, *The Lost World*. The hilarious escapades of a French officer, Brigadier Etienne Gerard, and the brutal world of prizefighters described in *Rodney Stone* illustrate the range of Doyle's imagination and the depth of his research.

Doyle was also a keen boxer and sportsman, and carried this spirit into his daily life, which found him unafraid to fight injustice wherever he saw it. Throughout much of his adult life he was fascinated by the possibility of psychic phenomenon, eventually becoming a devoted spiritualist, certain that the dead lived on in another plane. Doyle himself lives on today as the creator of some of the best-loved fictional characters of all time.